H Clarke

Fabulae Aesopi Selectae or, Select Fables of Aesop

With an English translation, more literal than any yet extant, designed for the

readier instruction of beginners in the Latin tongue

H Clarke

Fabulae Aesopi Selectae or, Select Fables of Aesop
With an English translation, more literal than any yet extant, designed for the readier instruction of beginners in the Latin tongue

ISBN/EAN: 9783337075866

Printed in Europe, USA, Canada, Australia, Japan

Cover: Foto ©Andreas Hilbeck / pixelio.de

More available books at **www.hansebooks.com**

FABULÆ ÆSOPI Selectæ,

O R,

Select FABLES of ÆSOP;

W I T H

An *Englijh* TRANSLATION,

More LITERAL than any yet extant,

Defigned for the Readier INSTRUCTION
of BEGINNERS in the *Latin Tongue.*

By H. CLARKE,

TEACHER of the LATIN LANGUAGE.

The FIRST BOSTON EDITION, from a Copy of the lateſt
Edition printed in LONDON.

B O S T O N :
Printed by SAMUEL HALL, in State-Street.
1787.

P R E F A C E.

WHOEVER hath duly confidered the great Difficulty there is in our firft encountering with the Idioms of the *Latin* Tongue, the Variety of *Englifh* Words, which will fometimes anfwer to one *Latin* one, with the many Miftakes which Boys muft naturally be liable to, who cannot immediately form any tolerable Judgment of the Thing which They are engaged in ; muft furely, in fome Meafure, be brought to acknowledge, that the having Things explained and cleared up to their Underftandings, as They go along, is the beft and only Means of making Them eager and defirous to learn. And here, perhaps, It may be fomewhat of a real Help to throw the Language into a yet more eafy Light, and to defcend a little lower, than Others have hitherto fubmitted Themfelves to. For I will not refufe to own, that I am apprehenfive, the Fear of too great a Baldnefs in the Tranflation hath deterred even Thofe, who have carried this Affair farther than was at firft imagined it could ever have gone, from rendering it fo plain, that Children might ftill the more readily

come

come into the Knowledge of the Conſtruction, and form a better and quicker Idea of the different Parts of Speech.

Things relating to Inſtruction cannot well be made too eaſy ; but to write in the Terms of a Pedant, or in ſuch a Lowneſs, or Poverty of Expreſſion, as dwindleth almoſt into Nonſenſe, is a Hardſhip too great to be ſubmitted to by any Man of Spirit. But alas! Freedom of Stile is one Thing, and literal Tranſlation another ; and the beſt Way to commence an Acquaintance with any Language, is firſt to read a great deal of a verbal Tranſlation. When ſingle Words have been apprehended rightly, a Number of them may be readily put together, the remembering that ſuch a Word is *Latin* for ſuch a Thing affording Learners the greateſt Pleaſure and Incitement towards the making a Progreſs more conſiderable ; whereas, by attempting the Conſtruction of Phraſes too ſoon, they become loſt, and bewildered in a Maze.

It hath been thought proper therefore to make the *Engliſh* Words here to anſwer to the *Latin*, as grammatically as poſſible ; and, where more expreſſive Ones might often have been made Uſe of, Thoſe, which are moſt uſually met with, have been judged the moſt convenient ; the varying the Phraſe too

much

much at firſt tending rather to confound, than graft any Thing in the Memory.

* A new Edition of *Æſop*, with the *Latin* and *Engliſh* each in their diſtinct Columns, had been long ago wiſhed for ; but, as Mr. *Locke* had before ſuffered an Interlineary Verſion of it to be printed with his Name in the Title Page, it is highly probable, Nobody would venture to undertake ſuch a Thing ; altho' You are told in the *Preface*, that the Deſign was to help Thoſe, who had not the Opportunity or Leiſure to learn the *Latin Language* by *Grammar* ; which, conſequently, did not lead Him to have the *Engliſh* made with the greateſt grammatical Strictneſs to the *Latin*, and left Room for ſomething to be attempted, which might be afforded at an eaſier Rate, and what might better anſwer the Purpoſes of a Common School-Book.

Upon the whole, You have here a Collection of the greateſt Part of the *Fables* done in an eaſier Manner, than any yet extant ; and the farther You enter into the Book, You will find ſuch little Liberties taken in the *Expreſſion*, as may naturally ſuit with *tender Capacities*, whilſt the Judgment ripens by Degrees.

Beſides, the Advantage of the *Roman* and *Italick Characters*

Characters being alternately ufed for the better In-
ftruction of *Young Beginners*, this *Tranflation* is contrived to anfwer *Line* for *Line* throughout ; and Care
hath been generally taken to avoid the *Breaks* of
Words fo frequent in Things of this Nature, that it is
next to an Impoffibility now to miftake.

SELECTÆ

FABULÆ ÆSOPI.

SELECT

FABLES of ÆSOP.

FABLE I.

De GALLO.

Gallus, *dum* vertit *Stercorarium*, offendit *Gemmam*, inquiens, *Quid reperio Rem* tam *nitidam?* Si *Gemmarius* reperisset *Te*, Nihil *esset* lætius *Eo*, ut *Qui* sciret *Pretium:* Quidem *est* nulli *Usui* Mihi, nec æstimo *Magni;* imo *equidem* mallem *Granum* Hordei *omnibus* Gemmis.

MORALE.

Intellige *per* Gemmam *Artem* & *Sapientiam*; per *Gallum*, Hominem *stolidum* & *volup-*

Of the COCK.

A Cock, *whilst* he turns up a *Dunghill*, finds a *Jewel*, saying, *Why* do I find *a Thing* so *bright?* If *a Jeweller* had found *Thee*, Nothing *would be* more joyful *than He*, as *Who* would know *the Price:* Indeed *it is* of no *Use* to Me, *nor* do I esteem it at a great *Rate*; nay *indeed* I had rather have *a Grain* of Barley *than all* Jewels.

The MORAL.

Understand *by* the Jewel *Art* and *Wisdom*; by *the Cock*, a Man *foolish* and *volup-*

voluptarium ; nec *Stulti*
amant *liberales* Artes, *cum*
nefciant *Ufum* earum ;
nec Voluptarius, *quippe*
Volúptas *fola* placeat *Ei.*

voluptuous ;   neither   *Fools*
love   *liberal*   Arts,   *when*
they know not *the Ufe* of them ;
nor a voluptuous Man, *becaufe*
Pleafure *alone* pleafes him.

FABLE II.

De Cane & Umbra.

Of the Dog and the Shadow.

CAnis *tranans* fluvium,
vehebat Carnem *Rictu ;*
Sole *fplendente,* Umbra
Carnis lucebat *in* Aquis :
Quam Ille *videns,* & *avidè*
captans, *perdidit* Quod *erat*
in *Faucibus :* Itaq; *pertulfts*
Jacturâ &   Rei   &
Spei, *primum* ftupuit ; *de-*
inde recipiens *Animum* fic
elatravit : Mifer ! *Modus*
deerat   *tuæ* Cupiditati :
Erat fatis   *fuperque,*
ni   *defipuiffes.*   Jam,
per tuam *Stultitiam,* eft
minus Nihilo Tibi.
         Mox.
Sit   *Modus*   tuæ
Cupiditati, nè *amittas*
certa *pro* incertis.

A Dog *fwimming over* a River,
carried Flefh *in his Chaps ;*
the Sun *fhining,* the Shadow
of the Flefh fhone *in the Waters ;*
which he *feeing,* and *greedily*
catching at, *loft* what *was*
in *his Jaws :* Therefore *ftruck*
with the Lofs of the Thing *and*
his Hope, and while was amazed ;
afterwards taking *Courage* thus
he barked out : Wretch ! *Modera-*
tion was wanting *to thy* Defire :
There was enough, *and too much,*
unlefs *thou hadft been mad.* Now,
thro' thy *Folly,* there is
lefs than Nothing *for Thee.*
            Mor.
Let there be *Moderation* to thy
Defire,   left   thou   *lofe*
certain things *for* uncertain.

FABLE III.

De Lupo & Grue.

Of the Wolf and the Crane.

DUM *Lupus* vorat
Ovem, forte *Offa*
hæfere *in* Gulâ, ambit,
orat *Opem,* Nemo *opitulatur ;*
Omnes *dictitant,* eum *tuliffe*
Præmium *fuæ* Voracitatis :
Tandem multis *Blanditiis*
plu-

WHilft *a Wolf* devoureth
a Sheep, by chance *the Bones*
ftuck *in his Throat ; He goes about,*
afks *Help,* Nobody *affifts ;*
All *fay,* that he had got
the Reward *of his* Greedinefs :
At length, with many *Flatteries*
and

pluribufq; *Promiſſis*, inducit
Gruem, ut, *longiſſimo*
Collo *inſerto* in *Gulam*,
eximeret *Os* infixum.
Verum illuſit *Ei* petenti
Præmium, inquiens, *Inepta*,
abi, *non habes* ſat, *quòd*
vivis? *Debes* tuam *Vitam*
Mihi ; *ſi* vellem, *poteram*
præmordere *tuum* Collum. ·

and more *Promiſes*, He draws in
the *Crane*, that *her very long*
Neck *being thruſt* into *his Throat*,
She would pull out *the Bone* fixed in.
But He played upon *Her* aſking
a *Reward*, ſaying, *Fool*,
go away, *haſt thou not* enough, *that*
thou liveſt? *Thou oweſt* thy *Life*
to Me ; *if* I would, *I was able*
to bite off *thy* Neck.

MOR.

Quod *facis* ingrato,
perit.

MOR.

What *thou doeſt* for the ungrateful
periſheth.

FABLE IV.

De RUSTICO & COLUBRO.	*Of* the COUNTRYMAN *and* the SNAKE.

RUſticus *tulit* Domum
Colubrum repertum *in*
Nive, *prope* eneɛtum *Frigore;*
adjicit *ad* Focum :
Coluber recipiens · *Vim*,
Virufque, *deinde* non *ferens*
Flammam, *infecit* omne *Tu-*
gurium Sibilando. *Ruſticus*
corripiens *Sudem* accurrit,
& expoſtulat · *Injuriam*
cum *Eo* Verbis *Verberibuſq;*
Num *referret* has
Gratias? Num *eriperet*
Vitam *Illi*, Qui *dederat*
Vitam *Illi?*

A Countryman *brought* Home
a Snake found in
the Snow, *almoſt* dead *with Cold ;*
He · lays him *to* the Fire ;
The Snake recovering *Strength*,
and Poiſon, *then* not *bearing*
the Flame, *filled* all the *Cot-*
tage with Hiſſing. *The Countryman*
ſnatching a *Stake* runs up,
and expoſtulates *the Injury*
with *Him* in Words *and Blows;*
Whether *he would return* theſe
Thanks? Whether *He would take*
Life *from Him*, Who *had given*
Life *to Him?*

MOR.

Interdum *fit*, ut
obſint Tibi, *Quibus*
Tu *profueris* ; & *Ii* mere-
antur *malè* de *Te*, de *Quibus*
Tu *meritus ſis* benè.

MOR.

Sometimes *it happens*, that
they are hurtful to Thee, *whom*
Thou *haſt profited;* and *They* de-
ſerve ill of *Thee* of *Whom*
Thou *haſt deſerved* well.

B   FABLE

FABLE V.

De Apro & Asino.

DUM iners Afinus irri-
debat Aprum, Ille
indignans frendebat. Igna-
viffime, fueras quidem
meritus Malum ; fed etiamfi
fueris dignus Pænâ, tamen
Ego fum indignus, qui puni-
am Te. Ride tutus ; nam
es tutus ob Inertiam.

Mor.

Demus Operam, ut
eum audiamus, aut patiamur
indigna Nobis, nè dicamus,
aut faciamus indigna Nobis.
Nam mali & perditi ple-
rumq; gaudent, fi Quif-
piam bonorum refiflat
iis ; pendent Magni,
Se haberi dignos
Ultione. Imitemur Equos,
& magnas Beflias, Qui
prætereunt oblatrantes
Caniculos cum Contemptu.

Of the Boar and the Ass.

WHilft the fluggifh Afs laughed at the Boar, He
fretting gnafhed his teeth. Moft
flothful Wretch, thou haft indeed
deferved Evil ; but although thou
haft been worthy of Punifhment, yet
I am unfit, who may pu-
nifh Thee. Laugh fecure, for
thou art fafe for thy Sluggifhnefs.

Mor.

Let us give an Endeavour, that
when we hear, or endure
Things unworthy of us, We do not fay,
or do Things unworthy of Us.
For bad and loft Men generally rejoice, if Any
one of the good refift
them; they value it at a great Rate,
that they are accounted worthy
of Revenge. Let us imitate Horfes,
and great Beafls, who
pafs by barking
Curs with Contempt.

FABLE VI.

De Aquila & Cornicula.

AQuila naâa Cochle-
am, non quivit eruere
Pifcem Vi, aut Arte.
Cornicula accedens dat
Confilium, fuadet fubvolare,
& è fublimi præcipitare
Cochleam in Saxa ; nam
fic fore, ut Cochlea
frangatur. Cornicula
manet Humi, ut
præftofetur Cafum :
Aquila

Of the Eagle and the Jackdaw.

AN Eagle having got a Cockle, was not able to get out
the Fifh by Force, or Art.
The Jackdaw coming up gives
Counfel, perfuades her to fly up,
and from on high to throw down
the Cockle upon the Stones ; for that
fo it would be that the Cockle
would be broken. The Jackdaw
flays on the Ground, that
fhe may watch the Fall .
The Eagle

Aquila precipitat; Testa frangitur; Piscis subripitur a Cornicula; clusa Aquila dolet.

The Eagle throws it down; The Shell is broken; The Fish is snatched away by the Jackdaw; the deluded Eagle grieves.

MOR.

MOR.

Noli habere Fidem Omnibus & fac inspicias Consilium, quod acceperis ab Aliis; nam Multi consulti non consulunt suis Confultoribus, sed Sibi.

Be not willing to have Faith in all Men, and do you look into the Counsel, which you have received from others; for Many being consulted do not counsel for their Consultors, but for Themselves.

FABLE VII.

De CORVO & VULPECULA.

Of the CROW and the FOX.

COrvus nactus Prædam, strepitat in Ramis: Vulpecula videt Eum gestientem, accurrit: Vulpes, inquit, impertit Corvum plurima Salute. Sepenumero audiveram, Famam esse Mendacem, jam experior Re ipsa: Nam, ut fortè prætereo hac, suspiciens Te in Arbore, advolo, culpans Famam: Nam Fama est, Te esse nigriorem Pice, & video te candidiorem Nive. Sanè in meo Judicio vincis Cygnos, & es formosior albâ Hederâ. Quòd si, ut excellas in Plumis, ita & Voce, equidem dicerem te Reginam omnium Avium. Corvus illectus hac Assentiunculâ, apparat ad canendum. Verò Cafeus excidit e Rostro; Quo correpto Vulpeculâ, tollit

A Crow having got a Prey, makes a Noise in the Branches: the Fox sees Him rejoicing, runs up: The Fox, says he, compliments the Crow with very much Health. Very often had I heard, that Fame was a Liar, now I find it in the Fact itself: For, as by Chance I pass by this way, seeing You in the Tree, I fly to you, blaming Fame: For the Report is, that you are blacker than Pitch, and I see you whiter than Snow. Truly in my Judgment you surpass the Swans, and are fairer than the white Ivy. But if, as you excel in Feathers, you do so also in Voice, truly I should call you the Queen of all Birds. The Crow allured by this Flattery, prepares to sing. But the Cheese fell from his Beak; Which being snatched by the Fox, he

tollit Cachinnum : Tum demum Corvus, Pudore junĉto Jacturæ Rei, dolet.

MOR.

Nonnulli *funt* tàm *avidi* Laudis, *ut* ament *Affen-tatorem* cum *fuo* Probro & Damno. *Homunciones* hujus *Modi* funt *Predæ* Parafito. *Quòd* fi *vitâffes* Jactan-tiam, *facile* vitaveris *pestiferum* Genus *Affen-tatorum.* Si *Tu* velis *effe* Thrafo, *Gnatho* nufquam *deerit* Tibi.

he fets up a Laughter : *Then* at laft *the* Crow, Shame *being joined* to the Lofs *of the Thing,* grieveth.

MOR.

Some *are* fo *greedy* of Praife, *that* they love *a Flat-terer* with *their own* Difgrace *and* Damage. *Men* of *this Kind* are *a Prey* to the Parafite. *But if you had avoided* Boaft-ing, *eafily* would you have avoided *the peftilent* Race *of Flatter-ers.* If *Thou* art willing *to be* a Thrafo, *a Gnatho* never *will be wanting* to Thee.

FABLE VIII.

De CANE & ASINO.   Of the DOG and the ASS.

DUM *Canis* blandiretur *Hero* & *Familiæ,* Herus & Familia *demulcent* Canem. *Afellus,* videns *id,* gemit *altiffimè* ; Nam *cæpit* pigere *Sor-tis :* Putat *inique* compa-ratum, *Canem* effe gra-tum cunĉtis, *pafcique* herili *Menfâ,* & confequi Hoc Otio Ludoque : (*Sefe* con-trà *portare* Clitellas, *eâdi* Flagello, *effe* nunquam *otiofum,* & tamen *odiofum* cunĉtis. Si *hæc* fiant *Blanditiis,* ftatuit *fectari* eam *Artem,* quæ fit tam *utilis.*) Igitur quo-dam Tempore *tentaturus* Rem, *procurrit* obviam *Hero* redeunti *Domum,* fub-

WHilft *the Dog* fawned on *his Mafter* and *the Family,* the Mafter *and* the Family *ftroke* the Dog. *The Afs,* feeing *that,* groans *moft deeply ;* for he began to be weary *of his Con-dition :* He thinks it *unjuftly* or-dered, *that the Dog* fhould be ac-ceptable to all, *and be fed* from his Mafter's *Table,* and *that he fhould get* This by *Idlenefs* and Play : *that Himfelf* on the contrary *carried* the Dorfers, *was beaten* with the Whip, *was* never idle, and *yet* odious *to all.* If *thefe things are* done *by Fawnings,* he refolves to follow that *Art,* which is fo *profitable.* Therefore *on a cer-tain* Time about to try the Thing, *He runs* in the Way to his Mafter returning *Home,* caps

fubfilit, *pulfat* Un-
gulis. *Hero* exclamante,
Servi accurrère &
ineptus *Afellus*, qui *credidit*
Se *urbanum*, vapulat.

leaps on Him, *ftrikes him* with
his Hoöfs. *The Mafter* crying out,
the *Servants* ran to him, *and*
the filly *Afs*, who *thought*
Himfelf *courtly*, is beaten.

Mor.

Mor.

Omnes *non poffimus* omnia;
nec omnia *decent* omnes.
Quifque faciat, *quifque*
tentet *id*, quod *poteft*.

We all *cannot do* all things;
nor do all things *become* all Men.
Let every one do, *let every one*
try *that*, which *he is able*.

FABLE IX.

De Leone & quibufdam
aliis.

Of the Lion and fome other
Beafts.

LEO *pepigerat* cum
Ove quibufdamque
aliis, Venationem fore
communem. *Venantur*,
Cervus *capitur:* fingulis
incipientibus tollere *fingulas*
Partes, *ut* convenerat,
Leo irrugiit, *inquiens*, una
Pars eft *mea*, quia *fum*
digniffimus; *altera* item
eft mea, quia præftantif-
fimus *Viribus*; porrò
vendico tertiam, *quia* fu-
daverim *plus* in *capiendo*
Cervo; *denique*, nifi *con-
cefferitis* quartam, *eft* actum
de Amicitiâ. Socii
audientes hoc, *difcedunt*
vacui & taciti, *non* aufi
mutire contra *Leonem*.

THE Lion *had agreed* with
the *Sheep* and fome
others, that the Hunting *fhould be*
common. *They hunt*,
a Stag *is taken:* all
beginning to take *their fingle*
Parts, *as* had been agreed,
the *Lion* roared, *faying*, one
Part is *mine*, becaufe *I am*
the moft worthy; *another* alfo
is mine, *becaufe* I am moft ex-
cellent *in Strength*; moreover
I claim a third, *becaufe* I have
fweated *more* in *taking*
the Stag; *laftly*, unlefs *you will*
grant the fourth, *there is* an end
of Friendfhip. His Companions
hearing this, *depart*
empty *and* filent, *not* having dared
to *mutter* againft *the Lion*.

Mor.

Mor.

Fides *femper* fuit *rara:*
apud *hoc* Seculum *eft* rarior;
apud potentes *eft*, &
femper fuit, *rariffima*. Quocirca *eft* fatius *vivere* cum
Pari. Nam, *Qui* vivit
cum potentiore, *fæpe* habet

Faith *always* has been *rare:*
in *this* Age *it is* rarer;
among the Powerful *it is*, and
always has been, *moft rare*. Wherefore *it is* better *to live* with
an *Equal*. For, *He who* liveth
with one more powerful, *often* hath

ne-

a Ne-

neceſſe conccderc *de* ſuo *Jure.*	a *Neceſſity* to depart *from* his Right.

FABLE X.

De Leone & Mure.	Of the Lion and the Mouse.
LEO *defeſſus* Æſtu Curſuque quieſcebat *ſub* Umbrâ, *ſuper* viridi *Gramine*; Grege *Murium* percurrente *ejus* Tergum, *experrectus*, comprehendit *Unum* ex *illis.* Captivus *ſupplicat*, clamitat, · *Se* eſſe *indignum*, cui *Leo* iraſcatur. *Ille*, reputans *fore* Nihil *Laudis* in *Nece* tantillæ *Beſtiæ*, dimittit *Captivum.* Non *diu* poſtea, *Leo*, dum *currit* per *Saltum*, incidit *in* Plagas: *Rugit*, ſed *non poteſt* exire. *Mus* audit *Leonem* miſerabiliter *rugientem*, agnoſcit *Vocem*, repit *in* Cuniculos, *quærit* Nodos, *quos* invenit, *corroditque*; Leo· *evadit* e *Plagis.*	THE Lion *tired* with Heat *and running*, reſted ·under the Shade, *upon* the green *Graſs*; a Company *of Mice* running over *his* Back, *having a-roſe*, He takes One of *them.* The Captive *begs*, cries, *that He* was *unworthy*, whom *the Lion* ſhould be angry with. *He*, thinking *there would be* Nothing of *Praiſe* in *the Death* of ſo little *a Beaſt*, diſmiſſes *the Captive.* Not *long* after, *the Lion*, whilſt *He runs* thro' *the Foreſt*, falls *into* the Toils: *He roars*, but *cannot* get out. *The Mouſe* hears *the* Lion miſerably *roaring*, knows *the Voice*, creeps *into the* Holes, *ſeeks* the Knots, *which* He finds, *and gnaws;* the Lion *eſcapes* out of *the Toils.*
Mor.	**Mor.**
Hæc *Fabula* ſuadet *Clementiam* potentibus; *Etenim* ut *humanæ* Res *ſunt* inſtabiles, *Potentes* ipſi *interdum* egent *Ope* humillimorum; *quare* prudens *Vir*, etſi *poteſt*, timet *nocere* vel *vili* Homini; *ſed* Qui *non timet* nocere *alteri*, deſipit *valdè.* Quid *ita?* Quia, *etſi* jam *fretus* Potentiâ, *metuit* Neminem, *forſan*, poſthac *erit*,	This *Fable* recommends *Clemency* to the powerful; *For* as *human* Things *are* unſtable, *the Powerful* themſelves *ſometimes* want *the Help* of the loweſt; *wherefore* a prudent *Man*, altho' *he is able*, feareth *to hurt* even *a mean* Man; *but* He that *does not fear* to hurt *another*, plays the Fool *very much.* Why *ſo?* Becauſe, *altho'* now *having relied* on his Power, *be feareth* Nobody, *perhaps*, hereafter

erit,   ut   indiguerit   it will be, that *he may have wanted*
vel *Gratiâ* vilium *Homun-*   either *the Favour* of mean *Men,*
cionum, vel *metuerit* Iram.   or *have feared* their Anger.

FABLE XI.

De *ægroto* MILVO.

M* Ilvus decumbebat* Lecto *jam* fermè *moriens,* orat *Matrem* ire *precatum* Deos. *Mater* refpondet, *Nihil* Opis *fperandum* Illi à Diis, *quorum* facra *toties* violaviffet *fuis* Rapinis.

Of *the fick* KITE.

THE Kite lay in Bed *now* almoſt *dying,* begs *his Mother* to go *to pray to* the Gods. *The Mother* anſwers, *No* Help *was to be* hoped by him *from* the Gods, *whofe* facred Things *fo often* he had violated *by his* Rapines.

MOR.

Decet *nos* venerari *Deos* ; nam *illi* juvant *pios,* & *adverfantur* impios. *Neglecti* in *Felicitate,* non exaudiunt *Miferiâ.* Quare *fis* memor *eorum* in *fecundis* rebus, *ut* vocati *fint* præfentes *in* adverfis *rebus.*

MOR.

It becometh *us* to worſhip *the Gods* ; for *they* help *the pious,* and *withftand* the impious. *Neglected* in *Felicity,* they do not hear *in Mifery.* Wherefore *be* mindful *of them* in *profperous* things, *that* being called *they may be* prefent *in* adverfe *things.*

FABLE XII.

De RANIS & earum *Rege.*

G* ENS Ranarum,* cum *effet* libera, *fupplicabat* Jovem, Regem dari *fibi.* Jupiter *ridebat* Vota *Ranarum.* Illæ *tamen* inſtabant *iterum,* atque *iterum,* donec *perpellerent* ipſum. *Ille* dejecit *Trabem* ; ea *Moles* quaffat *Fluvium* ingenti *Fragore.* Ranæ *territæ* filent ; *venerantur* Regem ; accedunt propiùs *pedetentim* ;

Of the FROGS *and* their *King.*

THE Nation *of Frogs,* when *it was* free, *befought* Jupiter, *for a King* to be given *to them.* Jupiter *laughed at* the Wiſhes *of the Frogs.* They *neverthelefs* preffed him *again,* and *again,* until *they drove* him to it. *He* threw down *a Log* ; that *Mafs* ſhakes *the River* with a great *Noife.* The Frogs *affrighted* are filent ; *they reverence* their King ; *they* come nearer *Step by Step* ;

tandem, *Metu* abjecto, *insultant*, & *defultant*; iners *Rex* eft *Lufui* & *Contemptui*. Rurfum *lacef-funt* Jovem; *orant* Regem *dari* fibi, *qui* fit *ftrenuus*; quibus *Jupiter* dat Ciconiam. Is *perftrenuè* perambulans *Paludem*, vorat *quicquid* Ranarum *fit* obviam. *Igitur* Ranæ *fruftrà* queftæ fuerunt *de* Sævitia *hujus*. Jupiter *non audit*, nam *queruntur* & *hodie*: Etenim *Vefperi* Ciconiâ *eunte* Cubitum, *egreffæ* ex-*Antris* murmurant *rauco* Ululatu; *fed* canunt *furdo*. Nam *Jupiter* vult, *ut* quæ *deprecate funt* clementem *Regem*, *jam ferant* inclementem.

at length, *Fear* being thrown away, *they leap upon*, and *leap off, him*; the fluggifh *King* is *their Sport* and, *Contempt*. Again they *provoke* Jupiter; *they pray for* a King *to be given* to them, *who* may be *valiant*; to whom *Jupiter* gives *the Stork*. He *very nimbly* ftalking through *the Marfh* devours *whatever* of the Frogs *comes* in the way. *Therefore* the Frogs *in vain* have complained *of* the Cruelty *of him*. Jupiter *does not hear*, for *they complain* even *this Day*: For *in the Evening* the Stork *going* to Reft, *having come* out of *their Caves* they murmur *with a hoarfe* Croaking; *but* they fing *to one deaf*. For *Jupiter wills, that* they who *petitioned againft* a merciful *King*, now *bear* an unmerciful.

MOR.

Solet *evenire* Plebi, *ut* Ranis, *quæ*, fi *habet* Regem *paulo* manfuetiorem, *damnat* cum *Ignaviæ* & *Inertiæ*, & *optat*, aliquando *Virum* dari *fibi*: Contra, *fi* quando *nacta eft* ftrenuum *Regem*, damnat *Sævitiam* hujus, & laudat *Clementiam* prioris; *five* quòd *femper* pœnitet *nos* præfentium, *five* quòd *eft* verum *Dictum*, nova *effe* potiora *veteribus*.

MOR.

It is wont *to happen* to the common People, *as to* the Frogs, *who*, if *they have* a King *a little* milder, *condemn* him *of Idlenefs* and *Sluggifhnefs*, and *wifh* at fometime *for a Man* to be given *to them*? On the contrary, *if* at any time *they have got* an active King, they condemn *the Cruelty* of him, *and* praife *the Clemency* of the former; *either* becaufe *it always* repents *us* of the prefent, *or* becaufe *it is* a true Saying, that new things *are* better *then* old.

FABLE

FABLE XIII.

De COLUMBIS *&* MILVO.

COlumbæ olim gef-
sêre *Bellum* cum *Mil-
vo;* quem ut expug-
narent, *delegerunt* fibi
Accipitrem Regem. *Ille* factus *Rex,* agit *Hoftem,* non
Regem : rapit ac laniat
non fegniùs, ac Milvus. *Pæ-
nitet* Columbas *Incœp-
ti,* putantes, *fuiffe*
fatius *pati* Bellum *Mil-
vi,* quàm *Tyrannidem*
Accipitris.

MOR.

Pigeat *Neminem* fuæ
Conditionis nimiùm. *Ut*
Horatius *ait,* Nihil *eft* bea-
tum *ab* omni *Parte.*
Equidem *non optarem* mu-
tare *meam* Sortem, *modò* fit
tolerabilis. Multi, cùm quæ-
fiverint *novam* Sortem,
rurfus optaverunt *veterem.*
Sumus *ferè* omnes *ita* vario
Ingenio, ut *pœniteat*
Nofmet *noftri.*

Of the PIGEONS *and the* KITE.

THE Pigeons *formerly* carried on *a War* with *the
Kite,* whom *that* they might fub-
due, *they chofe* to themfelves
the Hawk King. *He* being
made *King,* acts *the Enemy,* not
the King : he tears *and* butchers
no flower, *than* the Kite. *It repents* the Pigeons *of their Undertaking,* thinking, *that it had been*
better *to endure* the War *of*
the Kite, than *the Tyranny*
of the Hawk.

MOR.

Let it repent *so Man* of his
Condition too much. *As*
Horace *fays,* Nothing *is* happy *from* every *Part.*
Truly *I would not wifh* to
change *my* Lot, *provided* it be
tolerable. Many, *when* they have
fought *a new* State,
again have wifhed for *the old.*
We are *almoft* all *of fo* various
a Temper, that *it repenteth*
Us ourfelves *of ourfelves.*

FABLE XIV.

De FURE *&* CANE.

CANIS *refpondit* Furi
porrigenti Panem *ut*
fileat, *Novi* tuas
Infidias, das *Panem,*
quò *definam* latrare, *fed*
odi *tuum* Munus ; *quippe* fi
ego tulero Panem, tu
exportabis cuncta
ex his *Tectis.*

Of the THIEF *and the* DOG.

THE Dog *anfwered* the Thief
holding out Bread *that*
he would be filent, *I know* thy
Treacheries, thou giveft *Bread,*
that *I may ceafe* to bark, *but*
I hate *thy* Gift ; *for* if
I fhall take *the Bread,* thou
wilt carry all the Things
out of thefe *Houfes.*

MOR.

C

MOR.

Mor.

Cave, *Causa* parvi *Commodi*, amittas *magnum.* Cave, *habeas* Fidem *cuivis* Homini; *non* funt *qui* non *tantum* dicunt *be-nignè*, fed & faciunt *be-nignè*, Dolo.

Mor.

Take heed, *for the Sake* of a fmall *Profit*, thou lofeft not *a great one.* Take heed, *that thou baft not* Faith *in every* Man; *for* there are *who* not *only* fay *kind-ly*, but *alfo* do *kind-ly*, with Deceit.

FABLE XV.

De Lupo & Sucula.

SUCULA *parturiebat*; Lupus *pollicetur*, Se fore Cuftodem *Fœtûs.* Secula *refpondit*, Se non egere Obfequio *Lupi*; fi, *Ille* velit haberi pius, *fi* cupiat *facere* id, quod eft *gratum*, abeat *longiùs*: Etenim *officium* Lupi *conftare* non *Præfen-tiâ*, fed *Abfentiâ.*

Of the Wolf and the Sow.

THE Sow *brought forth:* the Wolf *promifes*, that he *would be* the Keeper *of the Young.* The Sow *anfwered*, That fhe *did not want* the Service *of the Wolf;* if He is willing *to be accounted* affectionate, *if* he defires *to do that*, *which* is *grateful*, let him go *farther off:* For that *the Office* of the Wolf *confifted* not *in his Pre-fence*, but *Abfence.*

Mor.

Omnia *non funt* creden-da *Omnibus.* Multi *pollicen-tur* fuam *Operam*, non *Amore* tui, *fed* fui; *non* quærentes *tuum* Commo-dum, *fed* fuum.

Mor.

All things *are not* to be truft-ed *to all* Men. Many *pro-mife* their *Service*, not *out of Love* of you, *but* of themfelves; *not* feeking *thine* Advan-tage, *but* their own.

FABLE XVI.

De Partu *Montium.*

OLim *erat* Rumor, quòd Montes *parturi-rent.* Homines *accurrunt*, circumfiftunt, *expectantes* Quippiam *Monftri*, non *fine*

Of the Bringing forth of the Mountains.

FOrmerly *there was a* Rumour, *that* the Mountains *would bring forth.* The Men *run thither*, ftand round about, *expecting* fomething *of* a *Monfter*, not *without*

fine Pavore. *Tandem* Montes *parturiunt.* Mus *cum Omnes* ridebant.

without Fear. *At length* the Mountains *bring forth.* A Mouse *comes out,* then *All* laughed.

Mor.

Jactatores, cùm profitentur & oftentant *magna,* vix *faciunt* parva. *Quapropter* ifti *Thrafones* funt *Jure* Materia *Joci* & Scommatum. Hæc *Fabula* item *vetat* inanes *Timores.* Nam plerumquè Timor *Periculi* eft gravior *Periculo ipfo ;* imò *id, quod* metuimus, eft *fæpe* ridiculum.

Mor.

Braggers, *when* they profefs *and* boaft *great things,* fcarce *do* little things. *Wherefore* thofe *Thrafos* are *by Right* the Matter of *Jeft* and *Scoffs.* This *Fable* alfo *forbids* vain *Fears.* For commonly the Fear *of Danger* is *more grievous* than the Danger *itfelf ;* nay *that,* which *we fear,* is *often* ridiculous.

FABLE XVII.

De Leporibus &
Ranis.

Of the Hares *and.* the Frogs.

SYlvâ *mugiente* infolito *Turbine,* trepidi *Lepores* occiuunt *rapidè* fugere. *Cùm* Palus *obfifteret* fugientibus, *ftetère* anxii, comprehenfi Periculis *utrinque.* Quodque *effet* Incitamentum *majoris* Timoris, *vident* Ranas *mergi* in *Palude.* Tunc unus ex *Leporibus* prudentior *ac* difertior *cæteris* inquit, *Quid* inaniter *timemus ?* Eft *Opus* Animo *quidem :* Eft *Nobis* Agilitas Corporis, fed *Animus* deeft. Hoc Periculum *Turbinis* non eft *fugiendum,* fed contemnendum.

THE Wood *roaring* with an unufual *Whirlwind,* the trembling *Hares* begin *haftily* to fly away. *When* a Fen *ftopped them* flying, *they ftood* anxious, encompaffed with Dangers on *both fides.* And *what was* an Incitement *of greater* Fear, *they perceive* the Frogs *to be plunged in the Fen.* Then one of *the Hares* more prudent *and* more eloquent *than the reft* faid, *What* vainly *do we fear ?* There is *Need* of Courage indeed : There is *to us* Agility *of Body,* but *Courage* is wanting. *This* Danger *of the Whirlwind* is not *to be fled from,* but contemned.

Mor,

Mor.

Est *Opus* Animo in omni *Re.* Virtus *jacet* sine *Confidentiâ.* Nam *Confidentia* est *Dux* & *Regina* Virtutis.

Mor.

There is *Need* of Courage in every *Thing.* Virtue *lies dead* without *Confidence.* For *Daringness* is *the Leader* and *Queen* of Virtue.

FABLE XVIII.

De Hædo & Lupo.

CAPRA, *cùm* esset *itura* pastum, *concludit* Hædum Domi, monens *aperire* Nemini, *dum* ipsa *redeat.* Lupus, *Qui* audiverat *id* procul, *post* Discessum Matris, pulsat *Fores,* capiissat *Voce,* jubens *recludi.* Hædus *præsentiens* Dolum *inquit,* Non *aperio;* nam *etsi* Vox *caprissat,* tamen *equidem* video *Lupum* per *Rimas.*

Of the Kid and the Wolf.

THE Goat, *when* she was *about to go to* feed, *shuts up* the Kid *at Home,* warning her *to open* to Nobody, *till* she return. The Wolf, *Who* had heard *that* afar off, *after* the Departure *of the Mother,* knocks at *the Doors,* acts the Goat *in Voice,* ordering them *to be opened.* The Kid *perceiving* the Cheat *says,* I do not open; for altho' the Voice *acts the Goat,* yet indeed I see a *Wolf* thro' *the Chinks.*

Mor.

Filii, *obedite* Parentibus, nam est *utile;* & decet Juvenem *auscultare* Seni.

Mor.

Children, *obey* your Parents, for it is *profitable;* and *it becometh* a Young Man *to hearken* to an Old Man.

FABLE

FABLE XIX.

De RUSTICO & ANGUE.

Of the COUNTRYMAN and the SNAKE.

QUIDAM *Rußicus* nutriverat *Anguem*; aliquando *iratus* petit *Beßiam* Secùri. *Ille* evadit, *non* fine *Vulnere.* Poßea *Rußicus* deveniens *in* Paupertatem *ratus eß* id *Infortuñii* accidere *Sibi* propter *Injuriam* Anguis. *Igitur* fupplicat, *ut* re-deat. *Illa* ait, *Se* ignof-cere, *fed* nolle *redire*; neque *fore* fecurum *cum* Ruftico, *cùm* fit *tanta* Securis *Domi*; Dolorem *vulneris* defiiffe, *tamen* Memoriam *fupereffe.*

A CERTAIN *Countryman* had nourifhed *a Snake*; on a time *being angry* He ftrikes *the Beaß* with an Ax. *He* efcapes, *not* without *a Wound.* Afterwards *the Countryman* coming *into* Poverty *thought* that *Misfortune* happened *to him* for *the Injury* of the Snake. *Therefore* he entreats, *that* He would return. *He* fays, *that* he for-gave, *but* was unwilling *to return;* nor *could he be* fecure *with* the Countryman, *when* there is *fo great* an Ax *at Home;* that the Pain *of the Wound* was worn away, *yet* the Memory remained.

MOR.

Eft *vix* tutum *habere* Fidem *Ei*, Qui *femel* folvit *Fidem.* Condonare *Injuriam,* id *fanè* eft *Mifericordiæ;* fed *cavere* fibi, & decet, & eft *Pru-dentiæ.*

MOR.

It is *fcarce* fafe *to have* Faith *in Him*, Who *once* has broke Faith. To forgive *an Injury,* that *indeed* is *the Part of Mercy;* but *to take heed* of One's felf, *both* becometh, *and* is *the Part of* Prudence.

FABLE XX.

De VULPECULA & CICONIA.

Of the Fox and the STORK.

VUlpecula *vocavit* Ciconiam *ad* Cœnam. *Effundit* Opfonium *in* Menfam, *Quod;* cùm *effet* liquidum,

THE Fox *called* the Stork *to* Supper. *She* pours out the Victuals *upon* the Table, *which*, when *it was* liquid,

liquidum, *Ciconiâ* tentante *Roſtro* fruſtrâ, *Vulpecula* lingit. *Eluſa* Avis *abit,* pudetque, *pigetque* Injuriæ. *Poſt* pluſculum *Dierum* redit, *invitat* Vulpeculam. *Vitreum* Vas erat ſitum *plenum* Opſonii ; *quod* Vas, *cùm* eſſet *arĉti* Gutturis, *licuit* Vulpeculæ *videre,* &*eſurire,* non *guſtare.* Ciconia *facilè* exhauſit *Roſtro.*

liquid, *the Stork* endeavouring *with her Bill* in vain, *the Fox* licks up. *The deluded* Bird *goes away,* and is aſhamed, *and vexed* at the Injury. *After* ſome *Days* ſhe returns, *invites* the Fox. *A Glaſs* Veſſel *was* placed *full* of Viĉtuals ; *which* Veſſel, *when* it was *of a narrow* Neck, *it was lawful* for the Fox *to ſee,* and *hunger,* not *to taſte.* The Stork *eaſily* drew it out *with her Beak.*

MOR.

Riſus *meretur* Riſum ; *Jocus* Jocum ; *Dolus* Dolum ; *&* Fraus *Fraudem.*

Laughter *deſerves* Laughter ; a *Jeſt* a Jeſt ; a Trick a Trick ; *and* Deceit *Deceit.*

FABLE XXI.

De Luro *&* piĉto *Capite.*

Of the Wolf *and* the painted *Head.*

LUPUS *verſat,* & *miratur* humanum *Caput* repertum *in* Officinâ *Sculptoris,* ſentiens *habere* nihil *Senſûs,* inquit, O pulchrum *Caput,* eſt in Te *multum* Artis, *ſed* Nihil *Senſûs.*

THE Wolf *turns about,* and *admires* a human *Head* found *in* the Shop *of a Carver,* perceiving it *to have* nothing *of Senſe,* he ſays, O fair *Head,* there is in Thee *much* of Art, *but* Nothing *of Senſe.*

MOR.

Externa *Pulchritudo,* ſi *interna* adſit, *eſt* grata ; *ſin* carendum eſt *alterutrâ,* præſtat *carere* externâ, quàm internâ : *nam* illa *ſine* hâc *interdum* incurrit *Odium,* ut *Stolidus* ſit eò odio-

Outward *Beauty,* if *the inward* be preſent, *is* pleaſing ; *but if* we muſt want *either,* it is better *to want* the outward, *than* the inward ; *for* that *without* this *ſometimes* incurs *Hatred,* that a *Fool* is *by ſo much* the

odiofior,   *quò* the more odious; *by how much*
formofior.   the more handfome.

FABLE XXII.

De GRACULO.   *Of* the JACKDAW.

GRACULUS *ornavit Se Plumis* Pavonis; *deinde* visus *pulchellus* Sibi *contulit* Se *ad* Genus [1] *Pavonum*, *fuo Genere* faftidito. *Illi* tandem *intelligentes* Fraudem, *nudabant* ftolidam *Avem* Coloribus, & affecerunt *cum* Plagis.

THE JACKDAW *adorned* Himfelf *with the Feathers* of the Peacock ; *then* feeming *pretty* to Himfelf *he betook* Himfelf *to* the Race *of the* Peacocks, his own *Race* being defpifed. *They* at length *underftanding* the Cheat, *ftripped* the foolifh *Bird* of his Colours, *and* belaboured him *with* blows.

MOR.   MOR.

Hæc *Fabula* notat *eos*, qui *gerunt* fe *fublimiùs*, quàm *eft* æqunm ; *qui* vivunt *cum* iis, *qui* funt & ditiores, & *magis nobiles ;* quare *fape* fiunt *inopes*, & *funt* Ludibrio.

This *Fable* denotes *thofe*, who carry themfelves *more loftily*, than is fit ; *who* live *with* thofe, *who* are *both* more rich, *and* more *noble ;* wherefore *often* they become *poor*, and are for a Laughing-ftock.

FABLE XXIII.

De RANA & BOVE.   *Of* the FROG *and* the Ox.

RAna *cupida* æquandi *Bovem* diftentabat *fe.* Filius *hortabatur* Matrem *defiftere* Cæpto, *inquiens*, Ranam *effe* nihil *ad* Bovem. *Illa* intumuit *fecundùm.* Natus *clamitat.* Ma-

A Frog *defirous* of equalling an Ox ftretched *herfelf.* The Son *advifed* the Mother *to defift* from the Undertaking, *faying*, that a Frog *was* nothing *to* an Ox. *She* fwelled a *fecond* time. The Son cries *out*, Mo-

Mater, *licèt* crepes, *nun-quam* vinces *Bovem.* Autem, *eùm* intumuiſſet *tertiùm,* erepuit.

Mother, *altho'* you burſt, *never* will you exceed *the Ox.* But, *when* ſhe had ſwelled *a third time,* ſhe burſt.

Mor.

Mor.

Quiſque *habet* ſuam' *Dotem.* Hic *excellit* Formâ, *Ille* Viribus. *Hic* pollet *Opibus,* Ille *Amicis.* Decet *Unumquemq;* eſſe *contentum* ſuo. *Ille* valet *Corpore,* Tu *Ingenio:* Quocirca *Quiſque* conſulat *Semet,* nec *invideat* Superiori, *Quod* eſt *miſerum ;* nec *optet* certare, *Quod* eſt *Stultitiæ.*

Every one *has* his *Gift.* This Man *excels* in Beauty, *That* in Strength. *This* is powerful *in Riches,* That *in Friends.* It becometh *Every one* to be *content* with his own. *He* is ſtrong *in Body,* Thou *in Wit:* Wherefore *let Every one* conſult *Himſelf,* nor *envy* a Superior, *Which* is *a miſerable thing ;* nor *wiſh* to contend, *Which* is *the Part of Folly.*

FABLE XXIV.

De Æquo & Leone.

Of the Horse and the Lion.

LEO *venit* ad *comedendum* Equum ; *autem* carens *Viribus* præ *Senectâ,* cœpit *meditari* Artem : *profitetur* Se *Medicum :* moratur Equum Ambage *Verborum.* Hic *opponit* Dolum *Dolo ;* fingit, *Se* nuper *pupugiſſe* Pedem *in* ſpinoſo *Loco ;* orat, *ut* Medicus *inſpiciens* educat *Sentem.* Leo *paret.* At *Equus,* quantâ *Vi* potuit, *impingit* Calcem *Leoni,* & *continuò* conjicit *Se* in *Pedes.* Leo *vix* tandem *rediens* ad *Se,* nam

THE Lion *cometh* to *eat* the Horſe ; *but* wanting *Strength* thro' *old Age,* he began *to meditate* an Art : *He profeſſes* Himſelf *a Phyſician :* He ſtays *the Horſe* with a Circuit *of Words.* He *oppoſes* Deceit *to Deceit :* He feigns, *that he* lately *had pricked* his Foot *in* a thorny *Place ;* He prays, *that* the Phyſician *looking into it* would draw out *the Thorn.* The Lion *obeys.* But *the Horſe,* with how great *Force* he could, *ſtrikes* his Heel *upon the Lion,* and *immediately* betakes *Himſelf* to *his Heels.* The Lion *ſcarce* at length *returning* to *Himſelf,* for

ham *fuerat* propè *txanimatus* Ictu, *inquit*, fero *Pretium* ob *Stultitiam*, & *is* meritò *effugit;* nam *ultus* *eſt* Dolum *Dolo.*

for *he had been* almoſt dead with the Blow, *ſays,* I bear *a Reward* for *my Folly,* and *he* deſervedly *has fled away ;* for *he has revenged* Deceit *with Deceit.*

Mor.

Simulatio *eſt* digna *Odio,* & *capienda* Simulatione. *Apertus* Hoſtis *non eſt* timendus ; *ſed* qui *ſimulat* Benevolentiam, *cùm* ſit *Hoſtis,* is *quidem* eſt *timendus,* & *eſt* digniſſimus *Odio.*

Mor.

Diſſimulation *is* worthy *of Hatred,* and *to be taken with* Diſſimulation. *An open* Enemy *is not* to be feared ; *but* he who *pretends* Benevolence, *when* he is *an Enemy,* he *indeed* is *to be feared,* and *is* moſt worthy *of Hatred.*

FABLE XXV.

De Avibus & Quadrupedibus.

Of the Birds *and* the four-footed Beaſts.

ERAT *Pugna* Avibus cum Quadrupedibus. *Erat* utrinque *Spes,* utrinque *Metus,* untrinque *Periculum:* autem *Veſpertilio* relinquens *Socios,* deficit *ad* Hoſtes. *Aves* vincunt, *Aquilâ* Duce & Auſpice ; *verò* damnant *Transfugam* Veſpertilionem, *uti* nunquam *redeat* ad *Aves,* uti *nunquam* volet *Luce.* Hæc *eſt* Cauſa *Veſpertilioni,* ut *non volet,* niſi *Noctu.*

THere was *a Battle* to the Birds with the four-footed Beaſts. *There was* on both ſides *Hope,* on both ſides *Fear,* on both ſides *Danger :* but the *Bat* leaving *his Companions,* revolts *to* the Enemies. *The Birds* overcome, *the Eagle* being Captain and Leader ; *but* they condemn *the Runaway* Bat, *that* he never *return* to *the Birds,* that *he never* fly *in the Light.* This *is* a Reaſon *for the Bat,* that *he fly not,* unleſs *in the Night.*

Mor.

Qui *renuit* eſſe *Particeps* Adverſitatis & Periculi *cum*

Mor.

He that *refuſes* to be *Partaker* of Adverſity *and* Danger *with*

cum	Sociis,	erit	with his Companions, *shall be*
expers	*Prosperitatis*,	destitute	of their Prosperity,
& *Salutis*.		and Safety.	

FABLE XXVI.

| *De* Sylva *&* Rus- | *Of* the Wood *and the* Coun- |
| TICO. | TRYMAN. |

QUO *Tempore* erat *Sermo* etiam *Arboribus*, Rusticus *venit* in *Sylvam*, rogat, *ut* liceat *tollere* Capulum *ad suam* Securim. Sylva annuit. Rusticus, Securi aptatâ, *cœpit* succidere *Arbores.* Tum, *&* quidem *serò* pœnituit Sylvam suæ *Facilitatis*, doluit *esse* Seipsam Causam sui *Exitii*.

AT what *Time* there was a *Speech* even *to Trees*, a Countryman *came* into *the Wood*, asks, *that* it may be lawful *to take* a Handle *to* his *Ax.* The Wood *consents.* The Countryman, *the Ax* being fitted, *began* to cut down *the Trees.* Then, and indeed *too late* it repented *the Wood* of her *Easiness*, it grieved her *to be* Herself the *Cause* of her own *Destruction.*

Mor.

Vide, *de* Quo *merearis* benè : *fuére* multi, *Qui* abusi sunt *Beneficio* accepto *in* Perniciem *Autoris*.

Mor.

See, *of* whom *thou mayest deserve* well : *there have been* many, *Who* have abused *a Benefit* received *to the* Destruction *of the Author.*

FABLE XXVII.

| *De* Lupo *&* Vulpe. | *Of* the Wolf *and the* Fox. |

LUPUS, *cùm* esset *satìs* Prædæ, *degebat* in *Otio*. Vulpecula *accedit*, sciscitatur Causam Otii. Lupus sensit, *fieri* Insidias, *simulat* Morbum

THE Wolf, *when* there was enough of Prey, *lived* in *Idleness.* The Fox *comes* to him, demands *the Cause* of his Idleness. *The Wolf* perceived, *there were* Treacheries, *pretends* a Disease

bum *effe* Caufam, *orat* cafe *to be* the Caufe, *prays*
Vulpeculam *ire* precatum the Fox *to go* to pray *the*
Deos. Illa *dolens,* Dolum Gods. She *grieving,* that the Trick
non fuccedere, adit *Paftorem,* *did not fucceed,* goes to *the Shepherd,*
monet, *Latebras* advifes him, *that the Den*
Lupi *patere,* & *Ho-* of the Wolf *lay open,* and *the Ene-*
ftem fecurum *poffe* opprimi *my* being fecure *could be* deftroyed
inopinatò. Paftor *adori-* unawares. The Shepherd *rifes*
tur Lupum, *mactat.* Vul- upon the Wolf, *flays him.* The
pes *potitur* Antro & Prædâ ; Fox *obtains* the Den and the Prey ;
fed breve *fuit* Gaudium but fhort *was* the Joy
fui fceleris *illi* ; nam *paulò* of her Villainy *to her ;* for *a little*
pòft *idem* Paftor *capit* after *the fame* Shepherd *takes*
ipfam. her.

MOR.

Invidia eft *fæda* Res, &
interdum *perniciofa* quoque
Authori ipfi.

MOR.

Envy is *a foul* Thing, *and*
fometimes *pernicious* alfo
to the Author himfelf.

FABLE XXVIII.

De VIPERA & LIMA.

VIpera *offendens* Limam
in Fabricâ *cæpit*
rodere : *Lima* fubrifit, *in-*
quiens, Inepta, *Quid* agis ?
Tu contriveris *tuos*
Dentes *antequam* atteras
Me, Quæ *foleo* præmordere
Duritiem Æris.

Of the VIPER *and the* FILE.

A VIPER *finding* a File
in a Smith's Shop, *began*
to gnaw it : *The File* fmiled, *fay-*
ing, Fool, *What* doft thou do ?
Thou wilt have worn out *thy*
Teeth *before* thou weareft out
Me, who *am wont* to gnaw off
the *Hardnefs* of Brafs.

MOR.

Vide etiam atq; *etiam*
Quicum *habeas* Rem ;
Si acuas *Dentes*
in *fortiorem,* non nocu-
eris *illi,* fed *tibi.*

MOR.

See *again* and *again*
with whom *thou haft* an Affair ;
if thou whetteft *thy Teeth*
againft *a ftronger Man,* thou wilt
not have hurt *him,* but *thyfelf.*

FABLE

FABLE XXIX.

De Cervo.

CErvus, *conspicatus* se in perspicuo *Fonte*, probat *procera* & *ramosa* Cornua, *sed* damnat *Exilitatem* Tibiarum : *fortè* dum *contemplatur*, dum *judicat*, Venator *intervenit :* Cervus *fugit.* Canes *insectantur* fugientem ; *sed* cùm *intravisset* densam *Sylvam*, Cornua erant implicita *Ramis.* Tum *demum* laudabat *Tibias*, & *damnabat* Cornua, *Quæ* fecêre, *ut* esset *Præda* Canibus.

Of the STAG.

A Stag, *having beheld* himself in a clear *Fountain*, approves *his lofty* and *branched* Horns, *but* condemns *the Smallness* of his Legs. *By Chance*, whilst *he looks*, whilst *he judges*, the Huntsman *passes by* ; the Stag *flies away.* The Dogs *pursue* him flying ; *but* when he had *entered* a thick *Wood*, his Horns *were* entangled *in the Boughs.* Then *at last* he praised *his Legs*, and *condemned* his Horns, *which* made, *that* he was *a Prey* to the Dogs.

MOR.

Petimus *fugienda*, fugimus *petenda* ; Quæ *officiunt* placent. *Quæ* conferunt *displicent.* Cupimus *Beatitudinem*, priusquam *intelligamus*, ubi *sit :* Quærimus *Excellentiam* Opum, & Celsitudinem *Honorum* ; opinamur *Beatitudinem* sitam *in his*, in quibus *est* tam *multum* Laboris, & Doloris.

MOR.

We desire *Things to be shunned*, we fly *Things to be desired* ; what *hurt* please. *What* profit *displease.* We desire *Happiness*, before that *we understand*, where *it is ;* We seek *the Excellency* of Riches, and the Loftiness *of Honours ;* we think *Happiness* placed in these, *in which there is* so *much* of Labour, and Pain.

FABLE XXX.

De LUPIS & AGNIS.

A Liquando *fuit* Fœdus *inter* Lupos & Agnos, *Quibus* est *Discordia*

Of the WOLVES and the LAMBS.

O N a Time *there was* a League *between* the Wolves and the Lambs, *to whom* there is a *Discord*

Difcordia Naturâ. *Obfi-dibus* datis *utrinque,* Lupi *dedère* fuos *Catulos,* Ov*es* Cohortem Canum. *Ovibus* quietis & pafcentibus, *Lupuli* Defiderio *Matrum* edunt *Ululatus*: Tum *Lupi* irruentes *clamitant,* Fidem, *Fædufque* folutum, *laniantque* Oves *deftitutas* Præfidio *Canum.*

a *Difcord* by Nature. *Hofta-ges* being given *on both Sides,* the Wolves *gave* their *Whelps,* the Sheep *their Troop* of Dogs. *The Sheep* being quiet *and* feeding, *the little Wolves* by the Defire *of their Dams* fend forth *Howlings :* Then *the Wolves* rufhing on them *cry out,* that their Faith, *and League* was broken, *and butcher* the Sheep *deftitute* of their Guard *of Dogs.*

MOR.

MOR.

Eft *Infcitia,* fi *in* Fœdere *tradas* tua *Præfidia* Hofti ; *nam* qui *fuit* Hoftis, *forfan* nondum *defivit* effe *Hoftis* ; & *for-taffis* ceperit *Caufam,* cur *adoriatur* te *nudatum* tuo *Præfidio.*

It is *Folly,* if *in* a League thou - *delivereft* thy *Guards* to an Enemy ; *for* he who *has been* an Enemy, *perhaps* not yet has ceafed to be an *Enemy ;* and *perhaps* will take *Occafion,* why he may rife upon thee *ftript of* thy Guard.

FABLE XXXI.

De MEMBRIS & VENTRE.

Of the MEMBERS *and* the BELLY.

OLim *Pedes* & *Manus* incufabant *Ventrem,* quòd *Lucra* ipforum *vorarentur* ab *Eo* otiofo. *Jubent,* aut *laboret,* aut *ne putet* ali. *Ille* fupplicat *femel* atq; *iterum* ; tamen *Manus* negant *Alimentum* ; Ventre *exhaufto* Inediâ, *ubi* omnes *Artus* cœpêre *deficere* ; tum *tandem,* Manus *voluerunt* effe *offici-ofe,* verùm *id* ferò ; *nam* Venter

FOrmerly *the Feet* and *Hands* accufed *the Belly,* that *the Gains* of them were devoured by *him* being idle. *They* command, or *let him labour,* or *not think* to be maintained. *He* intreats *once* and *again* ; yet *the* Hands deny *Suftenance* ; the Belly *being exhaufted* with Want, *when* all *the Limbs* began *to fail ;* then *at laft* the Hands *were willing* to be *officious,* but *that* too late ; *for* the Belly

Venter *debilis* Defuetudine renuit Cibum. *Ita* cuncti *Artus*, dum *invident* Ventri, *pereunt* cum *pereunte* Ventre.

the Belly *weak* by Difufe *refufed* Meat. *Thus* all *the Limbs*, whilft *they* envy the Belly, *perifh* with *the perifhing* Belly.

Mor.

Societas *Membrorum* non differt *ab* humanâ *Societate*. Membrum *eget* Membro, *Amicus* Amico ; *quare* utamur *mutuis* Officiis, *mutuis* Operibus ; *nam* neq; *Divitiæ*, neque *Dignitates* tuentur *Hominem* fatìs. *Unicum* & *fummum* Præfidium *eft* Amicitia *Complurium*.

Mor.

The Society *of the Members* does not differ *from* human *Society*. A Member *wants* a Member, *a Friend* a Friend ; *wherefore* let us ufe *mutual* Offices, *mutual* Works ; *for* neither *Riches*, nor *Dignities* defend *a Man* enough. *The only* and *chief* Safeguard *is* the Friendfhip *of Many*.

FABLE XXXII.

De Simia *&* Vulpecula.

Of the Ape *and* the Fox.

SImia *orat* Vulpeculam, *ut* daret *Partem* Caudæ *fibi* ad *tegendas* Nates ; *nam* effet *Oneri* Illi, *Quod* foret *Ufui* & *Honori* Illi. *Illa* refpondet, *effe* Nihil *nimis*, & *Se* malle Humum verri *fuâ* Caudâ, *quàm* Nates Simiæ tegi.

THE Ape *prays* the Fox, *that* fhe would give *Part* of her Tail *to Her* to *cover* her Buttocks ; *for* that was *a Burden* to Her, *Which* would be *an Ufe* and *Honour* to Her. She anfwers, *that it was* Nothing *too much*, and *that fhe* had rather *that the Ground* fhould be brufhed *with her* Tail, *than that* the Buttocks *of the Ape* be covered.

Mor.

Sunt, *qui* egent ; *funt*, quibus *fupereft* ; tamen id eft *Moris* Nulli *Divitum*, ut *beet* Egenos *fuperfluâ* Re.

Mor.

There are, *who* want ; *there are*, to whom *there is overmuch* ; yet' that is *of a Cuftom* to no One *of the Rich*, that *he blefs* the Needy *with his fuperfluous* Store.

FABLE

FABLE XXXIII.

De Vulpecula & Muſſeła.   *Of* the Fox *and* the Weaſel.

VUlpecula *tenuis* longâ *Inediâ* fortè *repſit* per *anguſtam* Rimam *in* Cameram *Frumenti,* in *quâ* cùm *fuit* probè *paſta,* deinde *Venter* diſtentus *impedit* tentantem *egredi* rurſus. *Muſtela* procul *contemplata* luſtantem, *tandem* monet, *ſi* cupiat *exire,* redeat *ad* Cavum *macra,* quo *intraverat* macra.

THE Fox *ſlender* by long *Want* by chance *crept* through *a narrow* Chink *into* a Heap *of Corn,* in *which* when *ſhe was* well *fed,* then her *Belly* being ſtretched *hindered* her trying *to go out* again. *A Weaſel* afar off *having ſeen her* ſtriving, *at length* adviſes, *if* ſhe deſires *to go out,* ſhe would return *to* the Hole *lean,* at which *ſhe had entered* lean.

Mor.

Videas *complures* lætos *atque* alacres *in* Mediocritate, *vacuos* Curis, *expertos* Moleſtiis *Animi.* Sin *Illi* fuerint *faſti* divites, *videbis* eos *incedere* mœſtos ; *nunquam* porrigere *Frontem,* plenos *Curis,* obrutos *Moleſtiis* Animi.

Mor.

You may ſee *many* merry *and* chearful *in* Mediocrity, *void* of Cares, *free* from Troubles *of Mind.* But if *They* ſhall be *made* rich, *you ſhall* ſee them *go* ſad ; *never* to ſmooth *their Forehead,* full *of Cares,* overwhelmed *with Troubles* of Mind.

FABLE XXXIV.

De Equo & Cervo.   *Of* the Horse *and* the Stag.

EQuus *gerebat* Bellum *cum* Cervo ; *tandem* pulſus *è* Paſcuis *implorabat* humanam *Opem.* Redit *cum* Homine, *deſcendit* in *Campum,* viſtus *antea* jam *fit* Victor ; *ſed*

THE Horſe *carried on* War *with* the Stag ; *at length* being driven *out of* the Paſtures *He implored* human *Help.* He returns *with* a Man, *He deſcends* into *the Field,* he conquered *before* now *becomes* Conqueror ; *but*

sed tamen Hoste victo, & misso sub Jugum, est necesse, ut Victor ipse serviat Homini. Fert Equitem Dorso, Frænum Ore.

but yet *the Enemy* being conquered, and sent *under* the Yoke, *it is necessary, that* the Victor *himself* serve *the* Man. He bears *the Horseman* on his Back, *the Bridle* in his Mouth.

Mor.

Multi *dimicant* contra Paupertatem ; quâ *victâ* per *Industriam* & *Fortunam*, Libertas *Victoris* sæpe *interit* ; quippe Domini & *Victores* Paupertatis *incipiunt* servire *Divitiis* ; anguntur *Flagris* Avaritiæ, cohibentur Frænis Parcimoniæ ; nec *tenent* Modum *querendi*, nec *audent* uti *Rebus* partis, *justo* supplicio *quidem* Avaritiæ.

Mor.

Many *fight* against Poverty ; which *being overcome* by *Industry* and *Fortune*, the Liberty *of the Victor* often *perisheth* ; for *the* Lords and Conquerors of Poverty begin to serve *Riches* ; they are tormented *with the Whips* of Avarice, *they are restrained* with the Bridles *of Parsimony* ; nor *do they* hold a Mean *of getting*, nor *do they dare* to use *the Things* got, *a just* Punishment *indeed* of Covetousness.

FABLE XXXV.

De Duobus *Adolescentibus.*

Of Two *Young Men.*

DUO *Adolescentes* simulant, *sese* empturos *Carnem* apud *Coquum :* Coquo *agente* alias *Res*, Alter *arripit* Carnem è Canistro, dat Socio, *ut* occultet *sub* Veste. *Coquus,* ut *vidit* Partem *Carnis* subreptam *sibi*, cœpit *insimulare utrumq; Furti.* Qui *abstulerat*, pejerat *per* Jovem, *se* habere *Nihil* ; verò

TWO young Men pretend, *that they* would buy *Flesh* at a *Cook's :* The Cook *doing* other *Things*, One *snatches* Flesh *out of* a Basket, *gives it* to his Companion, *that he* may hide it *under* his Garment. *The Cook,* as soon as he *saw* Part *of the* Flesh stolen *from him*, began *to* accuse each *of Theft.* He that *had taken it away*, swears *by* Jove, *that* he had *Nothing* ; but

vero is, qui *habuit,* pejerat identidem, se *abstulif-se* Nihil. *Ad* Quos Coquus inquit, *quidem* nunc Fur latet, *sed* is, *per* quem *juraviftis,* infpexit, is fcit.

but *he,* who had *it,* fwears *again and again,* that he *had taken away* Nothing. *To* whom the *Cock* fays, *indeed* now the *Thief* lies hid, *but* he, *by* whom *you have fwore,* looked on, he knows.

MOR.

MOR.

Cùm *peccavimus,* Homines *non fciunt* id *ftatim;* at Deus videt omnia, qui *fedet* fuper *Cælos,* & *intuetur* Abyfios.

When *we have finned,* Men do not *know* it *prefently;* but God fees *all things,* who *fitteth* upon the *Heavens,* and looks into the Deeps.

FABLE XXXVI.

De CANE & LANIO.

Of the DOG *and* the BUTCHER.

CUM *Canis* abftuliffet Carnem Lanio *in* Macello, *continuò* conjecit *fefe* in *Pedes* quantum *potuit.* Lanius *perculfus* Jacturâ *Rei,* primùm *tacuit,* deinde *recipiens* Animum, *fic* acclamavit procul, O furaciffime, curre tutus, *licet* tibi *currere* impunè; *nam* nunc *es* tutus ob Celeritatem, autem pofthac *obferva-beris* cautiùs.

WHen *the Dog* had taken away *Flefh* from the Butcher *in* the Shambles, *immediately* he betook *himfelf* to *his Heels* as much as he could. The Butcher *ftruck* with the Lofs *of the Thing,* at firft held *his Peace,* afterwards *taking* Courage, *thus* he cried to him *afar off,* O moft thieving Cur, run fafe, *it is lawful* for thee *to run* unpunifhedly; *for* now thou art fafe *for* thy Swiftnefs, but hereafter *thou fhalt be obfer-ved* more cautioufly.

MOR.

MOR.

Hæc *Fabula* fignificat, *plerofque* Homines *tum* demum *fieri* cautiores, cùm acceperint *Damnum.*

This *Fable* fignifies, that *moft* Men then at length *become* more cautious, when they have received *Damage.*

E

FABLE.

FABLE XXXVII.

De AGNO & LUPO.   *Of* the LAMB *and* the WOLF.

LUpus *occurrit* Agno *comitanti* Caprum, *rogitat,* cur *Matre* relictâ, *potiùs* sequatur olidum Hircum, *suadetque,* ut *redeat* ad *Ubera* Matris *distenta* Lacte, *sperans,* fore *ita,* ut *laniet* abductum ; *verò* ille *inquit,* O *Lupe,* Mater *commisit* me huic. Huic *summa* Cura *servandi* est *data ;* obsequar *Parenti* potiùs quàm tibi, *qui* postulas *seducere* me *istis* Dictis, & mox *discerpere* subductum.

THE Wolf *meets* the Lamb *accompanying* the Goat, *he asks,* why *his Mother* being left, *he rather* follows *a stinking* Goat, *and advises,* that *he would return* to *the Dugs* of his Mother *stretched* with Milk, *hoping,* that it would be *so,* that *he may butcher* him drawn away ; *but* he *says,* O *Wolf,* my Mother *hath committed* me *to* him. To him *the chief* Care *of keeping* is *given ;* I shall obey *a Parent* rather *than* thee, *who* requirest *to seduce* me *with those* Sayings, *and* by and by *to tear me in pieces* drawn away.

MOR.   MOR.

Noli *habere* Fidem Omnibus ; nam *Multi,* dum *videntur* velle *prodesse* Aliis, *interim* consulunt Sibi.

Be unwilling *to have* Faith *in all Men ;* for *Many,* whilst *they seem* to be willing *to profit* Others, *in the mean time* consult *for Themselves.*

FABLE XXXVIII.

De Agricolâ &. Filiis.   *Of* the Husbandman *and* his Sons.

AGricola *habebat* complures *Filios,* Iique *fuêre* discordes *inter* Se, quos *Pater elaborans* trahere *ad* mutuum *Amorem,* Fasciculo ap-

AHusbandman *had* many Sons, and they *were* disagreeing *among* themselves, *whom* the Father *labouring* to draw *to* mutual *Love,* a little Faggot be-

appofito, jubet *fingulos* effringere *circumdatum* brevi *Funiculo :* Imbecilla *Ætatula* conatur *fruftrà :* Pater *folvit,* redditque *fingulis* Virgulam, *quam* cùm *pro* fuis *Viribus* quifque *facilè* frangeret ; *Inquit,* O *Filioli,* fic *Nemo* poterit *vincere* Vos *concordes ;* fed *fi* volueritis *fevire* mutuis *Vulneribus,* atque *agitare* inteftinum *Bellum,* eritis *tandem* Prædæ *Hoftibus.*

being put, commands *them* fingle to break it *bound* about with a fhort *Cord :* Their weak *Youth* endeavoureth in *vain :* The Father *loofes it,* and gives *to* each a .. *Twig,* which when *with* his *Strength* every one eafily broke ; He *faith,* O *Children,* thus *Nobody* will be able *to* conquer You *agreeing ;* but if ye fhall be willing *to* rage with mutual *Wounds,* and *to* drive on inteftine *War,* ye fhall be *at* length for a Prey *to* your Enemies.

MOR.

Hæc *Fabula* docet, *parvas* Res *crefcere* Concordiâ, *magnas* dilabi *Difcordiâ.*

MOR.

This *Fable* teaches, *that finall* Things *increafe* by Concord, *great* Things fall away *by Difcord.*

FABLE XXXIX.

De CARBONARIO & FULLONE.

Of the COLLIER *and* the FULLER.

CArbonaſius *invitabat* Fullonem, *ut* habitaret *fecum* in *eâdem* Domo. *Fullo* inquit, *mi* Homo, *iftud* non eft *mihi,* vel *Cordi,* vel *utile ;* nam *vereor* magnopere, *ne,* Quæ *eluam,* Tu *reddas* tam atra, quàm *Carbo* eft.

THE Collier *invited* the Fuller, *that* he would dwell *with* him in *the fame* Houfe. *The* Fuller faith, my Man, *that* is not *to* me, either *to* my Heart, or *profitable ;* for I fear greatly, *left* what Things *I wafh* clean, Thou *mayft* make as *black,* as *a Coal* is.

MOR.

Monemur *hoc* Apologo *ambulare* cum *in-*

MOR.

We are admonifhed *by this* Apologue *to* walk with *the*

inculpatis; monemur devitare Confortium fceleratorum Hominum, velut certam Peftem; nam quifque evadit talis, quales fi funt, quibufcum verfatur.

the unblamed; we are admonifhed to avoid the Company of wicked Men, as a certain Plague; for every one cometh out fuch, as they are, with whom he is converfant.

FABLE XL.

De AUCUPE & PALUMBO.

Of the FOWLER and the RING-DOVE.

AUceps videt Palumbum procul nidulantem in altiffimâ Arbore; adproperat; denique molitur Infidias; forte premit Anguem Calcibus; hic mordet. Ille exanimatus improvifo Malo, inquit, miferum Me! dum infidior Alteri, Ipfe difperco.

THE Fowler fees the Ring-Dove afar off making a Neft in a very high Tree; he haftens to him; finally he contrives Snares; by Chance he preffes a Snake with his Heels; he bites him. He terrified at the fudden Evil, fays, wretched Me! whilft I lay Snares for another, I myfelf perifh.

MQR.

MOR.

Hæc Fabula fignificat, Eos nonnunquam circumveniri fuis Artibus, Qui meditantur mala.

This Fable fignifies, that they fometimes are circumvented with their own Arts, who meditate evil Things.

FABLE XLI.

De AGRICOLA & CANIBUS.

Of the HUSBANDMAN and the DOGS.

AGricola, cùm hyemâffet in Ruri multos Dies, cæpit tandem laborare Penuriâ ne-

THE Hufbandman, when he had wintered in the Country many Days, began at length to labour with the Want of

neceffariarum Rerum, *inter-*
fecit Oves, *deinde* &
Capellas, poftremò *quoque*
maftat *Boves,* ut *habeat*
quo *fuftentet* Corpufculum,
penè exhauftum *Inedid.*
Canes *videntes* id *conftituunt*
quærere *Salutem* Fugâ;
etenim Sefe *non viéturos*
diutiùs, *quando* Herus *non*
pepercit Bobus *quidem,*
Quorum *Operâ* utebatur *in*
faciendo *ruftico* Opere.

of *neceffary* Things, *be kill-*
ed his Sheep, *afterwards* alfo
his Goats, laftly *alfo*
he flays *his Oxen,* that *be may have*
wherewith *he may fuftain* his Body,
almoft exhaufted *with Want.*
The Dogs *feeing* that *refolve*
to feek *Safety* by Flight;
for that they *fhould not live*
longer, *when* their Mafter *has not*
fpared his Oxen *ind ed,*
whofe *Labour* he ufed *in*
doing *his Country-*Work.

Mor.

Mor.

Si *vis* effe *falvus,*
decede *ab eo cito,* quem
vides redaftum *ad* eas
Anguftias, ut *confumat*
Inftrumenta *neceffaria* fuis
Operibus, quo *fuppleatur*
præfenti *Inedia.*

If *thou art willing* to be *fafe,*
withdraw *from* him *foon,* whom
thou feeft reduced *to* thofe
Straits, that he *confumes*
the Inftruments *neceffary* for his
Works, whereby *be may be fupplied*
for the prefent *Want.*

FABLE XLII.

De Vulpe & Leone.

Of the Fox and the Lion.

VUlpecula, *qua*
non folebat *videre*
Immanitatem *Leonis,* contemplata *id* Animal *femel*
atque *iterum* trepidabat, &
fugitabat. Cùm jam *tertiò*
Leo *obtulijfet* fefe obvi-
àm, Vulpes *non metuit*
Quicquam, *fed* confidenter
adit, & *falutat* illum.

THE Fox, *who*
was not wont *to fee*
the Fiercenefs *of the Lion,* having
viewed *that* Beaft *once*
and *again* trembled, *and*
fled. *When* now a *third Time*
the Lion *had offered* himfelf *in his*
Way, the Fox *feared not*
any Thing, *but* confidently
goes up to, and *falutes* him.

Mor.

Mor.

Consuetudo *facit* Nos omnes audaciores, *vel* apud *Eos,* Quos *vix* antea *ausi fuimus* afpicere.

Mor.

Cuftom *makes* Us all bolder, *even* among *Those,* Whom *fcarce* before *we have dared* to look upon.

FABLE XLIII.

De Vulpe *&* Aquilâ

Of the Fox *and* the Eagle.

PROLES *Vulpecula* excurrebat *foras;* comprehenfa *ab* Aquilâ implorat Fidem *Matris.* Illa accurrit, rogat *Aquilam,* ut dimittat Captivam *Prolem.* Aquila *nacta* Prædam *fubvolat ad Pullos.* Vulpes, *Face* correptâ, *quafi* effet *abfumptura* Munitionem *Incendio,* Cùm jam afcendiffet *Arborem,* inquit, *nunc* tuere *Te,* tuofque, *fi* potes. *Aquila* trepidans, *dum* metuit *Incendium,* inquit, *parce* Mihi, reddam *quicquid* habeo *tuum.*

THE Young *of the Fox* ran *abroad;* caught *by* the Eagle *fhe* implores the Help *of her Dam.* She runs up, afks *the Eagle,* that *fhe would difmifs* her Captive *Young.* The Eagle *having got* her Prey *flies away to her Young.* The Fox, *a Firebrand* being fnatched up, *as if* fhe was *about to deftroy* her Fortrefs *with Fire,* When now fhe had gotten upon *the Tree,* fays, *now* defend *Thyfelf,* and thine, *if* Thou canft. *The Eagle* trembling, *whilft* fhe fears *the Fire,* fays, *fpare* Me, I will reftore *whatfoever* I have *of thine.*

Mor.

Intellige *per* Aquilam *potentes,* atq; *audaces;* per *Vulpem* pauperculos, *Quos* Divites *fæpenumerò* opprimunt *per* Vim. *Verùm* læfi interdum probè *ulcifcuntur* Injuriam *acceptam.*

Mor.

Underftand *by* the Eagle *the potent,* and *bold;* by *the* Fox the Poor, *Whom* the Rich *oftentimes* opprefs *by* Force. *But* the Hurt fometimes foundly *revenge* the Injury *received.*

FABLE

FABLE XLIV.

De Agricolâ & | *Of* the Huſbandman *and*
Ciconiâ. | the Stork.

Gruibus *Anſeribuſque* depaſcentibus *Sata,* Ruſticus *pretendit* Laqueum. *Grues* capiuntur, *Anſeres* capiuntur, & Ciconia *capitur.* Illa *ſupplicat,* clamitans, *Seſe* innocentem, & eſſe *nec* Gruem, *nec* Anſerem, *ſed* optimam omnium Avium, *quippe* Quæ *ſemper* conſueverit *inſervire* Parenti *ſedulò,* & *alere* Eum *confeⱰum* Senio. *Agricola* inquit, *probè* ſcio omnia hæc ; *verùm* poſtquam *cepimus* Te *cum* *nocentibus,* morieris *quoque* cum *Eis.*

THE Cranes *and the Geeſe* feeding on *the Corn,* the Countryman *ſets* a Gin. *The Cranes* are taken, *the Geeſe* are taken, *and* the Stork *is taken.* She *entreats,* crying, *that She* was innocent, *and* was *neither* a Crane, nor a Gooſe, *but* the beſt of *all* Birds, *as* Who *always* uſed *to ſerve* her Father *diligently,* and *to nouriſh* Him *worn out* with old Age. *The* Huſbandman ſays, *well* know I *all* theſe Things ; *but* ſince *we have* taken Thee *with the offending,.* thou ſhalt die *alſo* with *Them.*

Mor.

Qui *committit* Crimen, .& Is, *Qui* adjungit *Se* Socium *Sceleratis,* plectuntur *pari* Pœnâ.

Mor.

He that *committeth* a Crime, and He, *Who* joins *Himſelf* a Companion *to the Wicked,* are puniſhed *with equal* Puniſhment.

FABLE XLV.

De Opilione & | *Of* the Shepherd *and*
Agricolis. | the Countrymen.

PUER *paſcebat* Oves *editiore* Pratulo, *atq;* clamitans *terque,* quaterque *per*

A Boy *fed* his Sheep *upon a higher* Ground, *and* crying *both thrice,* and four times *in*

per Jocum, *Lupum* adeſſe, exciebat Agricolas undique: Illi illuſi ſæpius, dum non ſubveniunt imploranti *Auxilium*, Oves fiunt Præda *Lupo.*

in Jeſt, *that the Wolf* was there, he raiſed the Countrymen on all Sides : They *being deluded* too often, *whilſt* they do not *come* to him imploring *Help*, the Sheep become a Prey *to the Wolf.*

MOR.

Si *Quiſpiam* conſueverit mentiri, Fides non habebitur facile *Ei*, cùm occepe- rit narrare *verum.*

MOR.

If *any One* has been uſed *to lie,* Faith *will not be had* eaſily *in Him,* when he ſhall have begun to tell *the Truth.*

FABLE XLVI.

De Aquilâ & Corvo.

Of the Eagle *and* the Crow.

AQUILA devolat editiſſimâ Rupe, in *Tergum* Agni. *Corvus* videns *Id* geſtit, *veluti* Simia, imitari Aquilam, *dimittit* Se *in* Vellus *Arietis;* dimiſſus *impeditur;* impe- ditûs comprehenditur; comprehenſus *projicitur* Pueris.

THE EAGLE *flies down* from a very high *Rock,* on *the Back* of a Lamb. *The Crow* feeing *that* rejoiceth, *as* an Ape, *to imitate* the Eagle, *He drops* Himſelf *upon* the Fleece *of a Ram;* dropt down *He is entangled;* en- tangled he is taken; taken he is thrown to the Boys.

MOR.

Quiſque aſtimet Se ſuâ, non Virtute Aliorum. *Tentes* Id, *Quod* poſſis *facere.*

MOR.

Let every One eſteem Himſelf *by his own,* not *by the Virtue* of Others. *Attempt* That, *Which* thou mayſt be able *to do.*

FABLE

FABLE XLVII.

De invido CANE *&*
BOVE.

CANIS *decumbebat*
Præfepi *pleno* Fœni ;
Bos venit, *ut* comedat ;
Ille furrigens *Sefe* prohibet :
Bos inquit, *Dii* perdant
Te cum *ifthâc* tuâ *Invidiâ,*
Qui *nec* vefceris *Fæno,*
nec *finis* Me *vefci.*

Of the envious DOG *and*
the OX.

THE DOG *lay down*
in a Rack *full* of Hay ;
The Ox cometh, *that* He may eat ;
He raifing *Himfelf* hinders Him ;
The Ox fays, *May the Gods* deftroy
Thee with *that* thy *Envy,*
Who *neither* art fed *with Hay,*
nor *fufferest* Me *to be fed.*

MOR.

Plerique *funt* eó *Ingenio,*
ut *invideant* Ea
Aliis, Quæ *funt* nulli *Ufui*
Sibi.

MOR.

Many *are* of that *Temper,*
that *they envy* thofe Things
to Others, Which *are* of no *Ufe*
to Themfelves.

FABLE XLVIII.

De Corniculâ *&* Ove.

COrnicula *ftrepitat*
in *Dorfo* Oviculæ :
Ovis inquit, *Si* obftreperes
fic Cani, *ferres*
Infortunium. *At* Cornicula
inquit, fcio *Quibus* infultem,
molefta placidis, *amica*
fævis.

Of the Jackdaw *and* the Sheep.

THE Jackdaw *makes a Noife*
on *the Back* of the Sheep :
The Sheep fays, *If* thou made a Noife
thus to a Dog, *thou wouldeft bear*
the Damage. *But* the Jackdaw
faith, I know *Whom* I may infult,
troublefome to the mild, *friendly*
to the cruel.

MOR.

Mali *infultant* innocenti
& miti ; *fed* Nemo *irritat*
feroces *&* malignos.

MOR.

Evil Men *infult* the innocent
and mild ; *but* no One *irritates*
the fierce *and* mifchievous.

F FABLE

FABLE XLIX.

De Pavone & Lufciniâ.

PAVO *queritur* apud *Junonem*, Conjugem & Sororem *Jovis*, Lufciniam *cantillare* fuaviter, *Se* irrideri *ab* Omnibus *ob* raucam *Ravim.* Cui *Juno* inquit, *Lufcinia* longè *fuperat* in Cantu, *Tu* Plumis; *Quifque* habet *Suam* Dotem *à* Diis. *Decet* Unumquemq; *effe* conten-tum *fua* Sorte.

Of the Peacock *and* the Nightingale.

THE Peacock *complains* to *Juno,* the Wife *and* Sifter *of Jupiter*, that the Nightingale *fung* fweetly, *that He* was laughed at *by* All *for* his hoarfe *Squalling.* To whom *Juno* fays, *The Nightingale* by far *excels* in Singing, *Thou* in Feathers; *Every One* has *his* Gift *from* the Gods. *It becometh* Every One *to be* content *with his own* Lot.

MOR.

Sumamus *Ea,* Quæ *Deus* largitur, *grato* Animo, *neque* quæramus *majora.*

MOR.

Let us take *thofe Things*, Which God beftows, *with a grateful* Mind, nor let us feek *greater Things.*

FABLE L.

De feniculâ MUSTELA & MURIBUS.

MUstela *carens* Viribus *pre* Senio *non valebat* infequi *Mures* jam *ita*, ut *folebat*; cœpit *meditari* Dolum; *abfcondit* Se *in* Colliculo *Farine,* fic *fperans* fore, *ut* venetur *citra* Laborem. *Mures* accurrunt, & dum *cupiunt* efitare *Farinam,* Omnes *devorantur* ad *Unum* à *Muftelâ.*

Of the old WEASEL *and* the MICE.

THE WEASEL *wanting* Strength *thro'* old Age, *was not able* to purfue *the Mice* now *fo*, as *He was wont*; He began to meditate a Trick; *He hides* Himfelf *in* a Heap *of Meal,* thus *hoping* that it would be, *that* he may hunt *without* Labour. *The Mice* run to it, *and* whilft *they defire* to eat *the Meal,* They all *are* devoured to One by *the Weafel.*

MOR.

Mor.

Ubi *Quifquam* fuerit *de-flitutus* Viribus, *eft* Opus *Ingenio.* Lyfander *Laceda-monius* folebat *dicere* fub-inde, *quò* leonina *Pellis* non *perveniret,* Vulpinam *effe* affumendam.

Mor.

When *any One* fhall be *de-ftitute* of Strength, *there is* Need of *Wit.* Lyfander *the Laceda-monian* ufed *to fay* oft-en, *where* the Lion's *Skin* would not *reach,* that the Fox's *was to be* taken.

F A B L E LI.

De LEONE & RANA.   *Of* the LION *and* the FROG.

LEO, *cùm* audiret *Ranam* loquacem *magni,* putans *effe* aliquod *magnum* Animal, *vertit* Se *retro,* et *ftans* parum, *videt* Ranam *exeuntem* è *Stagno ;* Quam *ftatim* indignabundus *con-culcavit.* Pedibus, *inquiens,* non movebis *ampliùs* ullum *Animal* clamore, *ut* perfpiciat *Te.*

THE Lion, *when* he heard *the Frog* talking *at a great Rate,* thinking it *to be* fome *great* Beaft, turned Himfelf *back,* and *ftanding* a little, *He fees* the Frog going out of *the Pool ;* which *prefently* enraged *He trod - un-der* with his Feet, *faying,* Thou fhalt not move *any more* any *Animal* with thy Noife, *that* He may look at *Thee.*

Mor.

Fabula *fignificat,* quòd *apud* verbofos *Nihil* reperitur *præter* Linguam.

Mor.

The Fable *fignifies,* that among noify Men *Nothing* is found *except* a Tongue.

F A B L E LII.

De FORMICA & COLUMBA.   *Of* the PISMIRE *and* the DOVE,

FOrmica *fitiens* venit *ad* Fontem, *ut* biberet ; *fortè* incidit *in-*

THE Pifmire *thirfting* came *to* a Fountain, *that* fhe might drink ; *by chance* fhe fell *in-*

in Puteum. Columba superfidens Arborem imminentem Fonti, cùm conspiceret Formicam obrui Aquis, frangit Ramulum ex Arbore, Quem dejicit sine Morâ in Fontem. Formica confcendens Hunc fervatur. Auceps venit, ut capiat Columbam; Formica percipiens Id, mordet unum ex Pedibus Aucupis; Columba avolat.

into a Well. The Dove fitting upon a Tree hanging over the Fountain, when she faw the Pifmire overwhelmed in the Waters, breaks a little Branch from the Tree, Which she throws without Delay into the Fountain. The Pifmire getting upon This is faved. The Fowler comes, that he may take the Dove; the Ant perceiving That, bites one of the Feet of the Fowler; the Dove flies away.

Mor.

Fabula fignificat, cùm Bruta funt grata in Beneficios, eò magis Ii debent effe, Qui funt Participes Rationis.

Mor.

The Fable fignifies, when Brutes are grateful to Benefactors, by fo much the more They ought to be, Who are Partakers of Reafon.

FABLE LIII.

De Pavone & Picâ

Of the Peacock and the Magpie.

GENS Avium cùm vagaretur liberè, optabat Regem dari Sibi. Pavo putabat Se imprimis dignum, Qui eligeretur, quia effet formofiffimus. Hoc accepto in Regem, Pica inquit, O Rex, fi, Te imperante, Aquila cœperit infequi Nos perftrenuè, ut folet, quo Modo abiges Illam? quo Pacto fervabis Nos?

THE Nation of Birds, when they wandered freely, wifhed for a King to be given to Them. The Peacock thought Himfelf chiefly worthy, Who fhould be chofen, becaufe He was the moft beautiful. He being received for King, the Magpie fays, O King, if, You governing, the Eagle fhould begin to purfue Us ftrenuoufly, as fhe is wont, by what Method will you drive away Her? by what Means will you preferve Us?

Mor.

Mor.

In *Principe* Forma *non eſt* tàm *ſpectanda*, quàm *Fortitudo* Corporis & Prudentia.

Mor.

In *a Prince* Beauty *is not* ſo much *to be regarded*, as *Strength* of Body *and* Prudence.

FABLE LIV.

De Ægroto & **Medico.**

Of the **Sick Man** *and* the **Physician.**

MEdicus *curabat* Ægrotum ; *tandem* Ille *moritur ;* tum *Medicus* inquit *ad* Cognatos, *Hic* peribat *Intemperantiâ.*

A Phyſician *bad in cure* a Sick Man ; *at length* He *died ;* then *the Phyſician* ſaid *to* the Kinſmen, *This Man* periſhed *by Intemperance.*

Mor.

Niſi *Quis* reliquerit *Bibacitatem* & *Libidinem* mature, *aut* nunquam *perveniet* ad *Senectutem*, aut *eſt* habiturus *perbrevem* Senectutem.

Mor.

Unleſs *Any One* ſhall have left *Drunkenneſs* and *Luſt* timely, *either* He never *will arrive* to *old Age*, or *is* to have *a very ſhort* old Age.

FABLE LV.

De **Leone** *& aliis.*

Of the **Lion** *and* other Beaſts.

LEO, *Aſinus,* & *Vulpes* eunt *venatum* ; ampla *Venatio* capitur ; *capta* eſt *juſſa* partiri : *Aſino* ponente *Singulis* ſingulas *Partes*, Leo *irrugiebat*, rapit *Aſinum*, ac laniat. Poſtea *dat* id *Negotii* Vulpeculæ, *Quæ* aſtutior,

THE Lion, *the Aſs*, and *the Fox* go *to hunt* ; an ample *Prey* is taken ; *taken is commanded* to be parted : *The Aſs* putting *to each* their ſingle *Parts*, the Lion *roared*, he ſeized *the Aſs*, and *butchers him.* Afterwards *he gives* that *Buſineſs* to the Fox, *Who* more cunning, aſtutior, *càm* longè *optimâ* Parte *propoſitâ,* reſervaviſſet *vix* minimam, *Leo* rogat, *à* Quo ſic *docta?* Cui *Illa* inquit, *Calamitas* Aſini *docuit* Me.

more cunning, *when* by far *the beſt* Part *being propoſed,* ſhe had *reſerved ſcarce* a very ſmall one, the Lion aſks, *by* Whom *ſo taught?* To Whom *She* ſays, the Calamity of the Aſs *has taught* Me.

MOR.

Ille *eſt* Felix, *Quem* aliena *Pericula* faciunt *cautum.*

MOR.

He *is* Happy, *Whom* others *Dangers* make *cautious.*

FABLE LVI.

De HÆDO *&* LUPO.

Of the KID *and* the WOLF.

HÆdus *proſpectans* è *Feneſtrâ* audebat *laceſſere* Lupum *praetereuntem* Conviciis; *Cui* Lupus *ait,* Sceleſte, *Tu* non conviciaris *Mihi,* ſed *Locus.*

A KID *looking* out of a *Window* dared to *provoke* a Wolf *paſſing by* with Revilings; *to Whom* the Wolf *ſays,* Wretch, *Thou* doſt not revile *Me,* but *the Place.*

MOR.

Tempus *&* Locus *ſemper* addunt *Audaciam* Homini.

MOR.

Time *and* Place *always* add *Boldneſs* to a Man.

FABLE LVII.

De Leone *&* Caprâ.

Of the Lion *and* the Goat.

LEO *forte* conſpicatus *Capram* ambulantem *editâ* Rupe *monet,* ut *deſcendat* in *viride* Pratum: *Capra* inquit, *Fortaſſe* facerem, *ſi* Tu abeſſes; *Qui* non ſuades *Mihi*

THE Lion *by chance* having ſeen a *Goat* walking *on* a *high* Rock *adviſes,* that *ſhe would deſcend into the green* Paſture: The Goat ſays, *Perhaps* I ſhould do it *if* You was away; *Who* do not perſuade *Me*

Mihi iftud, · *ut* Ego *capiam* | *Me* to that, *that* I *may* take
ullam Voluptatem inde ; *fed* | any *Pleafure* - thence ; *but*
ut *Tu* habeas, *Quod* | that *Thou* mayft have, *What*
famelicus *vores.* | being hungry *Thou mayft devour.*

MOR. | MOR.

Ne habeas *Fidem* omnibus; | Do not have *Faith* in all ;
nam Quidam *non confulunt* | *for* Some *do not confult*
Tibi, *fed* Sibi. | for You, *but* for themfelves...

FABLE LVIII.

De VULTURE *aliifque* | *Of* the VULTURE *and other*
AVIBUS. | BIRDS.

VUltur *adfimulat,* Se | THE Vulture *feigns,* that He
celebrare annuum | would *celebrate* his annual
Natalem ; invitat *Avi-* | Birth-Day ; He invites *the little*
culas ad *Cænam ;* ferè | Birds to Supper ; almoft
omnes veniunt ; *accipit* | all come ; He *receives*
venientes *magno* Plaufu | them coming *with great* Applaufe
Favoribufque : Vultur | and Favours : The Vulture
laniat acceptas. | butchers *them* received.

MOR. | MOR.

Omnes *non funt* Amici, | All are *not* Friends,
Qui dicunt *blandè,* aut | Who fpeak *fairly,* or
fimulant, Se *facere* benig- | pretend, that They *will do* kind-
nè. | ly.

FABLE LIX.

De ANSERIBUS & | *Of* the GEESE *and*
GRUIBUS. | the CRANES.

ANferes *pafcebantur* | THE Geefe *were fed*
fimul *cum* Gruibus | at the fame time *with* the Cranes
eodem *Agro.* Grues | in the fame *Field.* The Cranes
confpicate | having *feen*

conspicatæ Rusticos, leves avolant; Anseres capiuntur, Qui impediti Onere Corporis, non poterant subvolare.

having seen the Countrymen, being light fly away; The Geese are taken, Who hindered with Burden of Body, were not able to fly away.

Mor.

Urbe expugnatâ ab Hostibus,. Inops facile subducit Se; at Dives captus servit. In Bello Divitiæ sunt magis Oneri quàm Usui.

Mor.

A City being besieged by Enemies, the poor Man easily withdraws Himself; but the Rich taken serves. In War Riches are more for a Burden than an Use.

FABLE LX.

De Anu & Ancillis.

Of the old Woman and her Maids.

QUædam *Anus* habebat Domi complures *Ancillas*, quas *quotidie* excitabat *ad* Opus *ad* Cantum *Galli*, Quem *habebat* Domi, *antequam* lucesceret. *Ancillæ* tandem *commotæ* Tædio *quotidiani* Negotii *obtruncant* Gallum, *sperantes* jam, *Illo* necato, *Sese* dormituras *usque* ad *Meridiem*; sed hæc *Spes* decepit *Eas*; nam *Hera*, ut *rescivit*, Gallum *interemptum*, deinceps *jubet* Eas *surgere* intempestâ Nocte.

A Certain *old Woman* had at Home many Maids, whom daily she rouzed *to* Work *at* the Crowing *of a* Cock, which *she* had at Home, *before that* it was light. *The Maids* at length *moved* with the Wearisomness *of their* daily Business *behead* the Cock, *hoping* now, He being killed, *that They* should sleep *even* to *Mid-day*; but this *Hope* deceived *Them*; for the *Mistress*, as soon *as she knew*, that the Cock *was killed*, thenceforwards *commands* Them *to rise* at Mid-night.

Mor.

Non *Pauci*, dum *student* evitare *Malum*, incidunt *in* gravius.

Mor.

Not *a few*, whilst *they study* to avoid *an Evil*, fall *into* a heavier.

FABLE

FABLE LXI.

De Asino & Equo.

Of the Ass and the Horse.

ASinus *putabat* Equum *beatum*, quòd *esset* pinguis, & degeret *in* Otio ; *verò* dicebat *Se* infelicem, *quòd* esset *macilentus*, & *strigosus*, & *quotidie* exerceretur *ab* immiti *Hero* in *ferendis* Oneribus. *Haud* multò *post* conclamant *ad* Arma ; *tum* Equus non repulit Frænum Ore, Equitem *Dorso*, nec *Telum* Corpore. *Asinus*, Hoc *viso*, agebat *magnas* Gratias *Diis*, quòd non *fecissent* Se *Equum*, sed *Asinum*.

THE Ass *thought* the Horse *happy*, becaufe *he was* fat *and* lived *in* Idlenefs ; *but* he called *Himself* unhappy, *becaufe* He 'was *lean*, and *raw-boned*, and *daily* was exercised *by* an unmerciful *Master* in *bearing* Burdens. *Not* much *after* they cry *to* Arms ; *then* the Horfe *drove not* back the Bridle *from his Mouth*, the Horfeman *from his Back*, nor *the Dart* from his Body. *The Ass*, This *being feen*, gave *great* Thanks *to the Gods*, that *they had* not made him a *Horfe*, but an *Afs*.

MOR.

Sunt *Miferi*, Quos *Vulgus* judicat *beatos* ; & non *Pauci* funt *beati*, Qui *putant* Se *miferrimos*. Sutor crepidarius *dicit* Regem *felicem*, non confiderans *in quantas* Res & Solicitudines *diftrahitur*, dum *interim* Ipfe *cantillat* cum *optimâ* Paupertate.

MOR.

They are *miferable*, Whom *the Vulgar* judges *happy* ; and not a *few* are *happy*, Who *think* Themfelves moft *miferable*. The Cobler *calls* the King *happy*, not *confidering* into *how great* Affairs *and* Troubles *he is drawn*, whilft *in the mean time* He *fings* with *his beft* Poverty.

G

FABLE

FABLE LXII.

De Leone & Tauro.

TAurus *fugiens* Leonem *incidit* in *Hircum*; Is *minitabatur* Cornu & caperatâ *Fronte*: Ad *Quem* Taurus *plenus* Irâ *inquit*, Tua *Frons* contracta in Rugas *non territat* Me; *sed* metuo immanem Leonem, *Qui* nisi *hæreret* me *Tergo* jam *scires* esse *non* ita *parvam* Rem *pugnare* cum *Tauro*.

Of the Lion *and* the Bull.

THE Bull *flying* the Lion *fell* upon *the Goat*; He *threatened* with his Horn *and* wrinkled *Brow*: To *Whom* the Bull *full* of Anger *said*, Thy *Brow* contracted *into* Wrinkles *does not affright* Me; *but* I fear a *vnst* Lion, *Who* unless *be stuck* to my *Back*, now *you should know* that it is *not* so *little* a Thing *to fight* with *a Bull*.

Mor.

Calamitas *non est* addenda *calamitosis*. Est *Miser* sat, *Qui* est *semel* miser.

Mor.

Calamity *is not* to be added *to the calamitous*. He is *miserable* enough, *Who* is *once* miserable.

FABLE LXIII.

De Testitudine & Aquila.

TÆdium reptandi occupaverat *Testitudinem*; si *Quis* tolleret *Eam* in *Cælum*, pollicetur *Baccas* rubri *Maris*. Aquila *sustulit* Eam; *poscit* Præmium; & fodit *Eam* non *habentem* Unguibus. *Ita*, Testudo, *Quæ* concupivit *videre* Astra, *reliquit* Vitam in Astris.

Of the Tortoise *and* the Eagle.

WEariness *of creeping* had seized *the Tortoise*; if *any One* would lift up *Her* into *Heaven*, She promises *the Pearls* of the red *Sea*. The Eagle *took up* Her; *demands* the Reward; *and* pierces *Her* not *having it* with her Talons. *Thus*, the Tortoise, *Which* desired *to see* the Stars, *left* her Life *in* the Stars.

Mor.

MOR.

Sis *contentus* tuâ *Sorte.*
Fuêre *Nonnulli,* Qui,
ſi manſiſſent *humiles,*
fuiſſent *tuti* ; faƈi *ſublimes,*
inciderunt *in* Pericula.

MOR.

Be *contented* with thy *Lot.*
There have been *Some,* Who,
if they had remained *low,*
would have been *ſafe;* become *high,*
have fallen *into* Dangers.

FABLE LXIV.

De CANCRO *&* ejus
MATRE.

Of the CRAB *and* his
MOTHER.

MAter *monet* Cancrum *retrogradum,* ut *eat* antrorſum. *Filius* reſpondet, *Mater,* I *præ,* ſequar.

THE Mother *adviſes* the Crab *going backwards,* that He *would go* forwards. *The Son* anſwers, *Mother,* go you *before,* I will follow.

MOR.

Reprehenderis *Nullum* Vitii, *cujus* Ipſe *queas* reprehendi.

MOR.

You ſhould reprehend *no One* of a Vice, *of which* You Yourſelf may *be* reprehended.

FABLE LXV.

De SOLE *&* AQUI-
LONE.

Of the SUN *and* the NORTH-
WIND.

SOL *&* Aquilo *certant,* Uter *ſit* fortior. *Eſt* conventum *ab* Illis experiri *Vires* in *Viatorem* ; ut *ſerat* Palmam, *Qui* excuſſerit *Manticam.* Boreas *aggre-ditur* Viatorem *horriſono* Nimbo ; *at* Ille *non deſiſtit* duplicare *Amiƈum* gradi-endo.

THE Sun *&* the North-Wind *ſtrive,* Whether *is* the ſtronger. *It is* agreed *by* Them to try *their Strength* upon a *Traveller* ; that *He bear* the Palm, *Who* ſhall have ſhaken off *his Cloak.* Boreas *ſets up-on* the Traveller *with* a *rattling* Cloud ; *but* He *does not deſiſt* to double *his Cloak* in going on.

endo. Sol *experitur* fuas *Vires,* Nimboque *paulatim* evi&o, *emittit* Radios. *Viator* incipit *æftuare,* fudare, *anhelare :* Tandem *nequiens* progredi *refidet* fub *frondofo* Nemore. *Ita* Vi&oria *contigit* Soli.

on. The Sun *tries* his *Strength,* and the Storm *little by little* being overcome, *fends forth* his Beams. *The Traveller* begins *to grow hot,* to fweat; *to pant :* At length *not being able* to go on. *He fits down* under *a fhady* Grove. *Thus* the Vi&ory *fell* to the Sun.

Mor.

Id *fæpe* obtinetur *Manfuetudine,* Quod *non poteft* extorqueri *Vi.*

Mor.

That *often* is obtained *by Gentlenefs,* which *is not able* to be extorted *by Force.*

FABLE LXVI.

De Asino.

Of the Ass.

ASinus *venit* in *Sylvam,* offendit *Exuvias* Leoni, *Quibus* indutus *venit* in *Pafcua,* territat *&* fugat *Greges & Armenta.* Venit, *Qui* perdiderat, *quæritat* fuum *Afinum.* Afinus, *Hero* vifo, *accurrit,* imò *incurrit* fuo *Rugitu.* At *Herus* Auriculis *prehenfis,* Quæ *extabant,* inquit, *Mi* Afelle, *poffis* fallere *Alios,* Ego *probè* novi *Te.*

THE Afs *comes* into *the Wood,* finds *the Skin* of a Lion, *with Which* being clad He *comes* into *the Paftures,* affrights *and* puts to Flight *the Flocks and Herds.* He comes, *Who* had loft him, *feeks* his *Afs.* The Afs, *his Mafter* being feen, *runs to him,* nay *runs upon Him* with his *Braying.* But *the Mafter* his Ears *being held,* Which *ftood out,* fays, *My* Afs, *thou mayft be able* to deceive *Others,* I *full well* know *Thee,*

Mor.

Ne *fimules* Te *effe,* Quod *non es ;* non *doctum,* cùm *fis* indoctus; *non jactes* Te *divitem* & *nobilem,* cùm *fis* pauper *&* ignobilis ; *etenim,* vero *comperto,* rideberis.

Mor.

Do *not feign* Thyfelf *to be,* What *thou art not ;* not *learned,* when *thou art* unlearned ; *do not boaft* Thyfelf *rich* and *noble,* when *Thou art* poor *and* ignoble ; *for,* the Truth *being found,* thou wilt be laughed at.

FABLE

FABLE LXVII.

De mordaci CANE.

DOminus *alligavit* Nolam Cani fubinde *mordenti* Homines, *ut* Quifq; `caveret` Sibi. Canis, ratus Id Decus *tributum* fuæ Virtuti, defpicit *fuos* Populares. *Aliquis* jam *gravis* Ætate & Auctoritate *accedit* ad *hunc* Canem, *monens* Eum, *ne erret ;* nam *inquit*, Ifta *Nola* eft *data* Tibi *in* Dedecus, *non* in Decus.

Of the biting DOG.

THE Mafter *tied* a little Bell *to the Dog* often *biting* Men, *that* every one *fhould take heed* to Himfelf. *The Dog,* thinking *That* an Ornament *given* to his Virtue, defpifes *his* Neighbours. One now grave with Age *and* Authority *comes* to this Dog, *advifing* Him, *that he err not ;* for *fays he,* That *little Bell* is *given* to Thee *for* a Difgrace, *not* for a Grace.

MOR.

Gloriofus interdum ducit *Id* Laudi *Sibi,* Quod *eft* Vituperio *Ipfi.*

MOR.

The Vain-glorious *fometimes* takes *That* for a Praife *to Himfelf,* Which *is* for a Difgrace *to Him.*

FABLE LXVIII.

De CAMELO.

CAmelus *defpiciens* Se *querebatur,* ·Tauros *ire* infignes *geminis* Cornibus ; Se inermem *effe* objectum *cæteris* Animalibus ; orat Jovem *donare* Cornua *Sibi :* Jupiter *ridet* Stultitiam Cameli, nec *modò* negat Votum Cameli, *verùm* & decurtat Auriculas *Beftiæ.*

Of the CAMEL.

THE Camel *defpifing* Himfelf *complained,* that the Bulls *went* remarkable *with two* Horns ; *that He* without Arms *was* expofed *to the other* Animals ; *He prays* Jupiter *to give* Horns *to Him :* Jupiter *laughs at* the Folly *of the Camel,* nor *only* denies *the Wifh* of the Camel, *but* alfo crops the Ears *of the Beaft.*

MOR.

FABLE LXIX.

De duobus AMICIS & URSO.

Of the two FRIENDS *and* the BEAR.

DUÔ *Amici* faciunt *Iter ;* Urfus *occurrit* in *Itinere ;* Unus *fcandens* Arborem *evitat* Periculum ; *Alter,* cùm non *effet* Spes *Fugæ,* procidens *fimulat* Se *mortuum.* Urfus *accedit,* & *olfacit* Aures & Os. *Homine* continente *Spiritum* & *Motum,* Urfus, *Qui* parcit *Mortuis,* credens *Eum* effe *mortuum,* abibat. *Poftea* Socio *percontante* quidnam *Beftia* dixiffet *Illi* accumbenti *in* Aurem, ait, Monuiffe *Hoc,* ne unquam *facerem* Iter *cum* Amicis *iftius* Modi.

TWO *Friends* make *a Journey ;* a Bear *meets them* in *the Road ;* One *climbing up* a Tree *fhuns* the Danger ; *The other,* when *there was not* Hope *of Flight,* falling down *feigns* Himfelf *Dead.* The Bear *comes,* and *fmells* to his Ears *and* Mouth. *The Man* holding in *Breath* and *Motion,* The Bear, *Which* fpares *the Dead,* believing *that He* was *dead,* went away. *Afterwards* the Companion *afking* what *the Beaft* had faid *to Him* lying down *in* his Ear, *He fays,* that He had advifed *This,* that I fhould not ever *make* a Journey *with* Friends *of this* Kind.

FABLE

FABLE LXX.

De Ruſtico & Fortunâ.　*Of* the Countryman *and* Fortune.

Rusticus, *cùm* araret, *offendebat* Theſaurum *in* Sulcis. *Fortuna* videns, *Nihil* Honoris *haberi* Sibi, *ita* locuta eſt *Secum :* Theſauro *reperto,* Stolidus *non eſt* gratus ; *at* eo *ipſo* Theſauro *amiſſo,* ſollicitabit *Me* primam *omnium* Votis & Clamoribus.

THE Countryman, *when* He ploughed, *found* Treaſure *in* the Furrows. *Fortune* ſeeing, *that Nothing* of Honour *was had* to Her, *thus* ſpake *with Herſelf :* Treaſure *being found,* the Fool *is not* grateful ; *but* that *ſelf-ſame* Treaſure *being loſt,* He will ſolicit *Me* firſt *of all* with Vows *and* Clamours.

MOR.
Beneficio *accepto,* ſimus *grati* Merenti *bene* de *Nobis ;* Etenim *Ingratitudo* eſt *digna* privari *etiam* Beneficio, *Quod* modò *acceperit.*

MOR.
A Benefit *being received,* let us be *grateful* to Him deſerving *well* of Us ; For *Ingratitude* is *worthy* to be deprived *even* of the Benefit, *Which* lately *it may have received.*

FABLE LXXI.

De PAVONE & GRUE.　*Of* the Peacock *and* the Crane.

PAVO & Grus *cænant* unà : *Pavo* jactat *Se,* oſtentat *Caudam :* Grus *fatetur* Pavonem *eſſe* formoſiſſimis *Pennis ;* tamen *Se* penetrare *Nubes* animoſo *Volatu,* dùm *Pavo* vix *ſupervolat* Tecta.

THE Peacock *and* the Crane *ſup* together : *The Peacock* boaſts *Himſelf,* ſhows *his Tail :* The Crane *confeſſes* the Peacock *to be* of moſt beautiful *Feathers ;* yet *that He* pierced *the Clouds* with a bold *Flight,* whilſt *the Peacock* ſcarce *flies over* the Houſes.

MOR.

Mor.

Nemo contempſerit Alterum : eſt cuique ſua Dos ; eſt cuique ſua Virtus : Qui caret tuâ Virtute, forſan habeat Eam, Quâ Tu careas.

Mor.

No man ſhould have deſpiſed Another : there is to every one his own Portion; there is to every one his own Virtue : He who wanteth thy Virtue, perhaps may have That Which thou mayſt want.

FABLE LXXII.

De Quercu & Arundine.

Of the Oak and the Reed.

Quercus effraĉta validiore Noto, præcipitatur in Flumen, &, dum fluitat, fortè hæret ſuis Ramis in Arundine ; miratur, Arundinem ſtare incolumem in tanto Turbine. Hæc reſpondet, Se eſſe tutam ſuâ Flexibilitate ; Se cedere Noto, Boreæ ; omni Flatui ; nec eſſe Mirum, quòd Quercus exciderit, Quæ concupivit non cedere, ſed reſiſtere.

THE Oak being broken by the ſtronger South Wind, is thrown into the River, and, whilſt She flows, by Chance ſticks by her Boughs upon a Reed ; ſhe wonders, that a Reed ſtood ſafe in ſo great a Whirlwind. She anſwers, that She was ſafe by her Flexibility ; that She yielded to Notus, to Boreas ; to every Blaſt ; nor was it a Wonder, that the Oak ſhould fall, Who deſired not to yield, but to reſiſt.

Mor.

Ne reſiſtas Potentiori, ſed vincas Hunc cedendo, & ferendo.

Mor.

Do not reſiſt One more powerful, but overcome Him by yielding, and bearing.

FABLE

FABLE LXXIII.

De LEONE & *Of* the LION *and*
VENATORE. the HUNTER.

LEO *litigat* cum
Venatore; præfert *suam*
Fortitudinem Fortitudini
Hominis. *Poſt* longa *Jur-*
gia Venator *ducit* Leonem
ad Mauſoleum, *in* Quo *Leo*
erat *ſculptus* deponens
Caput *in Gremium* Viri.
Fera negat *Id* eſſe *ſatis*
Indicii; *nam* ait, Homines
ſculpere *Quod* vellent;
quòd ſi Leones forent *Arti-*
fices; Virum jam iri
ſculptum ſub Pedibus
Leonis.

THE Lion *contends* with
the Hunter; He prefers *his*
Strength *to the Strength*
of Man. *After* long *Diſ-*
putes the Hunter *leads* the Lion
to a Tomb, *on* Which *a Lion*
was *carved* laying down
his Head on *the Lap* of a Man.
The Beaſt denies *that* to be *enough*
Proof; *for* he ſays, *that Men*
carved *What* they would;
but if *Lions* were *Arti-*
ficers, that the Man *now* would be
carved under *the Feet*
of the Lion.

MOR.

Quiſque, *quoad* poteſt,
& dicit, & facit *Id,* Quod
putat prodeſſe *ſuæ*
Cauſæ & Parti.

MOR.

Every One, *as much as* he is able,
both ſays, *and* does *That,* Which
he *thinks* to be profitable *to his*
Cauſe *and* Party.

FABLE LXXIV.

De PUERO & FURE. *Of* the BOY *and* the THIEF.

PUer *ſedebat* flens *apud*
Puteum; *Fur* rogat
Cauſam flendi; *Puer* dicit,
Fune rupto, Urnam
Auri *incidiſſe* in *Aquas.*
Homo *exuit* Se, *inſilit*
in *Puteum,* quærit. *Vaſe*
non *invento,* conſcendit,
atq;

A Boy *ſat* weeping *at*
a Well; *A Thief* aſks
*theCauſe*of his weeping;*theBoy*ſays,
the *Rope* being broke, *that an Urn*
of Gold *had fallen* into *the Waters.*
The Man *undreſſes* Himſelf, *leaps*
into *the Well,*ſeeks for it. *TheVeſſel*
not *being found,* He comes up,
and

H

atq; ibi nec invenit Puerum, nec suam Tunicam : Quippe Puer, Tunicá sublatá, fugerat.

and there neither does He find the Boy, nor his own Coat : For the Boy, the Coat being taken away, had fled.

MOR.

MOR.

Interdum falluntur, Qui solent fallere.

Sometimes they are deceived, Who are wont to deceive.

FABLE LXXV.

De RUSTICO & JUVENCO.

Of the COUNTRYMAN and the STEER.

RUSTICUS habebat Juvencum impatientem omnis Vinculi & Jugi : Homo astutulus resecat Cornua Bestiæ ; nam petebat Cornibus ; tum jungit non Currui, sed Aratro, ne , pulsaret Herum Calcibus, ut solebat. Ipse tenet Stivam, gaudens, effecisse Industriâ, ut jam foret tutus & à Cornibus, & ab Ungulis. Sed Quid evenit? Taurus subinde resistens spargendo Arenam opplet Os & Caput Rustici Eâ.

A COUNTRYMAN had a Steer impatient of every Chain and Yoke : The Man a little cunning cuts off the Horns of the Beast ; for he struck with his Horns ; then He joins him not to the Cart, but to the Plough, that he should not strike his Master with his Heels, as He was wont. He holds the Plough, rejoicing, that He had effected by Industry, that now he should be safe both from Horns, and from Hoofs. But What happened ? The Bullock frequently resisting by scattering the Sand fills the Mouth and Head of the Countryman with it.

MOR.

MOR.

Nonnulli sunt sic intractabiles, ut nequeant tractari ullâ Arte, aut Consilio.

Some are so intractable, that They cannot be managed by any Art, or Counsel.

FABLE

FABLE LXXVI.

De SATYRO & VIA-
: -TORE. '

Of the SATYR *and* the TRA-
VELLER.

SAtyrus, *Qui* olim *erat*
habitus *Deus* Nemo-
rum, *miſeratus* Viatorem
obrutum Nive, *atq*; enec-
tum *Algore*, ducit *in*
ſuum *Antrum* ; fovet
Igne. At, *dum* · ·ſpirat
in Manus, *percontatur*
Cauſam ; *Qui* reſpondens ·
inquit, ut *calefiant*. Poſtea, *cùm* accumberent,
Viator ſufflat *in* Pultem,
Quod interrogatus *cur* ſa-
ceret, *inquit*, ut *frigeſcat.*
Tum *continuò* Satyrus
ejiciens Viatorem *inquit*,
Nolo, *ut* Ille *ſit* in
meo Antro, *Cui* ſit *tam*
diverſum *Os.*

ASatyr, *Who* formerly *was*
accounted *a God* of the
Woods, *having pitied* a Traveller
covered with Snow, *and* almoſt
dead *with Cold*, leads Him *into*
his *Cave* ; cheriſhes Him
with a Fire. But, *whilſt* He breathes
into his Hands, *He enquires*
the Cauſe ; *Who* anſwering
ſays, that *they may be warm*. Afterwards, *when* they laid down,
the Traveller blows *into* his Porridge,
Which being aſked *why* He
did, *He ſaid*, that *It may grow cool.*
Then *immediately* the Satyr
caſting out the Traveller *ſays*,
I am not willing, *that* He *be* in
my Cave, *Who* has *ſo*
different *a Mouth.*

MOR.

MOR.

Evita *bilinguem* Hominem,
Qui eſt *Proteus* in *Sermone*. .

Avoid *a double-tongued* Man,
Who is a *Proteus* in *Diſcourſe.*

FABLE LXXVII.

De TAURO & MURE.

Of the BULL *and* the MOUSE.

MUS *momorderat*
Pedem *Tauri*, fu-
giens *in* ſuum *Antrum.*
Taurus *vibrat* Cornua,
querit Hoſtem, *videt* nuſ-
quam. *Mus* irridet *Eum* ;
inquit,

THE Mouſe *had bit*
the Foot *of the Bull*, flying into his Hole.
The Bull *brandiſhes* his Horns,
ſeeks his Enemy, *ſees him* no
where. *The Mouſe* laughs at *Him* ;
ſays

inquit, *quia es robustus,* | says He, *because* thou art *robust,*
ac *vastus,* idcirco *non con-* | and *big,* therefore *you should not*
tempseris Quemvis ; *nunc* | *have despised* any One ; *now*
eximius *Mus* læsit *Te,* & | a little *Mouse* has hurt *Thee,* and
quidem gratis. | *indeed* gratis.

MOR. | MOR.

Nemo *pendat* Hostem | Let no Man *rate* his Enemy
Flocci. | at a Lock of Wool.

FABLE LXXVIII.

De RUSTICO & | *Of* the COUNTRYMAN *and*
HERCULE. | HERCULES.

CURRUS *Rusti-* | THE Waggon *of a Country-*
ci hæret *in* profundo | *man* sticks *in* a deep
Luto.   Mox   *supinus* | *Clay.*   By and by *laying along*
implorat *Deum* Herculem ; | He implores *the God* Hercules ;
Vox intonat *è* Cœlo, | *a Voice* thunders *out of* Heaven,
Ineptè, flagella *tuos* Equos, | *Fool,*   whip   *thy*   Horses,
& Ipse *annitere* Rotis, | *and* Thyself *try* at the Wheels,
atq; *tum* Hercules *vocatus* | and *then* Hercules *being called*
aderit. | will be present.

MOR. | MOR.

Otiosa *Vota* profunt *Nil* ; | Idle *Vows* profit *Nothing* ;
Quæ *sanè* Deus *non audit.* | Which *indeed* God *does not hear,*
Ipse juva *Teipsum,* tum | *Thyself* help *Thyself,* then
Deus juvabit *Te.* | God will help *Thee.*

FABLE LXXIX.

De Cicadà & Formicà. | *Of* the Grashopper *and the* Pismire.

CUM *Cicada* cantet | WHEN *the Grashopper* sings
per Æstatem, *Formica* | in the Summer, *the Ant*
exercet *suam* Messem, *tra-* | exercises *her* Harvest, *draw-*
hens | ing

bens Grana *in* Antrum, *Quæ* reponit *in* Hyemem. *Brumâ* fæviente, *famelica* Cicada *venit* ad *Formicam*, & *mendicat* Victum. *Formica* renuit, *dictitans*, Sefe *laboravisse*, dum *Illa* cantabat.

ing the Grains *into* a Hole; *Which* She lays up *againft* Winter. The Winter raging, *the famished* Grashopper *comes* to *the Ant*, and *begs* Victuals. The *Ant* refuses, *saying*, that She *had laboured*, whilft *She* fung.

Mor.

Qui *eft* fegnis *in* Juventâ, *egebit* in *Senectâ* ; & Qui non *parcit*, mox *mendicabit.*

Mor.

Who *is* flothful *in* Youth, *shall want* in *Age* ; *and Who* doth not *spare*, by and by *shall beg.*

FABLE LXXX.

De Cane & Leone.

Of the Dog *and* the Lion.

CANIS *jocans* occurrit Leoni, quid *Tu* exhauftus *Inediâ* percurris Sylvas & *Devia* ? fpecta *Me* pinguem, & nitidum, *atque* confequor *Hæc*, non *Labore*, fed *Otio*. Tum Leo inquit, *Tu* quidem *babes* tuas *Epulas*, fed Stolide, habes *etiam* Vincula ; Efto *Tu* Servus, *Qui* potes fervire ; Ego *quidem*, fum liber, nec *volo* fervire.

A DOG *joking* meets a Lion, why *doft* Thou exhaufted *with* Want run thro' the *Woods* and *By-places* ? fee Me fat, and fleek, and I obtain *thefe Things*, not by *Labour*, but by *Idlenefs*. Then the Lion fays, *Thou* indeed *baft* thy Dainties, but Fool, Thou haft *alfo* Chains ; Be *Thou* a Slave, *Who* art able to ferve ; I *indeed*, am free, nor am *I willing* to ferve.

Mor.

Leo *refpondit* pulchrè : *Etenim* Libertas *eft* potior omnibus Rebus.

Mor.

The Lion *anfwered* beautifully : For Liberty *is* better than all Things.

FABLE

FABLE LXXXI.

De Piscibus.	Of the Fishes.

FLuvialis *Piscis* est *correptus* per *Vim* Fluminis *in* Mare, *ubi* efferens suam Nobilitatem, *pendebat* omne *marinum* Genus *vili.* Phoca *non tulit* Hoc, *sed* ait, Tunc *fore* Indicium *Nobilitatis,* si *coptus* portetur *ad* Forum *cum* Phocâ ; *Se* iri *emptum* à *Nobilibus,* autem *Illum* à *Plebe.*

A River *Fish* is *borne down* by *the Force* of the River *into* the Sea, *where* extolling *his* Nobility, *He valued* all *the Sea* Race *at a low Rate.* The Seal *bore not* This, *but* said, Then *would be* a Proof *of Nobility,* if *taken* He should be carried *to* Market *with* a Seal ; *that* He should be *bought* by *Nobles,* but *He* by *the common People.*

Mor.

Multi *sunt* sic *capti* Libidine *Gloriæ,* ut *Ipsi* jactent *Se.* Sed *Laus* sui *Oris* non datur *Homini* Laudi, *at* excipitur *cum* Risu *Auditorum.*

Mor.

Many are so *taken* with the Lust *of Glory,* that *They* boast *Themselves.* But *the Praise* of his own *Mouth* is not given *to a Man* for a *Praise, but* is received *with* the Laughter *of the Hearers.*

FABLE LXXXII.

De Pardo & Vulpeculâ.	Of the Leopard and the Fox.

PArdus, *Cui* est *pictum* Tergum, *cæteris* Feris, *etiam* Leonibus *despectis* ab *Eo,* intumescebat. *Vulpecula* accedit *ad* Hunc, suadet non superbire, *dicens* quidem, *Illi* esse *speciosam* Pellem, *verò* Sibi *esse* speciosam *Mentem.*

THE Leopard, *Who* has a *painted* Back, the other Beasts, *even* the Lions *being despised* by *Him,* was puffed up. The Fox comes *to* Him, persuades Him *not* to be proud, *saying* indeed, *that He* had a *fine* Skin, *but* He had a *fine Mind.*

Mor.

MOR.   MOR.

Eft *Difcrimen* & *Ordo*   There is *a Difference* and *Order*
Bonorum :   *Bona*   of good Things : *The Goods*
Corporis *præftant* Bonis   of the Body *excel* the Goods
Fortunæ ; fed *Bona* Animi   *of Fortune* ; but *the Goods* of the Mind
funt præferenda *His*.   *are* to be preferred *to Thefe*.

FABLE LXXXIII.

De VULPE & FELE.   *Of* the Fox *and* the CAT.

CUM *Vulpes* in *Collo-quio*, Quod *Illi* erat
cum Fele, *jactaret*, Sibi
effe varias *Technas*, adeò
ut haberet *vel* Peram
refertam : Dolis : *Autem*
Felis *refpondit*, Sibi *effe*
duntaxat *unicam* Artem, *Cui*
fideret, *fi* effet
Quid Difcriminis. *Inter* con-
fabulandum *repentè*
Tumultus *Canum* accurren-
tium *auditur :* Ibi *Felis*
fubfilit *in* altiffimam
Arborem ; interim *Vulpes*
cincta *Canibus* capitur.

WHEN *the Fox* in a *Dif-courfe,* Which *He* had
with the Cat, *boafted,* that He
had various *Shifts,* fo
that He had *even* a Budget
full of Tricks : *But*
the Cat *anfwered,* That She *had*
only one Art, *to which*
She trufted, *if* there was
any *Thing* of Danger. *In* the Dif-
courfe *fuddenly*
the Noife *of the Dogs* running *is heard :* Then *the Cat*
leaps *into* a very. high
Tree ; in the mean time *the Fox*
furrounded *by the Dogs* is taken.

MOR.   MOR.

Fabula *innuit*, nonnun-   The Fable *intimates*, that fome-
quam *unicum* Confilium,   times one Defign,
modò fit *verum*, & *efficax*, *fo that* it be *true*, and *effectual*,
effe *præftabilius* quàm *plures* is better than more
Dolos, & frivola *Confilia*.   Tricks, *and* frivolous *Defigns*.

FABLE

FABLE LXXXIV.

De RFGE & SIMIIS.　　*Of* the KING *and* the APES.

QUidam *Ægyptius* Rex *inflituit* aliquot *Simias,* ut *perdifcerent* Actionem *faltandi.* Nam, *ut* nullum *Animal* accedit *propiùs* ad *Figuram* Homjnis, *ita* nec *aliud* imitatur *humanos* Actus *aut* meliùs, *aut* libentiùs. *Itaque* protinus *edoctæ* Artem *faltandi,* *cæperunt* faltare, *indutæ* purpureis *Veſtimentis,* ac *perfonatæ* ; & *Spectaculum* jam *placebat* longo *Tempore* in *mirum* Modum ; *donec* Qnifpiam *è* Spectatoribus *facetus* abjecit *Nuces* in *Medium,* Quas *habebat* clanculum *in* Loculis. *Ibi* ftatim , Simiæ, fimul atque *vidiſſent* Nuces, *oblitæ* Choreæ, *cæperunt* eſſe *Id,* Quod *fuerant* antea, ac repentè *è* Saltatricibus *redièrunt* in Simias ; & *Perfonis* & *Veſtibus* dilaceratis, *pugnabaut* inter Se pro *Nucibus,* non *fine* maximo *Rifu* Spectatorum.

A Certain *Egyptian* King *appointed* fome *Apes,* that *they ſhould learn* the Action *of Dancing.* For, *as* no *Animal* cometh *nearer* to *the Figure* of a Man, *ſo* neither *any other* imitates *human* Actions *either* better, *or* more willingly. *Therefore* prefently *being taught* the Art *of Dancing,* They *began* to dance, *clothed* in purple *Veſments,* and *maſked ;* and the Sight now *pleaſed* for a long *Time* after *a wonderful* Manner ; *till* One *of* the Spectators *facetious* threw *Nuts* into *the Mid-dle,* Which he had privately *in* his Pockets. *Then* prefently *the Apes,* as foon as *They faw* the Nuts, *having forgot* the Dance, *began* to be *That,* Which *they had been* before, *and* fuddenly *from* Dancers *returned* into *Apes ;* and *their Maſks* and *Clothes* being torn, *they fought* among *Themfelves* for *the Nuts,* not *without* the greateſt *Laughter* of the Spectators.

MOR.

Hæc *Fabula* admonet, *Ornamenta* Fortunæ *non mutare* Ingenium *Hominis.*

MOR.

This *Fable* admoniſheth, *that the Ornaments* of Fortune *do not change* the Difpofition *of a Man.*

FABLE

FABLE LXXXV.

De ASINO & VIATO-RIBUS.

DUO *Quidam*, cùm *fortè* invenirent *Asinum* in *Sylvâ*, cœperunt *contendere* inter *Se*, Uter *Eorum* abduceret *Eum* Domum, *uti* fuum ; *nam* videbatur *pariter* objectus *Utriq;* à *Fortunâ*. In-terim, *Illis* altercantibus *invicem*, Afinus *abduxit* Se, *ac* Neuter *potitus eft* Eo.

MOR.

Quidam *excidunt* à *præfentibus* Commodis, *Quibus* nefciunt *uti* ob *Infcitiam*.

Of the ASS and the TRAVEL-LERS.

TWO *certain Men*, when *by chance* they found an *Afs* in a *Wood*, began to *contend* between *Themfelves*, Whether *of them* fhould lead *Him* Home, *as* his own ; *for* he feemed *equally* offered to *Either* by *Fortune*. In the mean time, *They* wrangling by *Turns*, the Afs *withdrew* Himfelf, *and* Neither *obtained* Him.

MOR.

Some *fall* from *prefent* Advantages, *Which* they know not how *to ufe* thro' *Ignorance.*

FABLE LXXXVI.

De CORVO & LUPIS.

CORVUS *comitatur* Lupos *per* ardua *Juga* Montium ; *paftu-lat* Partem *Prædæ* Si-bi, *quia* fecutus effet, *&* non deftituiffet *Eos* ullo *Tempore*. Deinde *eft* re-pulfus à Lupis, *quia* non minùs *voraret* Exta *Luporum*, fi *occiderentur*, quàm *Exta* cæterorum *Animalium*.

Of the CROW and the WOLVES.

THE CROW *accompanies* the Wolves *thro'* the high *Tops* of the Mountains ; *He demands* a Part *of the Prey* for Him-felf, *becaufe* he had followed, *and* had not forfook *Them* at any *Time*. Then *he is* re-pulfed *by* the Wolves, *becaufe* no lefs *would he devour* the Entrails *of the Wolves*, if they *fhould be flain,* than *the Entrails* of other *Animals.*

I

MOR.

Mor.

Non *Quid* agamus *est* semper *inspiciendum;* sed quo Animo *simus,* cùm agamus.

Mor.

Not *What* We may do *is* always *to be looked into;* but of *What* Mind *We be,* when *We do it.*

FABLE LXXXVII.

De Mure nato *in* Cistâ.

Of the Mouse born *in* the Chest.

MUS *natus* in *Cistâ* duxerat *ferè* omnem *Vitam* ibi, *pastus* Nucibus, *Quæ* solebant *servari* in *Eâ.* Autem, *dum* ludens *circa* Oras *Cistæ* decidisset, *&* quæreret *Ascensum,* reperit *Epulas* lautissimè *paratas,* Quas cùm cœpisset *gustare,* inquit, *Quàm* stolidus *fui* hactenus, *Qui* credebam *esse* Nihil in toto Orbe *melius* meâ *Cistulâ?* Ecce! *quàm* vescor *suavioribus* Cibis *hìc!*

A Mouse *born* in *a Chest* had led *almost* all *his Life* there, *fed* with Nuts, *Which* were wont *to be kept* in *It.* But, *whilst* playing about the Edges *of the Chest* He fell down, *and* tried at *getting up,* He found *Dainties* most sumptuously *prepared,* Which *when* He had began *to taste,* He said, *How* foolish *have I been* hitherto, *Who* believed *there was* nothing in the whole World *better* than my *Chest?* Behold! *how* I am fed *with sweeter* Meats *here!*

Mor.

Hæc *Fabula* indicat, *Patriam* non *diligendam* ita, *ut* non adeamus ea *Loca,* ubi *possimus* esse *beatiores.*

Mor.

This *Fable* shows, *that a Country* is not *to be beloved* so, *that* We may not go *to those Places,* where *We may be able* to be *more happy.*

FABLE

De RUSTICO *impetrante,* *Of* the COUNTRYMAN *obtaining,*
ut *Triticum* nasceretur   that *Wheat* should grow
absque Aristis.   *without* Beards.

Quidam *Rusticus* im-
petraverat *à* Cerere,
ut Triticum *nasceretur* absq;
Aristis, ne *læderet*
Manus *Metentium* &
Triturantium ; Quod, *cùm*
inaruit, *est* . *depastum* à
minutis Avibus : *Tum* Rusticus *inquit,* Quàm *dignè*
patior ! *Qui* Causâ
parvæ commoditatis *perdidi*
etiam *maxima* Emolumen-
ta.

A Certain *Countryman* had obtained *from* Ceres,
that Wheat *should grow* without
Beards, that it might not *hurt*
the Hands *of the Reapers* and
Threshers ; Which, *when*
it grew ripe, *was eat up* by
the small Birds : *Then* the Countryman *said,* How *worthily*
I suffer ! *Who* for the Sake
of a small Commodity *have lost*
even *the greatest* Advantages.

MOR.

MOR.

Fabula *indicat,* parva
Incommoda pensanda
majori Utilitate.

The Fable *shows,* that small
Disadvantages are to be weighed
with a greater Profit.

FABLE LXXXIX.

De ACCIPITRE *insequente*
COLUMBAM.

Of the HAWK *pursuing*
the PIGEON.

CUM *Accipiter* inse-
queretur *Columbam*
præcipiti *Volatu,* ingres-
sus *quandam* Villam *est*
captus *à* Rustico, *Quem*
obsecrabat *blandè,* ut
dimitteret Se ; *nam,*
dixit, *non læsi* Te.
Cui Rusticus *respon-*
dit, nec *Hæc* læserat *Te.*

WHEN *the Hawk* pur-
sued *the Pigeon*
with a speedy *Flight,* having entered a *certain* Village He *was*
taken *by* a Countryman, *Whom*
He besought *fairly,* that
He *would dismiss* Him ; *for,*
said He, - *I have not hurt* Thee.
To whom the Countryman an-
swered, nor *had She* hurt *Thee.*

MOR.

MOR.

Fabula *indicat*, Eos *puuiri* meritò, *Qui* conantur *ledere* innocentes.

MOR.

The Fable *shows*, that They *are punished* deservedly, *Who* endeavour *to hurt* the Innocent.

FABLE XC.

De RUSTICO *transituro* Amnem.

Of the COUNTRYMAN *about to pass over* a RIVER.

RUsticus *transiturus* Torrentem, *Qui* fortè excreverat *Imbribus*, quærebat *Vadum*, & cùm tentavisset *eam* Partem *Fluminis*, Quæ *videbatur* quietior, & placidior, *reperit* Eam *altiorem*, quàm *fuerat* opinatus ; *rursus* adinvenit *breviorem*, & *tutiorem* Partem ; *ibi* Fluvius *decurrebat* majori *Strepitu* Aquarum : *Tum* inquit *Secum*, Quàm *tutiùs* possumus *credere* nostram *Vitam* in *clamosis* Aquis, quàm in *quietis* & *silentibus*.

A Countryman *about to pass over* a Torrent, *Which* by Chance had increased *by the Showers*, fought *a Shallow*, and *when* He had tried *that* Part of the *River*, Which *seemed* more quiet, *and* smooth, *he found* It *deeper*, than He *had* thought ; again He came to *a shallower*, and *safer* Part ; *there* the River *ran down* with a greater *Noise* of Waters : *Then* He said *with Himself*, How more *safely* are we able *to trust* Our *Life* in *the* clamorous Waters, *than* in *the* quiet and *silent*.

MOR.

Admonemur *hâc* Fabulâ, *ut* extimescamus *Homines* verbosos, & minaces, *minùs* quàm *quietos.*

MOR.

We are admonished *by this* Fable, *that* We should fear *Men* verbose, *and* threatning, *less* than *the quiet.*

FABLE

FABLE XCI.

De Columba *&* Pica. *Of* the Pigeon *and* the Magpie.

Columbâ *interrogata* à Picâ, Quid *induceret* Eam, *ut* nidificaret *semper* in *eodem* Loco, *cùm* ejus *Pulli* femper *furriperentur* inde, *refpondit,* Simplicitas.

THE Pigeon *being afked by* the Pie, What *could induce* Her, *that* She built *always* in *the fame* Place, *when* Her *Young* always *were taken* from thence, *anfwered,* Simplicity.

Mor.

Mor:

Hæc *Fabula* indicat, *bonos* Viros *fæpe* decipi *facilè.*

This *Fable* fhows, *that good* Men *often* are deceived *eafily.*

FABLE XCII.

De Asino *&* Vitulo: *Of* the Ass *and* the Calf.

A Sinus *&* Vitulus, *cùm* pafcerentur *in* eodem *Prato,* præfentiebant *hoftilem* Exercitum *adventare* Sonitu *Campanæ.* Tum *Vitulus* inquit, O Sodalis, *fugiamus* hinc, *ne* Hoftes *abducant* Nos *Captivos* ; Cui *Afinus* refpondit, *Fuge* Tu, *Quem* Hoftes *confueverunt* occidere, *&* effe : *Nihil interest* Afini, *Cui* ubique *eadem* Conditio *ferendi* Oneris *est* propofita.

THE Afs *and* the Calf, *when* they were fed *in* the fame *Pafture,* perceived *an* Enemy's Army *to approach* by the Sound *of a Bell.* Then *the Calf* faid, O Companion, let us *fly* hence, *left* the Enemies *lead away* Us *Captives* ; To whom *the Afs* aufwered, *Fly* Thou, *Whom* the Enemies *have been* ufed to flay, *and* to eat : *It is no Interest* of the Afs, *to Whom* every where *the fame* Condition *of bearing* a Burden *is* offered.

Mor.

Mor.

Hæc *Fabula* admonet *Servos,* ne formident *mag-*

This *Fable* warns *Servants,* that they may not fear *greatly magnopere* mutare *Dominos,* modò *futuri* non fint *deteriores* prioribus.

greatly to change *their Lords,* provided that *the future* be not *worse* than the former.

FABLE XCIII.

De VULPE *&* MULIERI-BUS *edentibus* Gallinas,

Of the Fox *and* the Wo-MEN *eating* the Hens.

VUlpes *transiens* juxta *quandam* Villam, *conspexit* catervam *Mulierum* comedentem *alto* Silentio *plurimas* Gallinas *opiparè* affatas : *Ad* Quas *conversa* inquit, *Qui* Clamores *&* Latratus *Canum* effent contra Me, *si* Ego *facerem* Quod *Vos* facitis ? *Cui* quædam *Anus* refpondens inquit, Nos *comedimus* Quæ funt Noftra, verò Tu *furaris* aliena.

A FOX *paffing* near a *certain* Village, faw a Heap *of* *Women* eating in *deep* Silence very *many* Hens *daintily* roafted : *To* Whom *being turned* He faid, *What* Clamours *and* Barkings *of Dogs* would be *against* Me, *if* I *did* What *You* do ? *To* *whom* a certain *old* *Woman* anfwering faid, We eat What *are* Ours, *but* Thou *ftealeft* other Men's Things.

MOR.

Quod *eft* meum *non atti-net* ad *Te.* Ne *furare ;* efto *contentus* tuis *Rebus.*

MOR,

What *is* mine *does not be-long* to *Thee.* Do *not fteal ;* be *content* with thine own *Things.*

FABLE XCIV.

De pinguibus CAPONIBUS *&* macro.

Of the fat CAPONS *and* the lean one.

QUidam *Vir* nutricave-rat *complures* Capones *in* eodem *Ornithobofcio ;* Qui *omnes* funt *effecti* pingues *præter*

A Certain *Man* had brought up *very* *many* Capons *in* the fame *Coop ;* Who *all* were *made* fat *except*

præter Unum, *Quem* Fratres *irridebant,*ut *macilentum.* Dominus *accepturus* nobiles *Hospites* lauto & fumptuofo *Convivio,* imperat *Coquo,* ut *interimat,* & *coquat* ex *His,* Quos *invenerit* pinguiores. *Pingues* audientes *Hoc* afflictabant *Sefe,* dicentes, *O fi* Nos *fuiffemus* macilenti !

except One, *Which* his Brethren laughed at, as *lean.* The Mafter *about to receive* noble *Guefts* in a neat and fumptuous *Banquet,* commands *the Cook,* that *He fhould kill* and *cook* out of *Thefe,* which *He fhould find* the fatter. *The fat* hearing *This* afflicted *Themfelves,* faying, *O if* We had been lean !

MOR.

Hæc *Fabula* eft *conficta* in *Solamen* Pauperum, *quorum* Vita *eft* tutior, *quàm* Vita *Divitum.*

MOR.

This *Fable* was *invented* for *the Comfort* of the Poor, *whofe* Life is fafer, *than* the Life *of the Rich.*

FABLE XCV.

De CYGNO canente *in* Morte, *reprehenfo* Ciconiâ.

Of the SWAN finging *in* Death, *reprehended* by the Stork.

CYgnus *moriens* interrogabatur *à* Ciconiâ, *cur* in *Morte,* Quam *cætera* Animalia *adeò* exhorrent, *emitteret* Sonos *multò* fuaviores, *quàm* in omni Vitâ ; *cùm potiùs deberet* effe *mæftus.* Cui *Cygnus* inquit, *Quia* non *cruciabor* ampliùs *Curâ* quærendi *Cibi.*

THE Swan *dying* was afked *by* the Stork, *why* in *Death,* Which *other* Animals fo fear, He fent forth Sounds *much* fweeter, *than* in all his Life ; *when* rather *He* ought to be *fad.* To whom *the Swan* faid, *Becaufe* I fhall not *be tormented* longer *with the Care* of feeking *Meat.*

MOR.

Hæc *Fabula* admonet, ne *formidemus* Mortem ; *Quâ* omnes *Miferiæ* præfentis *Vitæ* præciduntur.

MOR.

This *Fable* admonifhes, that *We* do *not fear* Death ; *by Which* all *the Miferies* of the prefent *Life* are cut off.

FABLE

FABLE XCVI.

De TRABE & BOBUS trahentibus Eam.

ULmea *Trabs* conquerebatur *de* Bubus, *dicens,* O *Ingrati,* Ego *alui* Vos *multo* Tempore *meis* Fiondibus; *vero* Vos *trabitis* Me *vestram* Nutricem *per* Saxa , & Luta. *Cui* Boves ; *Nostra* Suspiria & Gemitus & Stimulus, *Quo* pungimur, *possunt* docere *Te;* quod *inviti* trahimus *Te.*

MOR.

Hæc *Fabula* docet *Nos,* ne excandescamus *in* Eos, *Qui* lædunt *Nos,* non *suâ* Sponte.

Of the BEAM *and* the OXEN *drawing* It.

AN Elm *Beam* complained *of* the Oxen, *saying,* O *ungrateful,* I *have fed* You *a long* Time *with my* Leaves ; *but* You draw Me *your* Nourisher *thro'* Stones *and* Dirt. *To Whom* the Oxen ; *Our* Sighs *and* Groans *and* the Goad, *with which* We are pricked, *are able* to teach *Thee,* that *unwilling* We draw *Thee.*

MOR.

This *Fable* teaches *Us,* that we should not be hot *against* Them, *Who* hurt *Us,* not *of their own* Accord.

FABLE XCVII.

De Anguillâ *conquerente,* quòd *infestaretur* magìs, *quàm* Serpens.

ANguilla *interrogabat* Serpentem, *cur,* cùm *essent* similes; *atq;* cognati, *Homines* tamen *insequerentur* Se *potiùs,* quàm *Illam :* Cui *Serpens* inquit, *quia* rarò *lædunt* Me impunè.

Of the Eel *complaining,* that *He was infested* more *than* the Serpent.

THE Eel *asked* the Serpent, *why,* seeing that *They were* alike, *and* Kinsfolk, Men yet *pursued* Him *rather* than *Her :* To whom *the Serpent* said, *because* seldom *do They* hurt Me *unpunished.*

MOR.

MOR.

Hæc *Fabula* indicat, *Eos* folere *lædi* minùs, *Qui* ulcifcuntur.

MOR.

This *Fable* fhows, *that They* are wont *to be hurt* lefs, *Who* revenge.

FABLE XCVIII.

De . ASINO, SIMIA, & TALPA.

Of the ASS, *the* APE, *and the* MOLE.

A Sino *conquerente*, quòd *careret* Cornibus ; *verò* Simia, *quòd* Cauda *deeffet* Sibi ; *Talpa* inquit, *Tacete*, cùm *videas* Me *effe* captum *Oculis.*

T HE Afs *complaining*, that He *wanted* Horns ; *but* the Ape, *that* a Tail *was wanting* to Him ; *The Mole* faid, *Hold your Peace*, when *you* fee Me *to be* deprived *of Eyes.*

MOR.

Hæc *Fabula* pertinet *ad* Eos, *Qui* non funt *contenti* fuâ Sorte ; Qui, fi *confiderarent* Infortunia *Aliorum*, tolerarent *fua* æquiore *Animo.*

MOR.

This *Fable* pertains *to* Them, *Who* are not *content* with their own *Condition ;* Who, if *They* confidered the Misfortunes *of Others*, would bear *their own* with a more patient *Mind.*

FABLE XCIX.

De NAUTIS *implorantibus* Auxilium *Sanctorum.*

Of the MARINERS *imploring* the Help *of the Saints.*

Q Uidam *Nauta* deprehenfus *in* Mari *fubitâ* & *atrâ* Tempeftate, *cæteris* ejus *Sociis* implorantibus Auxilium diverforum *Sanctorum*, inquit, *Nefcitis* Quod *petitis ;* Etenim, *antequam* ifti *Sancti* conferant

A Certain *Mariner* overtaken *at* Sea *with a fudden* and *dark* Tempeft, *the reft* of his *Companions* imploring the Help of different *Saints*, faid, *Ye know not* What *ye afk ;* For, *before that* thofe *Saints* can betake

K

rant *Se* ad *Deum* pro *nostrâ* Liberatiône, obruemur bâc *imminenti* Procellâ. *Confugite* igitur *ad Eum, Qui* Absque *Adminiculo Alterius* poterit *liberare* Nos *à* tantis *Malis.* Igitur, *Auxilio* Omnipotentis *Dei* invocato, *illico* Procella *cessavit.*

take *Themselves* to *God* for our Deliverance, *We shall be overwhelmed* in this *imminent* Storm. *Fly* therefore *to* Him, *Who* without *the Help of Another* shall be able *to deliver* Us *from* so great *Evils.* Therefore, *the Help* of Almighty *God* being invoked, *presently* the Storm *ceased.*

Mor.

Ne confugito *ad* imbecilliores, *ubi* Auxilium *potentioris* potest *haberi.*

Mor.

Do not fly *to* the weaker, *where* the Help *of a more powerful* may *be had.*

FABLE C.

De Piscibus *desilientibus* è *Sartagine* in *Prunas.*

Of the Fishes *leaping* out of *the Frying-Pan* into *the Coals.*

PIsces *adhuc* vivi *coquebantur* in *Sartagine* ferventi *Oleo :* Unus *Quorum* inquit, *Fratres,* Fugiamus *hinc,* ne pereamus. Tum *Omnes* pariter *exilientes* è *Sartagine* deciderunt *in* ardentes *Prunas.* Igitur *affecti* majore *Dolore* damnabant *Consilium,* Quod *ceperant,* dicentes, *Quanto* atrociori *Morte* nunc *perimus !*

FIshes *yet* alive *were cooked* in a *Frying-Pan* with scalding *Oil :* One *of Which* said, *O Brethren,* Let us fly *hence,* that we may not perish. Then *All* in like Manner *leaping* out of *the Frying-Pan* fell *upon* the burning *Coals.* Therefore *affected* with greater *Pain* They condemned *the Counsel,* Which *They had taken,* saying, *By how much* a more cruel *Death* now do *We perish !*

Mor.

Hæc *Fabula* admonet *Nos,* ut *vitemus* præsentia *Pericula* ita, *ne incidamus* in *graviora.*

Mor.

This *Fable* admonishes *Us,* that *We avoid* the present *Dangers* so, *that we do not fall* into *more grievous.*

FABLE

FABLE CI.

De Quadrupedibus *ineun-*
tibus Societatem *cum*
Piscibus *adverfus* Aves.

Of the Four-footed Beasts *enter-*
ing into an Alliance *with*
the Fishes *against* the Birds.

Quadrupedés, *cùm*
Bellum *effet* indictum
Sibi ab *Avibus*, ineunt
Fædus cum *Piscibus*,
ut *tuerentur* Se *eo-*
rum Auxilio *à* Furore
Avium. Autem, *cùm* ex-
pectarent *optata* Auxilia,
Pisces negant, *Se* posse
accedere ad *Se* per *Terram.*

THe Four-footed Beasts, *when*
War *was* proclaimed against
Them by *the Birds*, enter into
a League with *the Fishes*,
that *they would defend* Them *with*
their Help *from* the Fury
of the Birds. But, *when* They expected *the defired* Succours,
the Fishes deny, *that They* are able
to come to them *by Land.*

Mor.

Hæc *Fabula* admonet *Nos*,
ne faciamus *Eos* So-
cios *Nobis*, Qui, *cùm* sit
Opus, non possunt *adeffe*
Nobis.

Mor.

This *Fable* advifes *Us*,
that We do not make *Them* Companions *to Us*, Who, *when* there is
Need, are not able *to be prefent*
to Us.

FABLE CII.

De Viro, Qui *accessit* ad
Cardinalem nuper *creatum*
Gratiâ *gratulandi.*

Of a Man, Who *went* to
a *Cardinal* lately *created* for
the Sake *of congratulating Him.*

Quidam *Vir* admodum
facetus, audiens *suum*
Amicum *adfumptum* ad *Dig-*
nitatem Cardinalatûs,
accessit ad *Eum* Gratiâ gra-
tulandi : Qui *tumidus*
Honore, *diffimulans*
agnofcere *veterem* Amicum,
interrogabat, Quifnam *effet.*
Cui

A Certain Man very
facetious, hearing *that his*
Friend *was preferred* to *the Dig-*
nity of the Cardinalfhip,
went to *Him* for the Sake *of con-*
gratulating Him : Who *puffed up*
with the Honour, *diffembling*
to know *his* old Friend,
afked, Who *He was.*
To

Cui *ille* inquit, *ut* erat *promptus* ad *Jocos,* Miferefco *Tui* & *Cæterorum,* Qui *perveniunt* ad *Honores* hujus *Modi ;* etenim, *quamprimum* eftis affecuti *Dignitates* hujus *Modi,* ita *amittitis* Vifum, *Auditumq;* & *cæteros* Senfus, *ut* non *amplius* dignofcatis *priftinos* Amicos.

To Whom *He* faid, *as* He was *ready* at *Jefts,* I pity *Thee* and *Others,* Who *arrive* to *Honours* of this *Kind ;* for, *as foon as* Ye have obtained *Dignities* of this *Kind,* fo do *you lofe* Sight, *and Hearing,* and *the other* Senfes, *that* no *longer* do ye diftinguifh *old* Friends.

Mor.

Hæc *Fabula* notat *Eos,* Qui *fublati* in *altum* defpiciant *veteres* Amicitias.

Mor.

This *Fable* denotes *Thofe,* Who *raifed up* on *high* defpife *ancient* Friendfhips.

FABLE CIII.

De Aquilâ & Picâ.

Of the Eagle *and* the Magpie.

PIca *interrogabat* Aquilam, *ut* acciperet *Se* inter *fuos* Familiares & Domefticos ; *quando* mereretur *Id,* cùm *Pulchritudine* Corporis, *tum* Volubilitate *Linguæ* ad *peragenda* Mandata. *Cui Aquila* refpondit, *facerem* Hoc, *ni* vererer, *ne* efferres *cuncta* tuâ *Loquacitate,* Quæ *fiant* intra *meam* Tegulam.

THE Magpie *afked* the Eagle, *that* She would receive *Her* among *her* Familiars *and* Domefticks ; *feeing that* She deferved *That,* both *by Beauty* of Body, *and* Volubility *of Tongue* to *difpatch* Commands. *To whom* the Eagle anfwered, *I fhould do* This, *unlefs* I feared, *left* Thou fhouldft bear abroad *all Things* by *thy Talkativenefs,* Which *may be done* within *my* Roof.

Mor.

Hæc *Fabula* monet, *linguaces* & *garrulos* Homines *non habendos* Domi.

Mor.

This *Fable* advifes, *that* talkative and *prating* Men *are not to be had* at Home.

FABLE

FABLE CIV.

De Turdo *ineunte* Amicitiam *cum* Hirundine.

Of the Thrush *entering into* Friendship *with* the Swallow.

TUrdus gloriabatur, Se contraxisse Amicitiam *cum* Hirundine ; *Cui* Mater inquit, Fili, es Stultus, si credas, Te posse convivere cum Eâ, cùm Uterq; Veſtrûm soleat appetere diversa Loca ; etenim Tu delectaris frigidis Locis, Illa tepidis.

THE Thrush boaſted, that He had contracted a Friendship with the Swallow ; To whom the Mother said, Son, Thou art a Fool, if Thou believe that Thou art able to live with Her, seeing that Each of you is wont to desire different Places ; for Thou art delighted with cold Places, She with warm.

MOR.

Monemur hâc Fabulâ, ne faciamus Eos Amicos Nobis, Quorum Vita disſentit à noſtrâ.

MOR.

We are advised by this Fable, that We do not make Them Friends to Us, Whose Life diſſereth from ours.

FABLE CV.

De quodam Divite & Servo.

Of a certain Rich Man and his Servant.

ERat quidam Dives habens Servum tardi Ingenii, Quem solebat nuncupare Regem Stultorum : Ille sæpe irritatus his Verbis ſtatuit referre par Hero ; etenim semel converſus in Herum inquit, Utinam eſſem Rex Stultorum ; etenim nullum Imperium in toto Orbe Terrarum eſſet latiùs meo ;

THere was a certain rich Man having a Servant of a ſlow Wit, Whom He uſed to call the King of Fools : He often irritated at theſe Words reſolved to return the like to his Maſter ; for once turned upon his Maſter he said, I wish I was the King of Fools ; for no Empire in the whole Globe of Lands would be wider than

meo ; & *Tu* quoque *fub-* *effes* meo *Imperio.*

than mine ; and *Thou* alfo *wouldft* *be under* my *Empire.*

MOR.

Fabula *indicat,* Stultum *fæpe* loqui *opportunè.*

MOR.

The Fable *fhows,* that a Fool *often* fpeaks *pertinently.*

FABLE CVI.

De Urbanis CANIBUS *in-* *fequentibus* Villaticum.

Of the City DOGS *purfu-* ing the Village One.

COmplures *urbani* Canes *infequebantur* quendam *villaticum* præcipiti *Curfu ;* Quos *Ille* diu *fugit ;* nec *aufus eft* repugnare : At ubi *converfus* ad *Eos* infequentes *fubftitit,* & *Ipfe* quoque *cæpit* oftendere *Dentes,* Omnes *pariter* fubftiterunt, *nec* Aliquis *Urbanorum* audebat *appro-* *pinquare* Illi. *Tunc* Impe- rator Exercitûs, *Qui* fortè *aderat* ibi, *converfus* ad *fuos* Milites, *inquit,* Commilito- nes, *Hoc* Spectaculum *ad-* *monet* Nos, *ne* fugiamus, *cùm* videamus *præfentiora* Pericula *imminere* Nobis *fugientibus,* quàm *repug-* *nantibus.*

MANY City Dogs *purfued* a certain *Village one* with a hafty *Courfe ;* Whom *He* a long while *fled from ;* nor *dared* to refift : But when *turned* to *Them* purfuing *He ftopped,* and *He* alfo *began* to fhow his *Teeth,* They All *equally* ftopped, *nor* any One *of the City ones* dared *to ap-* proach Him. *Then* the General of an Army, *Who* by Chance *was* there, *turned* to his Soldiers, *faid,* Fellow-Sol- diers, *This* Sight *ad-* *monifhes* Us, *that we do not* fly, *when* We fee *more prefent* Dangers *to threaten* Us *flying,* than *refift-* ing.

FABLE

FABLE CVII.

De TESTUDINE *&* RANIS.	*Of the* TORTOISE *and the* FROGS.

TESTUDO *conspicata* Ranas, *Quæ* pasceban-tur *in eodem Stagno,* adeò *leves,* agilesque, *ut* facilè *prosilirent* quòlibet, *&* saltarent *longissimè,* accusa-bat *Naturam,* quòd *procreâsset* Se *tardum* Animal, *& impeditum* maximo One-*re,* ut *neque* posset *movere* Se *facilè,* & *assiduè* premeretur *magnâ* Mole. At, *ubi* vidit *Ranas* fi-eri *Escam* Anguillarum, & *obnoxias* vel *levissimo* Ictui, *aliquantulùm* recrea-ta *dicebat,* Quantò *est* meliùs *ferre* Onus, *Quo sum* munita *ad* omnes *Ictus,* quàm *subire* tot *Discrimina* Mortis ?

THE Tortoise *having seen* the Frogs, *Which* were fed *in* the fame Pool, *fo light,* and nimble, *that* easily *They leaped* any where, *and* jumped *very far,* accu-fed *Nature,* that *She* had made Her *a slow* Animal, *and* hindered with the greateft *Bur-den,* that *neither* was She able *to move* Herself *easily,* and *daily* was pressed *with a great* Weight. But, *when* She faw *the Frogs* be-come *the Food* of the Eels, and *obnoxious* even *to the lightest* Blow, *a little* comfort-ed *she said,* By how much *is it* better *to bear* a Burden, *by Which I am* fortified *to* all *Blows,* than *to undergo* fo many *Dangers* of Death ?

MOR.	MOR.

Hæc *Fabula* indicat, *ne* feramus *ægrè* Dona *Naturæ,* Quæ *sæpe* funt *majori* Commodo *Nobis,* quàm *Nos* valeamus *intel-ligere.*

This *Fable* shows, *that we should not* bear *discontentedly* the Gifts *of* Nature, Which *often* are *a greater* Advantage *to Us,* than *We* may be able *to under-stand.*

FABLE

FABLE CVIII.

De GLIRIBUS *volentibus* eruere *Quercum.*

GLires *deflinaverant* eruere *Quercum,* glandiferam *Arborem,* Dentibus; quò habent *Cibum* paratiorem, *ne cogerentur* toties aſcendere & deſcendere *Gratiâ* Victûs. Sed Quidam *ex* His, *Qui* longè anteibat cæteros *Ætate,* & *Experientiâ* Rerum, abſterruit Eos, dicens, Si nunc interficimus *noſtram* Nutricem, *Quis* præbebit *Alimenta* Nobis, *ac* Noſtris *Annis futuris ?*

Of the DORMICE *willing* to over-turn *the Oak.*

THE Dormice *had deſigned* to over-turn *the Oak,* an Acorn-bearing *Tree,* with their Teeth ; that they might have *Food* readier, *that They might not be forced* ſo often to aſcend and deſcend *for the Sake* of Food. But One *of* Theſe, *Who* by far *excelled* the reſt *in Age,* and *Experience* of Things, deterred Them, *ſaying,* If *now* We deſtroy Our Nouriſher, *Who* will afford *Nouriſhments* to Us, and Ours *for future Years ?*

Mor.

' Hæc *Fabula* monet, *prudentem* Virum *debere* intueri *non* modò *præſentia,* verùm *longè* proſpicere *futura.*

Mor.

This *Fable* adviſes, *that a prudent* Man *ought* to look into *not* only *preſent Things,* but *aſar off* to foreſee *the future.*

FABLE CIX.

De CANE & HERO.

QUidam *habens* Canem, quo diligeretur *Illo* magìs, *ſemper* paſcebat Eum ſuis *Manibus,* & *ſolvebat* ligatum ; *autem* jubebat *ligari* & *verberari* à *Servo,* ut *Beneficia* viderentur

Of the DOG *and the* MASTER.

A Certain Man *having* a Dog, *that* He ſhould be beloved by *Him* more, *always* fed *Him* with his own *Hands,* and *loosed* Him bound ; *but* ordered Him *to be bound* and beat by *a Servant,* that *the Benefits* ſhould

viderentur *esse* collata *in* Illum *à* Se, *autem* Male-facta *à* Servo. Autem *Canis* ferens *ægrè*, Se *assiduè* ligari, & verberari, *aufugit* ; &, *cùm* increpa-retur *à* Domino, *ut* ingra-tus, & immemor *tantorum Beneficiorum*, Qui *fugisset* à *Se*, à *Quo* fuisset *semper* dilectus, & pastus, autem nunquam *ligatus*, & verberatus, respondit, *Puto* Id *Factum* à *Te*, Quod Servus *facit* tuo *Jussu*.

should seem *to be* conferred *upon* Him *by* Himself, *but* the ill Turns *by* the Servant. But *the Dog* bearing *unkindly*, that He daily was bound, *and* beat, *fled away* ; and, *when* He was blamed *by* the Master, *as* un-grateful, *and* unmindful *of so great Benefits*, Who *had fled* from *Him*, by *Whom* He had been always beloved, *and* fed, but never bound, and beaten, He answered, *I think* That *done* by *Thee*, Which a Servant *doth* by thy *Command*.

.Mor.

Fabula *indicat*, Eos *habendos* Malefactores, *Qui* fuêre *Causa* Maleficio-rum. ⸗

Mor.

The Fable *shows*, that Those are *to be accounted* Evil Doers, *Who* have been *the Cause* of evil Deeds.

F A B L E CX.

De Avibus *timentibus* Scarabæos.

Of the Birds *fearing* the Beetles.

M Agnus *Timor* inces-serat *Aves*, ne Scarabæi *occiderent* Eas *Balistâ*, à *Quibus* audive-rant *magnam* Vim *Pila-rum* fuisse *fabricatam* in *Sterquilinio* summo *Labore*. Tum *Passer* inquit, *Noli-te* expavescere ; etenim quomodo *potuerunt* jacere *Pilas* volantes *per* Aëra in Nos, *cùm* vix *trahant* Eas *per* Terram *magno* Molimine ?

A Great *Fear* had seiz-ed *the Birds*, lest the Beetles *should kill* Them *with a Cross-Bow*, by *Whom* They had heard *a great* Power *of Bul-lets* had been *forged* on *a Dunghill* with very great *Labour*. Then *the Sparrow* said, *Be not wil-ling* to fear ; *for* how *shall they be able* to cast *Bullets* flying *thro'* the Air *upon* Us, *when* scarce *they can draw* Them *on* the Ground *with great* Labour ?

L

Mor.

MOR.

Hæc *Fabula* admonet *Nos*, ne extimefcamus *Opes* Hoftium, *Quibus* videmus *Ingenium* deeffe.

MOR.

This *Fable* admonifhes *Us*, that We fear not *the Riches* of Enemies, *to Whom* We fee that *Wit* is wanting.

FABLE CXI.

De URSO & APIBUS.

Of the BEAR *and* the BEES.

URSUS *ictus* ab *Ape* eft percitus *tantâ* Irâ, *ut* difcerperet *tota* Alvearia *Unguibus*, in *Quibus* Apes *mellificaverant.* Tunc *univerfæ* Apes, cùm viderent *fuas* Domos dirui, Cibaria auferri, Filios necari, fubito *Impetu* invadentes Urfum, penè *necavére* Aculeis; *Qui* vix elapfus ex *Manibus* Eorum, *dicebat* Secum, *Quantò* erat *meliùs* tolerare *Aculeum* unius *Apis,* quàm *concitare* tot *Hoftes* in *Me* meâ *Iracundiâ?*

A BEAR *being ftung* by *a Bee* was ftirred *with fo great* Anger, *that* He tore *all* the Hives *with his Paws,* in *Which* the Bees *had made Honey.* Then *all* the Bees, *when* they faw *their* Houfes *overturned,* their Maintenances *taken away,* their Young *killed,* with a fudden *Onfet* attacking *the Bear,* almoft *killed Him* with their Stings; *Who* fcarce *having flipt* out of *the Hands* of Them, *faid* with Himfelf, *By how much* was *it better* to bear *the Sting* of one *Bee,* than *to raife up* fo many *Enemies* againft *Me* by my *Anger?*

MOR.

Hæc *Fabula* indicat *effe* longè *meliùs* fuftinere *Injuriam* Unius, *quàm,* dum *volumus* punire *Unum,* comparare *multos* Inimicos.

MOR.

This *Fable* fhows *it to be* far *better* to fuftain *the Injury* of One, *than,* whilft *We are willing* to punifh *One,* to get *many* Enemies.

FABLE

FABLE CXII.

De MILITE & duobus EQUIS.

MIles *habens* optimum *Equum*, emit *Alium* nequicquam *parem* Illi Bonitate, Quem nutriebat multò *diligentiùs*, quàm *priorem.* Tum *Posterior* ait *sic* priori, *Cur* Dominus *curat* Me impensiùs, quàm *Te ;* cùm *sim* comparandus *Tibi* neque *Pulchritudine*, neq; *Robore*, neque *Velocitate ?* Cui *Ille* inquit, Hæc est Natura Hominum, *ut* sint *semper* benigniores *in* novos Hospites.

Of the SOLDIER and the two HORSES.

A Soldier *having* a very good *Horse*, bought *Another* not at all *equal* to Him *in* Goodness, Whom *He* nourished much more *diligently*, than *the former.* Then *the Latter* said *thus* to the former, *Why* does my Master *mind* Me *more* diligently, than *Thee ;* seeing that I am to be compared *to Thee* neither in *Beauty*, nor Strength, nor *Swiftness ?* To Whom *He* said, *This* is *the Nature* of Men, *that* they are *always* more kind *to* new Guests.

MOR.

Hæc *Fabula* indicat *Amentiam* Hominum, *Qui* solent *anteponere* nova *veteribus*, etiamsi *sint* deteriora.

MOR.

This *Fable* shows *the Madness* of Men, *Who* are wont *to prefer* new Things to old, altho' *they* are worse.

FABLE CXIII.

De Aucupe & Fringillâ.

AUCEPS *tetenderat* Retia *Volucribus*, & *effuderat* largam *Escam* Illis *in* Areâ ; *tamen* non capiebat *Aves* pascentes ; *quia* videbantur *paucæ* Sibi ;

Of the Fowler and the Chaffinch.

THE Fowler *had stretched out* his Nets *to the Birds*, and had poured out much *Food* to Them *in* a void Place ; *yet* He did not take *the Birds* feeding ; *because* they seemed *Few* to Him ;

Sibi ; *Quibus* paftis, *ac* avolantibus, *Aliæ* adveniunt *paftum* ; Quas quoq; neglexit *capere* propter *Paucitatem*. Hoc *Ordine* fervato *per* totum *Diem*, ac *Aliis* advenientibus, *Aliis* abeuntibus, *Illo* femper ex-*pectante* majorem *Prædam*, tandem *cæpit* advefpe-rafcere : *Tunc* Auceps, *Spe* amiffâ *capiendi* mul-tas, *cùm* jam *effet* Tempus *quiefcendi*, attrahens *fua* Retia, *cepit* tantùm *unam* Fringillam, *quæ* infelix *Avis* remanferat *in* Areâ.

to Him ; *Which* being fed, *and* flying away, *Others* come *to feed* ; Which *also* He neglected *to take* for their *Fewnefs*. This *Order* being kept *thro'* the whole *Day*, and *Others* coming, *Others* going away, *He* always ex-*pecting* a greater *Prey*, at length *it began* to grow Evening : *Then* the Fowler, the *Hope* being loft *of taking* ma-ny, *when* now *it was* Time *of refting*, drawing up *his* Nets, *took* only *one* Chaffinch, *which* unhappy *Bird* had remained *in* the void Place.

Mor.

Hæc *Fabula* indicat, *Eos* fæpe *vix* poffe *capere* pauca, *Qui* volunt *comprehendere* omnia.

Mor.

This *Fable* fhows, *that they* often *fcarce* are able *to take* a few Things, *Who* are willing *to take* all Things.

FABLE CXIV.

De Sue & Cane.

Of the Swine and the Dog.

SUS *irridebat* odori-fequum *Canem*, Qui adulabatur Domino *Mur-mure* & *Caudâ*, à *Quo* fuerat *inftructus* ad aucupa-toriam Artem *multis Verberibus* & *Vellicationibus* Aurium : *Cui* Canis *inquit*, Infane, *nefcis* Quæ *fum* confecutus *ex* illis *Verberibus* ; etenim *per Ea* vefcor fuaviffimâ Carne

THE Swine *laughed at* the Scent-following *Dog*, Who *flattered* the Mafter *with a Mur-mur* and *his Tail*, by *Whom* He had been *inftructed* for *the fow-ling* Art *with many* Stripes and *Plucks* of the Ears : *To whom* the Dog *faid*, Mad Wretch, *That knoweft not* What *I have* obtained *from* thofe Stripes ; for *by* Thofe I am fed *with the moft fweet* Flefh

Carne Perdicum & Flesh of Partridges and
Coturnicum. Quails.

MOR. MOR.

Hæc Fabula admonet Nos, ne feramus iniquo Animo Verbera Præceptorum, Quæ confueverunt esse Causa multorum bonorum.

This Fable admonishes Us, that We should not bear with an impatient Mind the Stripes of Masters, Which have used to be the Cause of many good Things.

FABLE CXV.

De TRABE increpante Pigritiam Boûm.

Of the BEAM blaming the Slowness of the Oxen.

TRabs, Quæ vehebatur Curru, increpabat Boves, ut lentulos, dicens, Pigri, currite, nam portatis leve Onus : Cui Boves responderunt, Irrides Nos ? Ignoras, quæ Pœna manet Te. Nos deponemus hoc Onus citò : autem tum Tu cogeris sustinere, quoad rumparis. Trabs indoluit, nec ausa est amplius lacessere Boves Conviciis.

THE Beam, which was carried in a Waggon, blamed the Oxen, as slow, saying, Ye slow Wretches, run, for ye carry a light Burden ; To whom the Oxen answered, Dost Thou laugh at Us ? Thou knowest not, what Punishment waits Thee. We shall lay down this Burden quickly : but then Thou shalt be forced to bear, until thou mayest be broken. The Beam grieved, nor dared longer to provoke the Oxen with Revilings.

MOR. MOR.

Hæc Fabula monet Quemlibet, ne insultet Calamitatibus Aliorum, cùm Ipse possit subjici majoribus.

This Fable adviseth any One, that He insult not the Calamities of Others, when He Himself may be subject to greater.

FABLE

FABLE CXVI.

De Carduele & Puero.

CArduelis *interrogata* à *Puero*, à *Quo* fuerat *habita* suis *Deliciis*, & *nutrita* suavibus *Cibis*, cur *egressa* Caveâ nollet regredi, inquit, Ut *possim* pascere meo Arbitratu, *non* tuo.

Of the Linnet and the Boy.

THE Linnet *being asked* by *the Boy*, by *Whom* She had been *held* in his *Delights*, and *nourished* with sweet *Meats*, why *having gone out* of the Cage *She was unwilling* to return, said, That *I may be able* to feed *at my* Pleasure, *not* at thine.

Mor.

Hæc *Fabula* indicat, *Libertatem* Vitæ anteponendam cunctis *Deliciis*.

Mor.

This *Fable* shows, *that Liberty* of Life *is to be preferred before* all *Delights.*

FABLE CXVII.

De Scurrâ & Episcopo.

SCurra *accedens* ad *quendam* Episcopum, *divitem* quidem, *sed* avarum, *Calendis* Januarii, *petebat* aureum *Numisma* Nomine *Strenæ:* Antistes *dixit,* Hominem *insanire,* Qui *crederet,* tantam *Pecuniam* dari *Sibi* in *Strenam.* Tum *Scurra* cœpit *efflagitare* argenteum *Nummum;* sed, *cùm* Ille *diceret,* Hoc *videri* nimiùm *Sibi,* orabat, *ut* traderet *Sibi* æreum *Quadrantem:* Sed *cùm* non posset *ex-*

Of the Jester and the Bishop.

A Jester *coming* to *a certain* Bishop, *rich* indeed, *but* covetous, *on the Calends* of January, *asked* a Golden Piece *of Money* in the Name *of a New-Year's Gift:* The Prelate said, that the Man *was mad,* Who *believed,* that so much *Money* would be given *Him* for a *New-Year's Gift.* Then *the Jester* began *to ask* some Silver *Money;* but, *when* He said, that This *seemed* too much *to Him,* He entreated, *that* He would give *Him* a brass *Farthing:* But *when* he was not able *to*

extorquere Hunc *ab* Epifco-po, *inquit*, reverende *Pater*, imperti *Me* tuâ *Benedictione* pro *Strenâ :* Tunc *Epifcopus* inquit, *Fili*, flecte tua *Genua*, ut *benedicam* Tibi. At *Scurra* inquit, *Ego* nolo *tuam* tam *vilem* Benedicti-onem ; *etenim* fi *valeret* æreum *Nummum*, profectò *nunquam* concederes *Eam* Mihi.

to wring This *from* the Bi-fhop, *he faid*, reverend *Father*, reward *Me* with your *Bleffing* for *a New-Year's Gift :* Then the *Bifhop* faid, *Son*, bend thy *Knees*, that *I may blefs* Thee. But *the Jefter* faid, *I* will not have *thy* fo *cheap* Blef-fing ; *for* if *it availed* a brafs *Farthing*, truly *never* wouldft Thou grant *It* to Me.

MOR.

Hæc *Fabula* eft *confecta* contra *eos* Epifcopos *&* Sacerdotes, Qui *æftimant* Opes *&* Divitias *pluris* quàm *Sacra*, & *Myfteria* Ecclefiæ.

MOR.

This *Fable* is *made* againft *thofe* Bifhops *and* Priefts, Who *efteem* Wealth *and* Riches *more* than *the facred Rites*, and *Myfteries* of the Church.

FABLE CXVIII.

De Upupâ *honoratâ* in-dignè.

Of the Puet *honoured* un-worthily.

FErè *omnes* Aves *invi-tatæ* ad *Nuptias* Aqui-læ *ferebant* indigne, *Upupam* præferri *cæteris*, quia *effet* infignis *Coronâ*, & *ornata* verficoloribus *Pennis ;* cùm *femper* effet *folita* volitare *inter* Stercora *&* Sordes.

ALmoft *all* the Birds *being invi-ted* to *the Wedding* of the Ea-gle *bore it* unworthily, *that the Puet* was preferred *to the reft*, becaufe *fhe was* fine *with a Crown*, and adorned with various coloured Feathers ; when *always* She was *wont* to neftle *among* the Mud and Filth.

MOR.

Hæc *Fabula* arguit *Stul-titiam* Eorum, *Qui* in *ho-norandis* Hominibus *potiùs*

MOR.

This *Fable* reproves *the Fol-ly* of Them, *Who* in *honour-ing* Men *rather* are

foleant *obfervare* Nitorem
Veftium, & *Preftantiam*
Formæ, *quàm* Virtutes
& Mores.

are wont *to mind* the Splendour
of Cloaths, and *Excellency*
of Beauty, *than* Virtues
and Morals.

FABLE CXIX.

De SACERDOTE &
PYRIS.

Of the PRIEST *and*
the PEARS.

QUidam *gulofus* Sacerdos
proficifcens extra *Patri-*
am ad *Nuptias*, ad *Quas*
fuerat *invitatus*, reperit
Acervum Pyrorum in
Itinere, *Quorum* attigit
ne Unum *quidem ;* quin *po-*
tius habens *Ea* Ludibrio,
confperfit Urinâ ; *etenim*
indiguabatur, *Cibos* hujufmodi *offerri* in *Itinere*,
Qui *accefebat* ad *lautas*
Epulas. *Sed* cùm *offendiffet*
in *Itinere* quendam
Torrentem ita *auctum*
Imbribus, *ut* non pof-
fet *tranfire* Eum *fine*
Periculo *Vitæ*, conftituit
redire *Domum :* Autem *re-*
vertens jejunus *fuit* oppreffus
tantâ Fame, *ut* nifi
comediffet *illa* Pyra, *Quæ*
confperferat *Urinâ*, cùm
non *inveniret* Aliud,
fuiffet extinctus *Fame*.

A Certain *greedy* Prieft
going out of *his* Coun-
try to a *Wedding*, to *Which*
He had been *invited*, found
a *Heap* of Pears in
the Road, *of Which* He touched
not One *indeed ;* but *ra-*
ther having *Them* in Derifion,
He fprinkled them with Urine ; *for*
He refented, *that Meats* of this
Kind *fhould be offered* in *the Journey*,
Who *was going* to *fumptuous*
Dainties. *But* when *He had found*
in *the Way* a certain
Brook fo *increafed*
with the Showers, *that* He was
not able *to pafs over* It *without*
Danger *of Life*, He refolved
to return *Home :* But *re-*
turning fafting *He was* oppreffed
with fo great Hunger, *that* unlefs
He had eat *thofe* Pears, *Which*
He had fprinkled *with Urine*, when
He could not *find* any Thing elfe,
He had been dead *with Hunger*.

MOR.

Hæc *Fabula* admonet,
Nihil effe *contemnendum*,
cùm *Nihil* fit *tam* vile &
ab-

MOR.

This *Fable* advifes,
that *Nothing* is to be *defpifed*,
feeing that *Nothing* is fo vile and
ab-

abjectum, *Quod* non poffit
aliquando effe *Ufui*.

abject, *Which* may not
fometime be of *Ufe*.

FABLE CXX.

De Porco & Equo.

Of the Hog *and* the Horfe.

POrcus *confpiciens* Equum
Bellatoris, Qui *cata-*
phractus prodibat *ad* Pug-
nam, *inquit,* Stulte, *Quò*
properas ? *etenim* fortaffe
morieris in *Pugnâ.*
Cui *Equus* refpondit,
Cultellus adimet *Vitam* Tibi,
impinguato inter *Lutum* &
Sordes, cùm *gefferis*
Nihil dignum *Laude ;* verò
Gloria comitabitur *meam*
Mortem.

THE Hog *beholding* the Horfe
of a *Warriour,* Who *arm-*
ed went to Bat-
tle, *faid,* Fool, *Whither*
doft Thou haften ? *for* perhaps
Thou wilt die in the Fight.
To whom *the Horfe* anfwered,
A Knife will take *Life* from Thee,
fattened amongft *Mud* and
Filth, when *Thou fhalt have done*
Nothing worthy *of Praife ;* but
Glory fhall accompany *my*
Death.

Mor.

Hæc *Fabula* innuit, *effe*
honeftius *occumbere,* Rebus
geftis præclarè, *quàm*
protrahere *Vitam* actam
turpiter.

Mor.

This *Fable* hints, *that it is*
more honeft *to die,* Things
being carried famoufly, *than*
to protract *a Life* fpent
bafely.

FABLE CXXI.

De Coriario *emente* Pellem
Urfi nondum *capti* à
Venatore.

Of the Tanner *buying* the Skin
of a *Bear* not yet *taken* by
the *Huntfman.*

COriarius *accedens* ad
Venatorem emit *Pellem*
Urfi *ab* Eo, & protulit
Pecuniam pro *Eâ.* Ille *dixit,*
Sibi

THE Tanner *coming* to
the Hunter bought *the Skin*
of a Bear *of* Him, *and* proffered
Money for *It.* He *faid,*
that

M

Sibi *non esse* Pellem *Ursi* in *Præsentiâ;* cæterùm *po-stridie* profecturum *venatum,* &, *Urso* interfecto, *pollicetur,* Se *daturum* Pellem Illius *Ei.* Coriarius *profectus* in *Sylvam,* afcendit *altissimam* Arborem, *ut* inde *prospiceret* Certamen • *Ursi* & *Venatoris.* Venator *intrepidus* profectus *ad* Antrum, *ubi* Urfus *latebat,* Canibus *immissis,* compulit *Illum* exire, *Qui,* Ictu *Venatoris* évitato, *pro-stravit* Eum *Humi.* Tunc *Venator* fciens, *hanc* Feram *non fævire in* Cadavera, *fuo* Anhelitu *retento,* fimulabat *Se* mortuum. *Urfus* olfaciens, *cùm* deprehenderet *Illum,* nec *fpirantem* Nafo, nec Ore, *abfceffit.* Coriarius, *cùm* perfpiceret *Feram* abeffe, *ac* adeffe *Nihil* ampliùs *Periculi,* deducens *Se* ex *Arbore,* & *accedens* ad *Venatorem,* Qui *audebat* nondum *furgere,* monebat *Illum,* ut *furgeret:* deinde *interrogavit,* Quid *Urfus* effet locutus *Ei* ad *Aurem.* Cui *Venator* inquit, *Monuit* Me, *ne vellem* deinceps *vendere* Pellem *Urfi,* nifi *priùs* ceperim *Eum.*

that He *bad not* the Skin *of a Bear* at *prefent;* but *the* Day *after* He fhould go *to hunt,* and, *the* Bear being killed, *He promifes,* that He *would give the Skin* of it *to Him.* The Tanner *having gone* into *the Wood,* afcends *a very high* Tree, *that* thence *He might behold* the Engagement *of the Bear* and *the Hunter.* The Hunter *unaffrighted* having gone *to* the Cave, *where* the Bear *lay hid,* the Dogs *being fent in,* forced *Him* to go out, *Who,* the Blow *of the Hunter* being avoided, *beat* Him *on the Ground.* Then *the Hunter* knowing, *that this* Beaft *did not* rage *on* Carcaffes, *his* Breath *being held,* feigned *Himfelf* dead. *The Bear* fmelling, *when* he held *Him,* neither *breathing* at the Nofe, nor Mouth, *went away.* The Tanner, *when* He perceived *the Beaft* to be gone, *and* that there was *Nothing* more *of Danger,* letting down *Himfelf* out of *the Tree,* and *coming* to *the Hunter,* Who dared not yet *to arife,* advifed *Him,* that *He fhould arife:* then He *afked,* What *the* Bear had fpoke *to him* in *his Ear.* To whom *the* Hunter faid, *He warned* Me, *that I fhould not be willing* hereafter *to fell* the Skin *of a Bear,* unlefs *I firft* fhall have taken *Him.*

MOR.

MOR.

Hæc *Fabula* indicat, *incerta* non *habenda pro* certis.

MOR.

This *Fable* shows, *that uncertain Things* are not to be accounted *for* certain.

FABLE CXXII.

De·Eremitâ & Milite.

Of the Hermit·*and* the Soldier.

QUidam *Eremita,* Vir *sanctissime* Vitæ, *hortabatur* Militem, *ut* feculari *Militiâ* relictâ, *Quam* Pauci *exercent* absque *Offensâ* Dei, *& Difcrimine Vitæ,* tandem *traderet* Se *Quieti* Corporis, *&* confuleret *Saluti* Animæ. *Cui* Miles *inquit,* Pater, *faciam* quod *mones;* nam *eft* verum, *quòd* hoc *Tempore* Milites *neque* audent *exigere* Stipendia, *licèt* fint *exigua,* neque *prædari.*

A Certain *Hermit,* a Man *of most holy* Life, *advifed* a Soldier, *that* fecular *Warfare* being left, *Which* Few *exercife* without *Offence* of God, *and* Hazard *of Life,* at length, *he would give* Himfelf *to Quiet* of Body, *and* would confult *for Safety* of Soul. *To Whom* the Soldier *faid,* Father, *I will do* what *You advife;* for *it is* true, *that* at this *Time* Soldiers *neither* dare *to afk* Pay, *altho'* it be *fmall,* nor *to plunder.*

MOR.

Hæc *Fabula* indicat, *Multos* renunciare *Vitiis,* quia *Illi* non poffunt *exercere* Illa *ampliùs.*

MOR.

This *Fable* shows, *that Many* renounce *Vices,* becaufe *They* are not able *to exercife* Them *longer.*

FABLE CXXIII.

De Viro & Uxore *biga-mis.*

Of the Man *and* Wife *twice married.*

QUidam *Vir,* fuâ *Uxore* defunctâ, *Quam* valde *dilexerat,* duxit *Alteram,* & *Ipfam* Viduam ; *Quæ* affi-duè *objiciebat* Ei *Virtutes* & *fortia* Facinora *prioris* Ma-riti : *Cui,* ut *refferret* Par, Ipfe *quoque* refe-rebat *probatiffimos* Mores, & infignem *Pudicitiam* de-functæ *Uxoris.* Autem *quodam* Die, *irata* fuo *Viro,* dedit *Partem* Capo-nis, *Quem* coxerat *in* Cœnam *Utrifq;* Pauperi *petenti* Eleemofynam, *dicens,* Do *Hoc* Tibi *pro* Animâ *mei* prioris *Viri ;* Quod *Maritus* audiens, *Paupere* accerfito *ab* Eo, dedit *reliquum* Caponis *Ei,* dicens, *Et* Ego *quoque* do *Hoc* Tibi *pro* Animâ *meæ* defunctæ *Uxoris.* Sic *Illi,* dum *Alter* cupit *nocere* Alteri, *tandem* non habu-erunt *Quod* cœnarent.

A Certain *Man,* his *Wife* being dead, *Whom He* very much *had loved,* married *Another,* and *Her* a Widow ; *Who* dai-ly *objected* to Him *the Virtues* and *valiant* Deeds *of her former* Huf-band : *To Whom,* that *He might return* the Like, He *alfo* relat-ed *the moft approved* Morals, *and* remarkable *Modefty* of his dead *Wife.* But *on a cer-tain* Day, *being angry with* her *Hufband,* She gave *Part* of a Ca-pon, *Which* fhe had cooked *for* the Supper *of Each,* to a poor Man *afking* an Alms, *faying,* I give *This* to Thee *for* the Soul *of* my former *Hufband ;* Which *the Hufband* hearing, *the poor Man* being called *by* Him, gave *the reft* of the Capon *to Him,* faying, *And* I *alfo* give *This* to Thee *for* the Soul *of* my departed *Wife.* Thus *They,* whilft *One* defires *to* hurt the other, *at length* had not *What* They might fup on.

MOR.

Hæc *Fabula* monet, *non effe* pugnandum *contra* Eos *Qui* poffunt *vindicare* Se *optimè.*

MOR.

This *Fable* advifes, *that it is not* to be fought *againft* Thofe *Who* are able *to revenge* Themfelves *very well.*

FABLE

FABLE CXXIV.

De LEONE & MURE.

Of the LION *and* the MOUSE.

LEO, *captus* Laqueo *in* Sylvâ, *cùm* videret *Se* ita *irretitum,* ut *non.* *poſſet* explicare *Se* inde, *rogavit* Murem, *ut,* Laqueo *abroſo* ab *Eo,* liberaret *Eum,* promittens, *Se* non futurum *immemorem* tanti *Beneficii ;* Quod *cùm* Mus *feciſſet* promptè, *rogavit* Leonem, *ut* traderet *Filiam* Sibi *in* Uxorem : *Leo* non abnuit, *ut* faceret *Rem* gratam *ſuo* Benefaĉtori. *Autem* nova *nupta* veniens *ad* Virum, *cùm* non videret *Eum,* Caſu *preſſit* Illum *ſuo* Pede, & contrí-vit.

THE LION, *taken* in a Snare *in* the Wood, *when* He ſaw Himſelf ſo entangled, that He was not able to extricate Himſelf thence, aſked the Mouſe, *that,* the Snare *being gnawed* by *Him,* He would free *Him,* promiſing, *that He* would not be *unmindful* of ſo great *a Benefit ;* Which *when* the Mouſe *had done* readily, *He* aſked the Lion, *that* He would give *his Daughter* to Him *to* Wife : *The Lion* refuſed not, *that* He might do *a Thing* grateful *to his* Benefaĉtor. But the new *married Lady* coming *to* the Huſband, *when* She did not ſee *Him,* by Chance *preſſed* Him *with Her* Foot, and trod him to Pieces.

MOR.

Hæc *Fabula* indicat, *Matrimonia* & *cætera* Conſortia *improbanda,* Quæ *contrahuntur* ab *Imparibus.*

MOR.

This *Fable* ſhows, *that Marriages* and *other* Fellowſhips *are to be condemned,* Which *are contraĉted* by *Unequals.*

FABLE CXXV.

De ULMO & SILERE.

Of the ELM *and* the OSIER.

ULmus, *nata* in *Ripâ* Fluminis, *irridebat* Siler *proximum* Sibi, *ut* debile & infirmum, quòd

THE Elm, *born* on *the Bank* of a River, *laughed at* the Oſier *next* to Him, *as* weak *and* infirm, becauſe

quòd flecteretur *ad* omnem *vel* leviſſimum *Impetum* Undarum ; *autem* extolle-bat *ſuam* Firmitatem *&* Robur *magnificis* Verbis ; quòd inconcuſſa *pertulerat* aſſiduos *Impetus* Amnis multos Annos. ' *Autem* Ulmus *tandem* perfracta *maximâ* Violentiâ *Undarum*, trahebatur *ab* Aquis : Cui Siler *ridens*, inquit, *Vicina*, Cur *deſeris* Me ? *Ubi* nunc *eſt* tua *Fortitudo ?*

becauſe it would be bent *at* every *even* the lighteſt *Force* of the Waters ; *but* She extol-led *her own* Steadineſs *and* Strength *with magnificent* Words ; *becauſe* unſhook *ſhe had bore* the daily *Attacks* of the River *many* Years. *But* the Elm *at laſt* being broken *by the very great* Violence *of the Waters*, was drawn along *by* the Waters : *To which* the Oſier *laughing*, ſaid, *Neighbour*, Why *doſt thou forſake* Me ? *Where* now *is* thy *Fortitude ?*

Mor.

Fabula *indicat* Eos *eſſe* ſapientiores, *Qui* cedunt *potentioribus*, quàm *Qui* volentes *reſiſtere* ſuperan-tur *turpiter*.

Mor.

The Fable *ſhoweth* Thoſe *to be* more wiſe, *Who* yield *to the more powerful*, than *They Who* willing *to reſiſt* are over-come *baſely*.

FABLE CXXVI. •

De Cerâ *appetente* Duritiem.

Of the Wax *deſiring* Hardneſs.

CEra *ingemiſcebat*, Se *eſſe mollem*, & *procreatam* penetrabilem *cuicunque* le-viſſimo *Ictui*. Autem *videns* Lateres *factos* ex *Luto*, molliores *multò*, Se *perve-niſſe* in *tantam* Duritiem *Calore* Ignis, *ut* per-durarent *multa* Secula, jecit Se *in* Ignem, *ut* conſeque-retur *eandem* Duritiem ; *ſed* ſtatim *liquefacta* in *Igne* eſt *conſumpta*.

THE Wax *grieved*, that It *was ſoft*, and made penetrable. *to every* the lighteſt *Blow*. But *ſeeing* the Bricks *made* of *Clay*, ſofter *by much*, that they came to *ſo great* Hardneſs *by the Heat* of the Fire, *that* They laſted *many* Ages, *It caſt* itſelf *into* the Fire, *that* it might obtain *the ſame* Hardneſs ; *but* preſently *being melted* in *the Fire* it was *conſumed*. Mor.

MOR.

Hæc *Fabula* admonet, *ne appetamus,* Quod *eſt* denegatum *Nobis* à *Naturâ.*

MOR.

This *Fable* adviſes, that *we deſire not,* What is denied *Us* by *Nature.*

F A B L E CXXVII.

De Agricolâ *affectante* Militiam, & Mercaturam.

Of the Huſbandman *affecting* Warfare, *and* Merchandiſe.

QUidam *Agricola* ferebat *ægrè,* Se *aſſiduè* volvere *Terram,* nec *pervenire* ad *magnas* Divitias *ſuis* perpetuis *Laboribus ;* cùm *videret* nonnullos *Milites,* Qui *ita* auxerant *Rem* Bello, *ut* incederent *bene* induti, & nutriti *lautis* Epulis *agerent* beatam *Vitam.* Igitur *ſuis* Ovibus *venditis* cum *Capris* ac *Bobus,* emit : *Equos* & *Arma,* & *profectus eſt* in *Militiam ;* Ubi, *cùm* eſſet *pugnatum* malè *à* ſuo *Imperatore,* non *ſolùm* perdidit *Quæ* habebat, *ſed* etiam *recepit* multa *Vulnera.* Quare, *Militiâ* damnatâ, *ſtatuit* exercere *Mercaturam,* ut in Quâ *exiſtimabat* eſſe *majus* Lucrum, & minorem *Laborem.* Igitur *Prædiis* venditis, *cùm* impleviſſet *Navim* Mercibus, *cæperat* navigare ; *ſed,* cùm *eſſet* in

A Certain *Huſbandman* bore it *ill,* that He *daily* ſtirred up the *Earth,* nor *arrived* to *great* Riches *by his* perpetual *Labours ;* when *He ſaw* ſome *Soldiers,* Who *ſo* had increaſed *an Eſtate* in the War, *that* They went *well* clothed, *and* fed *with ſumptuous* Dainties *led* a happy *Life.* Therefore *his* Sheep *being ſold* with *the Goats* and *Oxen,* He bought *Horſes* and *Arms,* and *went* into the *War ;* Where, *when* it was *fought* unſuccefsfully *by* his *General,* He not *only* loſt *What Things* He had, *but* alſo *received* many *Wounds.* Wherefore, *War* being condemned, *He reſolved* to exerciſe *Merchandiſe,* as in what He thought there was *greater* Gain, *and* leſs *Labour.* Therefore *his Farms* being ſold, *when* He had filled a *Ship* with Wares, *He had begun* to ſail ; *but,* when *He was* in

in *Alto*, magnâ *Tempeſtate* coörtâ, *Navis* ſubmerſa eſt, & Ipſe *cum* cæteris, *Qui* erant *in* Eâ, *Omnes* periêre *ad* Unum.

in *the Deep*, a great *Tempeſt* having aroſe, *the Ship* was ſunk, *and* He *with* the reſt, *Who* were *in* It, *All* periſh'ed *to* One.

Mor.

Hæc *Fabula* admonet, *Quemlibet* debere *eſſe* contentum *ſuâ* Sorte, *cùm* Miſeria *ſit* parata *ubique*.

Mor.

This *Fable* adviſes, that every One ought *to* be content *with* his own Lot, *when* Miſery *is* ready *every where*.

FABLE CXXVIII.

De Asino & Scurra.

Of the Ass *and* the Jester.

A Sinus *ferens* indignè, *quendam* Scurram *honorari* & amiciri pulchris *Veſtibus*, quia *edebat* magnos *Sonos* Ventris, *acceſſit* ad *Magiſtratus*, petens *ne vellent* honorare *Se* minùs, *quàm* Scurram; *Et cùm Magiſtratus* admirantes *interrogarent*, cur *duceret* Se *ita* dignum *Honore*, inquit, *Quia* emitto *majores* Crepitus *Ventris*, quàm *Scurra*, & *eos* abſque *Fœtore*.

THE Aſs *bearing it* unkindly, *that a certain* Jeſter *was honoured* and *clothed* in fair *Garments*, becauſe *He made* great *Sounds* of Belly, *went* to the *Magiſtrates*, deſiring *that they would not* honour *Him* leſs, *than* the Jeſter; *And* when the *Magiſtrates* admiring *aſked*, why *He thought* Himſelf *ſo* worthy *of Honour*, He ſaid, *Becauſe* I ſend out *greater* Noiſes *of Belly*, than *the Jeſter*, and *thoſe* without *Stink*.

Mor.

Hæc *Fabula* arguit *Eos*, *Qui profundunt* ſuas *Pecunias* in *leviſſimis* Rebus.

Mor.

This *Fable* reproves *Thoſe*, Who *lay out* their *Monies* in *the lighteſt* Things.

FABLE

FABLE CXXIX.

De Amne *laceſſente* ſuum *Fontem* Conviciis.

Of the River *provoking* his *Spring* with Reproaches.

Quidam *Amnis* laceſſebat *ſuum* Fontem *Conviciis*, ut *inertem*, quòd *ſtaret* immobilis, *nec* haberet *ullos* Piſces, *autem* commendabat *Se* plurimùm, *quòd* crearet *optimos* Piſces, *&* ſerperet *per* Valles *blando* Murmure. *Fons* indignatus *in* Amnem, *velut* ingratùm, *repreſſit* Undas. *Tunc* Amnis, *privatus* & *Piſcibus* & *dulci* Sono, *evanuit.*

A Certain *River* provoked *his* Spring *with Reproaches*, as *ſluggiſh*, becauſe *He ſtood* immoveable, *nor* had *any* Fiſh, *but* commended *Himſelf* very much, *becauſe* he bred *the beſt* Fiſhes, *and* 'crept *thro'* the Vallies *with* a *pleaſant* Murmur. *The Spring* angry *at* the River, *as* ungrateful, *kept back* the Waters. *Then* the River, *deprived* both of *the Fiſhes* and *the ſweet* Sound, *vaniſhed away.*

MŌR.

Hæc Fabula notat *Eos, Qui arrogant* bona, *Quæ* agúnt, *Sibi, & non* attribuunt *Deo, à Quo,* ceu *à* largo *Fonte,* noſtra *Bona* procedunt.

MOR.

This *Fable* marketh *Thoſe,* Who *arrogate* the good Things, *Which* They do, *to Themſelves,* and do not attribute Them *to God,* from *Whom,* as *from* a large Fountain, our good Things proceed.

FABLE CXXX.

De maligno *Viro* & *Dæmone.*

Of the wicked *Man* and *the Devil.*

Quidam *malignus* Vir, *cùm* perpetraviſſet *plurima* Scelera, *&* ſæpius *captus,* & *concluſus* Carcere, *teneretur* arctiſſimè *per-*

A Certain *wicked* Man, *when* He had committed *many* Wickedneſſes, *and* often *being* taken, *and ſhut* in Priſon, *was* detained very cloſely *with*

N

pervigili Cuſtodiâ, implorabat Auxilium Dæmonis, Qui ſæpenumero affuit Illi, & liberavit Eum è multis Periculis. Tandem Dæmon apparuit Ei iterum deprehenſo, & imploranti ſolitum Auxilium, habens magnam Faſcem Calceorum pertuſorum ſuper Humeros, dicens, Amice, non poſſum eſſe Auxilio Tibi ampliùs; etenim peragravi tot Loca pro liberando Te, ut contriverim omnes hos Calceos, & etiam nulla Pecunia ſupereſt Mihi, Quâ valeam comparare alios; quare peribis.

with a watchful Guard, implored the Help of the Devil, Who oftentimes was with Him, and freed Him out of many Dangers. At length the Devil appeared to Him again taken, and imploring the uſual Help, having a great Bundle of Shoes worn out upon his Shoulders, ſaying, Friend, I am not able to be a Help to Thee longer; for I have travelled thro' ſo many Places for freeing Thee, that I have worn out all theſe Shoes, and moreover no Money remains to Me, with Which I may be able to get others; wherefore thou ſhalt periſh.

Mor.

Hæc Fabula admonet, ne exiſtimemus noſtra Peccata fore ſemper impunita.

Mor.

This Fable adviſes, that we ſhould not think our Sins will be always unpuniſhed.

FABLE CXXXI.

De Avibus volentibus eligere plures Reges.

Of the Birds being willing to chooſe more Kings.

AVes conſultabant de eligendis pluribus Regibus, cùm Aquila ſola non poſſet regere tantas Greges Volucrum, & feciſſent ſatìs Voto, niſi deſtitiſſent à Conſilio Monitu Cornicis, Quæ, cùm Cauſa interrogabatur, cur

THE Birds conſulted about chooſing more Kings, ſeeing that the Eagle alone was not able to rule ſo great Flocks of Birds, and They had done enough to their Wiſh, unleſs They had deſiſted from the Counſel by the Advice of the Crow, Who, when the Cauſe was aſked, why

cur *non* duceret *plures* Reges *eligendos,* inquit, quia *multi* Sacci *implentur* difficiliùs, *quàm* unus.

why *She did not* think *more* Kings *were to be chosen,* said, because *many* Bags *are filled* more difficultly, *than* one.

MOR.

Hæc *Fabula* docet *esse* longè *meliùs* gubernari *ab* Uno, *quàm* à *multis* Principibus.

MOR.

This *Fable* teaches it *to be* by far *better* to be governed *by* One, *than* by *many* Princes.

FABLE CXXXII.

De Muliere, *Quæ* dicebat, Se *velle* mori *pro* suo *Viro.*

Of the Woman, *Who* said, that She *was willing* to die *for* her *Husband.*

Quædam *Matrona,* admodum *pudica* & amanti∫∫ima Viri, *ferebat* ægrè, *Maritum* detineri *adver∫â* Valetudine : lamentabatur, ingemi∫cebat, &, ut *te∫taretur* suum *Amorem* in *Virum,* rogabat *Mortem,* ut, *∫i* e∫∫et *ereptura* Maritum *Sibi,* potiùs *vellet* occidere *Se,* quàm *Illum.* Inter *hæc* Verba, *cernit* Mortem *venientem* horribili *A∫pectu,* Timore *Cujus* preterrita, & .jam *pænitens* sui *Voti,* inquit, *Ego* non sum, *Quem* petis ; *jacet* in Lecto, *Quem* veni∫ti occi∫ura.

A Certain *Matron,* very *cha∫te* and mo∫t loving of her Husband, bore it ill, *that the Husband* was kept down *by bad* Health : *She lamented,* She grieved, *and,* that *She might te∫tify* Her *Love* to *her Husband,* She asked *Death,* that, *if* He was *about to* ∫natch her Husband *from Her,* He rather *would* kill *Her,* than *Him.* Among *the∫e* Words, *She beholds* Death coming with a horrible *A∫pect,* with the Fear *of Whom* being affrighted, *and* now repenting of Her *Vow,* She said, *I* am not He, *Whom* Thou ∫eeke∫t ; *He lies* in *the* Bed, Whom *thou come∫t* about to kill.

MOR.

MOR.

Hæc *Fabula* indicat, *Neminem* effe *adeò* amantem *Amici*, Qui *non malit* effe *bene* Sibi, *quàm* Alteri.

MOR.

This *Fable* fhows, *that no* One is *fo* loving *of a Friend*, Who *had not rather* it was *well* to Him, *than* Another.

FABLE CXXXIII.

De Adolefcente *canente* in *Funere* Matris.

Of the young Man *finging at the Funeral* of his Mother.

QUidam *Vir* profequebatur *defunctam* Uxorem, *Quæ* efferebatur *ad* Sepulchrum *Lachrymis* & *Fletibus ;* verò *ejus* Filius *canebat*, Qui, *cùm* increparetur *à* Patre, *ut* amens, *Qui* cantaret *in* Funere *Matris*, *cùm deberet* effe *mæftus*, & *flere* unà *Secum*, inquit, *Mi* Pater, *fi* conduxifti *Sacerdotes*, ut *canerent*, cur *irafceris* Mihi *concinenti* gratis ? *Cui* Pater *inquit*, Tuum *Officium*, & *Sacerdotum* non eft *idem*.

A Certain *Man* followed his *dead* Wife, *Who* was borne *to* the Grave *with Tears* and *Weepings ;* but *his* Son *fung*, Who, *when* he was blamed *by* the Father, *as* mad, *Who* could fing *at* the Burial *of a Mother*, when *he ought* to be *fad*, and *to weep* together *with Him*, faid, *My* Father, *if* You have hired *Priefts*, that *they might fing*, why *are you angry* with Me *finging* gratis ? *To whom* the Father faid, Thy *Office*, and *that of the Priefts* is not *the fame*.

MOR.

Hæc *Fabula* indicat, *Omnia* non effe *decora* Omnibus.

MOR.

This *Fable* fhows, that *all Things* are not *decent* for All Men.

FABLE

FABLE CXXXIV.

De zelotypo Viro, Qui dede-
rat Uxorem cuſtodiendam.

Of the jealous *Man,* Who *had*
given his Wife *to be guarded.*

Z Elotypus *Vir* dederat
Uxorem, Quam com-
pererat vivere parum pudi-
cè, cuidam Amico, *Cui*
fideret *plurimùm,* cuſtodiendam, *pollicitus* ingentem
Pecuniam, ſi obſervaret Eam
ita diligenter, *ut* nullo
Modo violaret conjuga-
lem Copulam. *At* Ille, *ubi*
expertus eſſet *hanc*
Cuſtodiam *nimis* difficilem
aliquot Dies, & comperiſſet
ſuum Ingenium *vinci* Ver-
futiâ *Mulieris,* accedens ad
Maritum, *dixit,* Se
nolle gerere *hanc* tam
duram Provinciam *ampliùs ;*
quandoquidem *ne* Argus
quidem, Qui *fuit* totus
oculatus, poſſet *cuſtodire* impudicam *Mulierem :* Ad-
didit prætereâ, ſi ſit neceſſe,
Se' malle deferre
Saccum *plenum* Pulicibus *in*
Pratum quotidie integro
Anno, &, Sacco ſoluto,
paſcere Eos inter Herbas,
& Veſpere redu-
cere omnes Domum, quàm
ſervare impudicam Mulie-
rem uno Die.

A Jealous *Man* had given
his *Wife,* Whom *He had*
found to live but a little chaſte-
ly, *to a certain* Friend, *to Whom*
He could truſt *very much,* to be
guarded, *having promiſed* much
Money, if *He could obſerve* Her
ſo diligently, *that* by no
Method She might violate *the con-*
jugal Tie. *But* He, *when*
He had experienced *this*
Charge *too* difficult
ſome Days, *and* had found
his Wit *to be overcome* by the Cunning *of the Woman,* going *to*
the Huſband, *ſaid,* that *He*
was unwilling to bear *this* ſo
hard a Province longer ;
ſeeing that *not* Argus
indeed, Who *was* all
eyed, could be able *to keep* an unchaſte Woman : He add-
ed moreover, if *it was* neceſſary,
that *He* had rather carry down
a Sack *full* of Fleas *into*
a Meadow *daily* for a whole
Year, and, *the Sack* being looſed,
to feed Them among the Graſs,
and in the Evening *to bring them*
back all *Home,* than
to keep an unchaſte Wo-
man one Day.

MOR.

Hæc *Fabula* indicat, *nullos*
Cuſtodes eſſe ita *diligentes,*
Qui

MOR.

This *Fable* ſhows, *that* no.
Guards are ſo *diligent,*
Who

Qui *valeant* cuſtodire Who *can be able* to keep
impudicas Mulieres.   *unchaſte* Women.

FABLE CXXXV.

De Viro *recuſante* Cly-   *Of* the Man *refuſing* Cly-
ſteres.   ſters.

QUidam *Vir*, Germanus
Natione, admodum *dives*,
ægrotabat ; *ad* curandum
Quem plures *Medici*
acceſſerunt, *(etenim* Muſcæ
convolant catervatim *ad*
Mel) *Unus* Quorum *dicebat*
inter *Cætera*, eſſe
Opus Clyſteribus, *ſi* vellet *convaleſcere ;* Quod
cùm Vir *audiret*, inſuetus
Medicinæ hujuſmodi, *percitus* Furore, *jubet*
Medicos *ejici*
Domo, *dicens*, Eos
eſſe infamos, *Qui*, cùm
Caput doleret, *vellent*
mederi *Podicem*.

A Certain *Man*, a German
by Nation, very *rich*,
was ſick ; *to* cure
Whom many *Phyſicians*
came, *(for* the Flies
fly in Heaps *to*
the Honey) *One* of Whom *ſaid*,
among *other Things*, that there was
Need of Clyſters, *if* He was
willing *to grow well ;* Which
when the Man *heard*, unuſed
to a Medicine of this Kind, *moved* with Anger, *He commands*
the Phyſicians *to be caſt out*
of the Houſe, *ſaying*, that They
were mad, *Who*, when
the Head grieved, *were willing*
to cure *the Breech*.

Mor.

Hæc *Fabula* indicat,
Omnia, quamvis *ſalutaria*,
videri *&* aſpera *&* obſu-
tura *inſuetis* & *inexper-
tis*.

Mor.

This *Fable* ſhows,
that all Things, altho' *healthful*,
ſeem *both* rough *and* hurtful *to the unaccuſtomed* and *inex-
perienced*.

FABLE CXXXVI.

De Afino *ægrotante,* & | *Of* the Afs *being fick,* and
Lupis vifitantibus *Eum.* | the *Wolves* vifiting *Him.*

A Sinus *ægrotabat,* & *Fama* exiverat, *Eum* moriturum *citò ;* Igitur, *cùm* Lupi *veniffent* ad *vifendum* Eum, *&* peterent *à* Filio, *quomodo* ejus *Pater* valeret, *Ille* refpondit *per* Rimulam *Ofii,* meliùs, *quàm* velletis.

THE Afs *was fick,* and *Fame* had gone out, *that He* would die *quickly ;* Therefore, when the Wolves *had come* to *fee* Him, *and* afked *of* the Son, *how* his *Father* did, *He* anfwered *thro'* the Chink *of the Door,* better, *than* Ye would have Him.

MOR.

Hæc *Fabula* indicat, *quòd* Multi *fingunt* ferre *Mortem* Aliorum *cum* Moleftiâ, *Quos* tamen *cupiunt* interire *celeriter.*

MOR.

This *Fable* fhows, *that* Many *feign* to bear the *Death* of Others *with* Trouble, *Whom* yet *They defire* to perifh *quickly.*

FABLE CXXXVII.

De Nuce, *Afino,* & | *Of* the Nut-tree, *the Afs,* and
Muliere. | the *Woman.*

QUædam *Mulier* interrogabat *Nucem,* nafcentem *Viam fecus,* Quæ impetebatur Saxis *à* Populo prætereunte, *quare* effet *ita* amens, *ut* quò *cæderetur* pluribus *&* majoribus *Verberibus,* eò *procrearet* plures *&* præftantiores *Fruftus ?* Cui *inquit,* Efne *immemor* Proverbii *dicen-*

A Certain *Woman* afked a *Nut-tree,* growing by the *Way-Side,* Which *was beaten* with Stones *by* the People paffing by, *why* It was fo mad, *that* by how much *It was beaten* with more *and* greater *Stripes,* by fo much *it yielded* more *and* better *Fruits ?* To whom *it faid,* Art thou *unmindful* of the Proverb *fay-*

dicentis ita, *Nux*, Afinus, *saying* thus, *A Nut-tree*, an Afs,
& Mulier, *funt* ligati *and* a Woman, *are* bound
fimili Lege. *Hæc* tria *by a like* Law. *Thefe* three
faciunt Nil *rectè*, fi *Verbera* do Nothing *rightly*, if *Blows*
ceffant. ceafe.

Mor.

Hæc *Fabula* indicat, This *Fable* fhows,
Homines fæpe *folere* con- *that Men* often *are wont* to
fodere *Se* propriis wound *Themfelves* with their own
Jaculis. *Darts.*

FABLE CXXXVIII.

De Afino, *non* inveniente   *Of* the Afs, *not* finding
Finem Laborum.   *an End* of his Labours.

A Sinus *angebatur* pluri- THE Afs *was grieved* very
mùm *hyberno* tempore, much *in winter* Time,
quòd afficeretur *nimio that* He was affected *with too much*
Frigore, *& haberet durum* Cold, and had hard
Victum *Palearum ;* quare Meat *of Chaff ;* wherefore
optabat vernam *Temperiem,* He *defired* the Spring *Seafon,*
& *teneras* Herbas. *Sed* and *the tender* Grafs. *But*
cùm *Ver* advenisset, *& * when *Spring* came, and
cogèretur *à* Domino, He was compelled *by* the Mafter,
Qui erat *Figulus,* deferre *Who was a Potter,* to carry
Argillam in *Aream,* & *Clay* into *the Yard,* and
Lignum ad *Fornacem,* & Wood to *the Furnace,* and
inde Lateres & Tegulas *ad thence* Bricks and Tiles *to*
diverfa *Loca ;* pertæfus diverfe *Places ;* tired
Veris, in *Quo* tolerabat *of the Spring,* in *Which* He bore
tot Labores, *fperabat fo* many Labours, *He hoped for*
Æftatem, *ut* Dominus Summer, *that* the Mafter
impeditus Messe *being hindered* by the Harveft
pateretur Eum *quiefcere ;* Sed *would fuffer* Him *to reft ;* But
tunc quoque, *cùm* compel- *then* alfo, *when* He was com-
leretur *ferre* Messes *in* pelled *to bear* the Corn *into*
Aream, & *inde* Triticum the Barn, and *thence* the Wheat
Domum, *nec* effet *Locus* Home, *nor* was there *Space*
Qui-   for

SELECT FABLES OF ÆSOP. 99

Quieti Sibi ; faltem fperabat Autumnum fore Finem Laborum : Sed, cùm ne tunc quoque cerneret Finem Malorum, cùm quotidie Vinum, Poma, & Lignum effent portanda, rurfus efflagitabat Nivem & Glaciem Hyemis, ut tunc faltem aliqua Requies contederetur Sibi à tantis Laboribus.

for Reft for Him ; at leaft He hoped that Autumn would be the End of his Labours : But, when not then alfo He perceived an End of Evils, feeing that daily Wine, Apples, and Wood were to be carried, again He longed for the Snow and Ice of Winter, that then at leaft fome Reft might be granted to Him from fo great Labours.

MOR.

Hæc Fabula indicat, effe nulla Tempora præfentis Vitæ, Quæ non funt fubjecta perpetuis Laboribus.

MOR.

This Fable fhows; that there are no Times of the prefent Life; Which are not fubject to perpetual Labours.

FABLE. CXXXIX.

De Mure, Qui volebat contrahere Amicitiam cum Fele.

Of the Moufe, Who was willing to contract a Friendfhip with the Cat.

COmplures Mures, commorantes in Cavo Parietis, contemplabantur Felem, Quæ incumbebat in Tabulato, Capite demiffo, & trifti Vultu. Tunc Unus ex Iis inquit, Hoc Animal videtur admodùm benignum, & mite ; etenim præfert quàndam Sanctimoniam ipfo Vultu ; volo alloqui Ipfam, & nectere indiffolubilem Amicitiam cum Eâ ; Quæ cùm dixiffet, & accefffet

MANY Mice, dwelling in the Hollow of a Wall, efpied a Cat, Who lay on the boarded Floor, with her Head hung down, and a fad Countenance. Then One of them faid, This Animal feems very kind and mild ; for She fhows a certain Sanctity in Her very Countenance ; I am willing to fpeak to Her, and to knit an indiffoluble Friendfhip with Her ; Which Things when He had faid, and had approached

O

set propiùs, erat captus, *& dilaceratus à* Fele. *Tunc Cæteri, videntes* Hoc, *aiebant* Secum, *profectò* non est *credendum* temerè *Vultui.*

proached nearer, *He was* taken, *and* torn to Pieces *by* the Cat. *Then* the Rest, *seeing* This, *said* with Themselves, *truly* It is not *to be trusted* rashly *to the Countenance.*

Mor.

Hæc *Fabula* innuit, *Homines* hon esse *judicandos* è *Vultu,* sed *ex* Operibus ; *cùm* atroces *Lupi* sæpe *delitescant* sub *ovinâ* Pelle.

Mor.

This *Fable* hints, *that Men* are not *to be judged* by *the Countenance,* but *by* Works ; *seeing that* fierce *Wolves* often *lie hid* under *a Sheep's* Skin.

FABLE CXL.

De Asino, *Qui* serviebat *ingrato* Hero.

Of the Ass, *Who* served *an ungrateful* Master.

A Sinus, *Qui* servivrat *ingrato* Hero *multos.* Annos *inoffenso* Pede, *semel,* ut *fit,* dum *esset* pressus *gravi* Sarcinâ, *&* incederet *salebrosâ* Viâ, *recidebat* sub *Onere.* Tum *implacabilis* Dominus compellebat Eum *surgere* multis *Verberibus,* nuncupans *ignavum & pigrum* Animal. *At* miser *Asinus* dicebat *Secum,* inter *hæc* Verbera, *Infelix* Ego, *Qui* sortitus sum *tam ingratum Herum !* Nam *quamvis* serviverim *Ei* multo *Tempore* sine *Offensâ,* tamen *non compensat* hoc *unum* Delictum *meis* tot *pristinis* Beneficiis.

THE Ass, *Who* had served *an ungrateful* Master *many* Years *with an inoffensive* Foot, *once,* as *it happens,* whilst *He was* pressed *with a heavy* Load, *and* went *in an uneven* Way, *fell* under *the Burden.* Then *the implacable* Master *compelled* Him *to rise* with many *Blows,* calling Him *an idle* and *dull* Animal. *But* the miserable *Ass* said *with Himself,* among *these* Stripes, *Unhappy* I, *Who* have got *so* ungrateful *a Master !* For *altho'* I have served *Him* a long *Time* without *Offence,* yet *He does not weigh* this *one* Fault *with my* so many *former* Benefits.

Mor.

MOR.

Hæc *Fabula* confiɔ̌a eſt in Eos, *Qui* immemores *Beneficiorum* collatorum Sibi, profequuntur *etiam* minimam *Offenfam* fui *Benefaɔ̌oris* in *Se* atroci *Pænâ.*

MOR.

This *Fable* was feigned *againſt* Thofe, *Who* unmindful *of* Benefits conferred on *Themfelves*, profecute. *even* the leaſt *Offence* of their *Benefaɔ̌or* on *Him* with a cruel *Puniſhment.*

FABLE CXLI.

De Lupo, *fuadente* Hiſtrici, *ut* deponeret *fua* Tela.

Of the Wolf, *perfuading* the Porcupine, *that* She would lay down *her* Darts.

LUpus *efuriens* intenderat *Animum* in *Hiſtricem*, Quam *tamen* non audebat *invadere*, quia *erat* munita *undique* Sagittis. Autem *Aſlutiâ* excogitatâ *perdendi* Eam, *cæpit* fuadere *Illi*, ne portaret *tantum* Onus *Telorum* Tergo *Tempore* Pacis, *quandoquidem* Sagittarii non *portarent* Aliquid, *nifi* cùm *Tempus* Prælii *inſtaret :* Cui *Hiſtrix* inquit, *Eſt* credendum *femper* effe *Tempus* præliandi *adverfus* Lupum.

THE Wolf *hungering* had bent *his Mind* upon *the Porcupine*, Which *nevertheleſs* He dared *not to attack*, becaufe *She was* fortified *every where* with Darts. But *a cunning* being thought on *of deſtroying* Her, *He began* to perfuade *Her*, that She would not carry *fo great* a Burden *of Darts* on her Back *in a Time* of Peace, *feeing that* the Archers *did not carry* any Thing, *unlefs* when *the Time* of Battle *approached :* To whom *the* Porcupine faid, *It is* to be believed *always* to be *a Time* of fighting *againſt* a Wolf.

MOR.

Hæc *Fabula* innuit, *fapientem* Virum *oportere* femper *effe* munitum *adverfus* Fraudes *Inimicorum*, & *Hoſtium.*

MOR.

This *Fable* hints, *that* a *wife* Man *ought* always *to be* fortified *againſt* Deceits *of* Enemies, and *Foes.*

FABLE

FABLE CXLII.

De Mure liberante Milvum.

MUS, conspicatus Milvum implicitum Laqueo *Aucupis*, misertus est *Avis*, quamvis *Inimicæ* Sibi ; *Vinculisque* abrosis *Dentibus*, fecit *Viam* Sibi evolandi. Milvus, immemor tanti *Beneficii*, ubi *vidit* Se *solutum*, corripiens *Murem* suspicantem *Nil* tale, lacerqvit Unguibus, & Rostro.

Mor.

Hæc *Fabula* indicat, malignos Viros *solere* rependere *Gratias* hujus *Modi* suis *Benefactoribus*.

Of the Mouse freeing the Kite.

THE Mouse, *having espied* the Kite *entangled* in the Snare *of the Fowler*, pitied the *Bird*, altho' *an Enemy* to Her ; *and the Bands* being gnawed *with her Teeth*, She made *a Way* for Her *of flying out*. The Kite, unmindful of so great *Benefit*, when *He saw* Himself *loosed*, seizing *the Mouse suspecting no such Thing, *tore Her* with her Claws, *and Bill.

Mor.

This *Fable* shows, that *wicked* Men are *wont* to repay *Thanks* of this *Kind* to their *Benefactors.*

FABLE CXLIII.

De Cochleâ *petente* à *Jove*, ut *posset* ferre *suam* Domum Secum.

CUM *Jupiter*, ab *Exordio* Mundi, elargiretur singulis *Animalibus* Munera, *Quæ* petiissent, *Cochlea* petiit ab Eo, ut. posset circumferre suam *Domum*. Interrogata à Jove, *quare* exposceret *tale* Munus ab Eo,

Of the Snail *desiring* of *Jupiter*, that *She might be able* to bear Her House *with Her.

WHEN *Jupiter*, from *the Beginning* of the World, *bestowed* on all *Animals* the Gifts, *Which* They had desired, *the* Snail desired *of* Him, *that* She might be able *to bear about* her *House.* Being asked *by* Jupiter, *why* She demanded *such* a Gift *from* Him,

Eo, *Quod* futurum erat grave, & *moleſtum* illi, inquit, malo ſerre tam grave Onus *perpetuò*, quàm non poſſe *vitare* malum *Vicinum*, cùm *Mihi* libuerit.

Him, *Which* would be heavy, and *troubleſome* to Her, She ſaid, I had rather *bear* ſo heavy a Burden *perpetually*, than *not* to be able *to avoid* a bad Neighbour, when *I* liſt.

MOR.

Hæc *Fabula* indicat, *Vicinitatem* Malorum ſugiendam omni *Incom̄modo*.

MOR.

This *Fable* ſhows, that the Neighbourhood of bad Men is to be avoided with every *Diſadvantage.*

F A B L E CXLIV.

De Herinaceo *ejiciente* Viperam *Hoſpitem.*

Of the Hedge-Hog *caſting out* the Viper her *Hoſt.*

HErinaceus, *præſentiens* Hyemem *adventare*, rogavit *Viperam*, ut *concederet* Locum Sibi in *ſuâ* Cavernâ *adverſus* Vim *Frigoris* ; Quod cùm Illa *feciſſet*, Herinaceus, *pervolvens* Se *huc* atque *illuc*, pungebat *Viperam* Acumine Spinarum, & torquebat vehementer ; *Illa* videns Se malè *tractatam* quando ſuſcepit *Herinaceum* Hoſpitio, orabat Eum *blandis* Verbis, ut exiret, cùm Locus *eſſet* nimis *anguſtus* duobus. *Cui* Herinaceus *inquit*, Exeat, *Qui* nequit *manere* hîc ; quare Vipera *ſentiens*, non eſſe *Locum* Sibi

THE Hedge-Hog, *perceiving* the Winter *to approach*, aſked *the Viper*, that *She would* grant a Place to *Him* in *her* Cavern *againſt* the Extremity *of the Cold ;* Which *when* She had done, the Hedge-Hog, *rolling* Himſelf *hither* and *thither*, pricked *the Viper* with the Sharpneſs *of his Darts*, and *tormented Her* vehemently ; *She* ſeeing *Herſelf* ill treated *when* She took *the Hedge-Hog* Gueſt-wiſe, *entreated* Him *with fair* Words, *that* He would go out, *ſeeing that* the Place *was* too narrow for both. *To - whom* the Hedge-Hog *ſaid*, Let Him go out, *Who* cannot *abide* here ; *wherefore* the Viper *perceiving*, there was not a *Place* for

Sibi *ibi*, ceſſit *illinc* ex *Hoſpitio*.

for Her *there*, departed *thence* out of *her Lodging*.

Mor.

Hæc *Fabula* indicat, *Eos* non eſſe *admittendos* in *Conſortium*, *Qui poſſunt* ejicere *Nos*.

Mor.

This *Fable* ſhows, *that They* are not *to be admitted* into *Fellowſhip*, Who *are able* to caſt out *Us*.

FABLE CXLV.

De quodam *Agricolâ* & *Poëtâ*.

Of a certain *Huſbandman* and a *Poet*.

QUidam *Agricola* accedens ad Poëtam, *cujus* Agros *colebat*, cùm *offendiſſet* Eum *ſolum* inter *Libros*, interrogabat *Eum*, quo *Paſto* poſſet *vivere* ita *ſolus?* Cui *Ille* inquit, *Tantùm* cœpi *eſſe* ſolus, *poſtquam* adveniſti *huc*.

A Certain *Huſbandman* coming *to* a Poet, *whoſe* Fields He *ploughed*, when He had *found* Him *alone* among *his Books*, aſked *Him*, by what *Means* He was able *to live ſo alone?* To whom *He* ſaid, *I only* began *to be* alone, *ſince* You came *hither*.

Mor.

Hæc *Fabula* indicat, *eruditos* Viros, *Qui* continuò *ſtipantur* Turbâ *doſtiſſimorum* Virorum, tunc eſſe *ſolos*, cùm *fuerint* inter *illiteratos* Homines.

Mor.

This *Fable* ſhows, *that learned* Men, *Who* continually *are thronged* with a Crowd *of* the *moſt learned* Men, *then* are *alone*, when *they are* amongſt *illiterate* Fellows.

FABLE

FABLE CXLVI.

De Lupo, *induto* Pelle Ovis, *Qui* devorabat Gregem.

Of the Wolf, *clothed* with the Skin *of* the Sheep, *Who* devoured *the Flock.*

Lupus, *indutus* Pelle Ovis, immifcuit Se Gregi Ovium, & quotidie occidebat *Aliquam* ex. *Eis :* Quod cùm Paftor *animadvertiffet,* fufpendit *Illum* in *altiffimâ* Arbore. *Autem* cæteris *Paftoribus* interrogantibus, cur fufpendiffet *Ovem,* aiebat, *Quidem* Pellis *eft* Ovis, *ut* videtis ; *autem* Opera *erant* Lupi.

A Wolf, *clothed* with the Skin *of a Sheep,* mixed *Himfelf* with a Flock *of Sheep,* and daily flew fome One of *Them :* Which *when* the Shepherd *had obferved,* He hanged *Him* on a *very high* Tree. *But* the other *Shepherds* afking, *why* He had hung *the Sheep,* He faid, *Indeed* the Skin *is* a Sheep's, *as* you fee ; *but* the Works *were* a Wolf's.

MOR.

Hæc *Fabula* indicat, *Homines* non effe *judicandos* ex *Habitu,* fed *ex* Operibus ; *quoniam* Multi *faciunt* Lupina *Opera* fub *Veftimentis* Ovium.

MOR.

This *Fable* fhows, *that Men* are not *to be judged* by *Habit,* but *by* Works ; *becaufe* Many do Wolves' *Works* under the *Clothings* of Sheep.

FABLE CXLVII.

De CANE *occidente* OVES *fui* Domini.

Of the DOG *killing* the SHEEP *of his* Mafter.

Quidam *Paftor* dederat *fuas* Oves *Cani* cuftodiendas, *pafcens* Illum *optimis* Cibis. *At* Ille *fæpe* occidebat *aliquam* Ovem ; *Quod* cùm *Paftor* animadvertiffet,

A Certain *Shepherd* had given *his* Sheep *to his Dog* to be kept, feeding Him *with the beft* Meats. *But* He *often* killed fome one Sheep ; *Which* when *the Shepherd* had obferved,

vertiſſet, *capient* Canem, | ſerved, *taking* the Dog,
volebat occidere _Eum._ | He *was willing* to kill _Him._
Cui *Canis* inquit, *Quare* | To whom *the Dog* ſaid, *Wherefore*
cupis. *perdere* Me? | doſt Thou deſire *to deſtroy* Me?
Sum unus *ex* tuis *domeſticis*; | I am one *of* thy *Domeſtics*;
potiùs *interfice* Lupum, *Qui* | rather *ſlay* the Wolf, *Who*
continuò *inſidiatur* tuo | continually *lays wait* for your
Ovili. Imò, *inquit* Pa- | Sheepfold. Nay, *ſays* the Shep-
ſtor, *Puto* Te *magis* dignum | herd, *I think* You *more worthy*
Morte, quàm *Lupum*: Etenim | *of Death*, than *the Wolf*; For
Ille profitetur *Se* meum | He profeſſes *Himſelf* my
Hoſtem palam; *verò* Tu, *ſub* | *Enemy* openly; *but* Thou, *under*
Specie *Amicitiæ*, quotidie | the Show *of Friendſhip*, daily
imminuis meum *Gregem*. | *diminiſheſt* my *Flock*.

MOR. MOR.

Hæc *Fabula* indicat, *Eos* | This *Fable* ſhows, *that They*
eſſe *puniendos* longè *magis*, | are to be *puniſhed* by *far more*,
Qui *lædunt* Nos *ſub* Specie | Who *hurt* Us *under* a Pretence
Amicitiæ, quàm *Qui* pro- | *of Friendſhip*, than *They Who* pro-
fitentur *Se* noſtros *Inimicos* | feſs *Themſelves* our *Enemies*
palam. | openly.

F A B L E   CXLVIII.

De ARIETE *pugnante* cum | *Of* the RAM *fighting with*
TAURO. | the BULL.

ERat *quidam* Aries | THERE was *a certain* Ram
inter Oves, *Qui* | among the Sheep, *Who*
habebat *tam* firmum *Caput* | had *ſo* firm *a Head*
& *Cornua*, ut *ſtatim* & | and *Horns*, that *preſently* and
facilè ſuperaret *ceteros* | *eaſily* He overcame *the other*
Arietes; *quare* cùm *inveniret* | Rams; *wherefore* when *he found*
nullum *Arietem* ampliùs, | no Ram *more*,
Qui auderet *obſiſtere* Sibi | *Who* dared *to withſtand* Him
occurſanti, elatus | running *againſt Him*, puffed up
crebris Victoriis, *auſus eſt* | with *frequent* Victories, *he dared*
provocare *Taurum* ad *Pug-* | to provoke *a Bull* to *Bat-*
nam; ſed *primo* Congreſſu, | *tle*; but *at the firſt* Onſet,
cùm |

cùm arietaviffet *in* Frontem *Tauri*, eft reper- cuffus *tam* atroci *Iĉtu*, ut *ferè* moriens, *diceret* hæc, *Stultus* Ego ! *quid* egi ? *Cur* aufus fum *laceffere* tam *potentem* Ad- verfarium, *Cui* Natura creavit Me *imparem ?*	*when* He had butted *againſt* the forehead *of the Bull*, He was ftruck back *with fo* cruel *a Blow*, that *almoſt* dying, He *faid* thefe words, *Fool* that I am ! *what* have I done ? *Why* dared I to *provoke* fo *powerful* an Ad- verfary, *to Whom* Nature hath created Me *unequal ?*

Mor.

Hæc *Fabula* indicat, *non effe* certandum *cum* poten- tioribus.	This *Fable* ſhows, *that it is not* to be ftrove *with* the more powerful.

FABLE CXLIX.

De Aquilâ *rapiente* Filios Cuniculi.	*Of* the Eagle *ſnatching* the Young of the Coney.

AQUILA, *nidulata* in *altiſſimâ* Arbore, ra- *puerat* Filios *Cuniculi*, Qui *pafcebatur* non *longè* illinc, *in* Prædam *fuorum* Pullorum ; *Quam* Cuni- culus *orabat* blandis *Verbis*, ut *dignaretur* reftituere *fuos* Filios *Sibi ;* At *Illa*, arbitrans *Eum* effe *pufillum* & *terreſtre* Animal, *dilacerabat* Eos *Unguibus*, Quos *apponebat* fuis *Pullis* epulandos *in* Confpeĉtu *Matris :* Tunc *Cuniculus*, commotus *Morte* fuorum *Filiorum*, haud permifit *hanc* Injuriam *abire* impu- nitam ; *etenim* effodit *Arborem*, radicitus, *Quæ* fufti-	THe Eagle, *having built a Neſt* in *a very high* Tree, *had ſnatch-* ed away the Young *of the Coney*, Who *was fed* not *far* from thence, *for* the Prey *of her* Young ; *When* the Co- ney *befought* with fair *Words*, that *She would vouchſafe* to reftore her Young *to Her ;* But *She*, fuppofing *Him* to be *a little* and *earthly* Animal, *tore* Them *with her Talons*, Which *She* put to her *Young* to eat *in* the Sight *of the Dam :* Then *the Coney*, moved *at the Death* of her *Young*, permitted not *this* Injury *to go* unpunifh- ed ; *for* She dug up the *Tree* by the Roots, *Which* fuftain-

P

ſuſtinebat *Nidum*, Quæ procidens levi *Impulſu* Ventorum, dejecit Pullos *Aquilæ* adhuc implumes in *Humum*, Qui depaſti à *Feris* præbuerunt *Solatium* Doloris *Cuniculo*.

ſuſtained *the Neſt*, which falling with a light *Blaſt* of the Winds, *threw down* the Young *of the Eagle*, as yet *unfledged*, upon *the Ground*, Who *being eat up* by *the Wild Beaſts* afforded *Comfort* of Grief *to the Coney.*

Mor.

Hæc *Fabula* indicat *Neminem* fretum *ſuâ* Potentiâ *debere* deſpicere *imbecilliores*, cùm *aliquando* infirmiores *ulciſcantur* Injurias *potentiorum.*

Mor.

This *Fable* ſhows, *that no Man* relying on *his* Power ought to deſpiſe *the Weaker*, ſeeing that *ſometimes* the Weaker *revenge* the Injuries *of the more powerful.*

FABLE CL.

De Lupo, *Piſce* Fluvii, *affectante* Regnum Maris.

Of the Pike, *a Fiſh* of the River, *affecting* the Dominion *of the Sea.*

ERAT *Lupus*, in quodam Amne, *Qui* excedebat *cæteros* Piſces *ejuſdem* Fluminis in *Pulchritudine, Magnitudine*, ac *Robore ;* unde *Omnes* admirabantur, & afficiebant *Eum* maximo *Honore ;* quare *elatus* Superbiâ *cæpit* appetere *majorem* Principatum. *Igitur* Amne *relicto*, in *Quo* regnaverat *multos* Annos, ingreſſus *eſt* Mare, *ut* vendicaret *Regnum* Ejus *Sibi ;* ſed *offendens* Delphinum *miræ* Magnitudinis, Qui

THERE was *a Pike*, in a certain River, *Who* exceeded the other Fiſhes of *the ſame* River *in* Fairneſs, Greatneſs, and Strength *;* whence *All* admired, and affected *Him* with the greateſt *Honour ;* wherefore *puffed up* with Pride *He began* to deſire *greater* Command. *Therefore* the River *being left*, in *Which* He had reigned *many* Years, *He entered* into the Sea, *that* he might challenge *the Dominion* of It *to Himſelf ;* but *finding* a Dolphin *of a wonderful* Greatneſs, *Who*

Qui regnabat *in* Illo, *eſt* | *Who* reign'd *in* It, *He was*
ita *infeƀatus* ab *Illo*, ut *au-* | ſo *purſued* by *Him*, that *flying*
fugiens vix *ingrederetur* | *away* ſcarce *could He enter into*
Oſtium *Amnis*, unde | the Mouth *of the River*, whence
auſus eſt exire *non ampliùs*. | *He durſt* to go out *no more.*

MOR.

Hæc Fabula admonet *Nos*, | This *Fable* admoniſhes *Us*,
ut *contenti* noſtris *Rebus*, | that *content* with our own *Things*,
ne appetamus, *Quæ* ſunt | We do not deſire, *What* are
longè majora *noſtris* Viribus. | *by far* greater *than our* Strength.

FABLE CLI.

De OVE *convitiante* | *Of the* SHEEP *railing on*
Paſtori. | the Shepherd.

OVis *convitiabatur* Pa- | A Sheep *railed on* a Shep-
ſtori, *quòd* non *con-* | herd, *that* not *con-*
tentus Lacte, *Quod* mul- | *tent* with the Milk, *Which* He
gebat *ab* Eâ *in* ſuum *Uſum*, | milked *from* Her *for* his own *Uſe*,
& *Uſum* Filiorum, | and *the Uſe* of his Children,
inſuper denudaret *Illam* | *moreover* He ſtripped *Her*
Vellere. *Tunc* Paſtor | of the Fleece. *Then* the Shepherd
iratus trahebat *ejus* Filium | *angry* dragged *her* Young one
ad Mortem. *Ovis* inquit, | *to* Death. *The Sheep* ſays,
Quid pejus *potes* facere | *What* worſe *are You able* to do
Mibi ? Paſtor *inquit*, ut | *to Me ?* The Shepherd *ſays*, that
occidam Te, *&* projiciam | *I may kill* Thee, and throw Thee out
devorandam Lupis *&* | *to be devoured* by the Wolves *and*
Canibus. *Ovis* ſiluit, | Dogs. *The Sheep* held her Peace,
formidans adhuc *majora* | *fearing* yet *greater*
Mala. | Evils.

MOR.

Hæc Fabula indicat, | This *Fable* ſhows,
Homines non debere *excan-* | that *Men* ought not *to grow*
deſcere in *Deum*, ſi *permittat* | *warm againſt* God, *if He permitteth*
Divitias *&* Filios *auferri* | Riches *and* Children *to be taken*
Ipſis ; *cùm* poſſit | from Them ; *when* He is able
inferre etiam *majora* Sup- | *to bring* even *greater* Puniſh-
plicia | ments

plicia *Ipfis* & *viventibus* ments *upon Them* both *living* & *mortuis.*   and *dead.*

FABLE CLII.

De Aurigâ & Rotâ   *Of* the Waggoner *and* the Wheel
Currûs *ftridente.*   of the Waggon *creaking.*

AUriga *interrogabat* Currum, *quare* Rota, *Quæ* erat *deterior,* ftrideret, *cùm* cæteri *non facerent* idem? *Cui* Currus *inquit,* Ægroti *femper* confueverunt *effe* morofi & queruli.

THE Waggoner *afked* the Waggon, *wherefore* the Wheel, *Which* was *worfe,* creaked, *when* the reft *did not do* the fame? *To whom* the Waggon *faid,* The Sick *always* have ufed *to be* morofe *and* complaining.

Mor.

Hæc *Fabula* indicat, *Mala femper folere* impellere *Homines* ad *Querimoniam.*

Mor.

This *Fable* fhows, *that Evils* always *are wont* to drive *Men* to *Complaint.*

FABLE CLIII.

De Viro *volente* experiri Amicos.   *Of* the Man *willing* to try his Friends.

QUidam *Vir* admodum *dives* & *liberalis,* habebat *magnam* Copiam *Amicorum,* Quos *fæpe* invitabat *ad* Cœnam; *ad* Quem accedebant libentiffimè. *Autem* volens *experiri,* an effent *fideles* Sibi in Laboribus & Periculis, *convocavit* Eos omnes, dicens, *Inimicos* effe obortos Sibi,

A Certain *Man* very *rich* and *liberal,* had *a great* Abundance *of Friends,* Whom *often* He invited *to* Supper; *to Whom They went* moft willingly. *But* willing *to try,* whether *They* would be *faithful* to Him in Labours *and* Dangers, *He called together* Them all, *faying, that Enemies* were *rifen up* againft Him,

Sibi, *Quos* ſtatuit *occidere;* quare, *Armis* correptis, *irent* Secum, ut *ulciſcerentur* Injurias *illatas* Sibi. *Tum* Omnes *cæperunt* excuſare *Se,* præter *Duos.* Igitur, *cæteris* repudiatis, *habuit* tantùm *Illos* Duos *in* Numero *Amicorum.*

againſt Him, *Whom* He reſolved *to kill;* wherefore, *Arms* being taken up, *they ſhould go* with Him, that *They might revenge* the Injuries *offered* to Him. *Then* All *began* to excuſe *Themſelves,* except *Two.* Therefore, *the reſt* being rejected, *He held* only *Thoſe* Two *in* the Number *of Friends.*

MOR.

Hæc *Fabula* indicat, ad-*verſam* Fortunam *eſſe* optimum *Experimentum* Amicitiæ.

MOR.

This *Fable* ſhows, *that* ad-*verſe* Fortune *is* the beſt *Experiment* of Friendſhip.

FABLE CLIV.

De Vulpe *laudante* Carnem *Leporis* Cani.

Of the Fox *praiſing* the Fleſh *of the Hare* to the Dog.

CUM *Vulpes* fugeretur à Cane, *&* jamjam *eſſet* capienda, *nec* cognoſcerat *ullam* aliam *Viam* evadendi, *inquit,* O *Canis,* quid *cupis* perdere *Me,* cujus *Caro* non poteſt *eſſe* ulli *Uſui* Tibi? *cape* potiùs *illum* Leporem; (*etenim* Lepus *aderat* propè) *cujus* carnem *Mortales* dicunt *eſſe* ſuaviſſimam. *Igitur* Canis, *motus* Conſilio *Vulpis,* Vulpe *omiſſâ,* infecutus eſt *Leporem;* Quem *tamen* non potuit *capere* ob *ejus* incredibilem *Velocitatem.* Poſt *paucos* Dies *Lepus*

WHEN *the Fox* was put to flight by the Dog, *and* juſt now *was* to be catched, *nor* knew *any* other *Way* of eſcaping, He *ſaid,* O *Dog,* why *doſt Thou deſire* to deſtroy *Me,* whoſe *Fleſh* cannot *be* of any *Uſe* to Thee? *take* rather *that* Hare; (*for* the Hare *was* nigh) *whoſe* Fleſh *Men* ſay is moſt ſweet. *Therefore* the Dog, *moved* with the Counſel *of the Fox,* the Fox *being let alone,* purſued *the Hare;* Which yet He could not *take* for her incredible *Swiftneſs.* After *a few* Days *the Hare*

Lepus conveniens *Vulpem* accufabat *Eam* vehementer, (*etenim* audièrat *ejus* Verba) quòd demonftrâffet *Se* Cani. *Cui* Vulpes *inquit*, Lepus, *quid* accufas *Me*, cùm *laudavi* Te *tantopere ?* Quid diceres, fi *vituperâffem* Te ?

the *Hare* meeting *the Fox* accufed *Her* vehemently, (*for* He had heard *her* Words) *becaufe* She had fhown *Him* to the Dog. *To whom* the Fox *faid*, O Hare, *why* do You accufe *Me*, when *I have* praifed Thee *fo greatly ?* What *would You fay*, if *I had difgraced* You ?

MOR.

Hæc *Fabula* indicat, *Homines* machinari *Perniciem* Aliis *fub* Specie *Laudationis.*

MOR.

This *Fable* fhows, that *Men* contrive *Deftruction* for Others *under* the Pretence of *Commendation.*

---

v

FABLE CLV.

De Lepore *petente* Calliditatem, *&* Vulpe *Celeritatem* à *Jove.*

Of the Hare *afking* Craftinefs, *and* the Fox *Swiftnefs* from *Jupiter.*

LEpus *&* Vulpes *petebant* à *Jove ;* Hæc, *ut* adjungeret *Celeritatem* fuæ *Calliditati ;* Ille, *ut* adjungeret *Calliditatem* fuæ *Celeritati :* Quibus *Jupiter* ita *refpondit ;* Elargiti fumus *Munera* fingulis *Animantibus,* ab *Origine* Mundi, *è* noftro *liberaliffimo* Sinu ; *fed* dediffe *Omnia* Uni *fuiffet* Injuria *Aliorum.*

THE Hare *and* the Fox *begged* of *Jupiter ;* This, *that* He would join *Swiftnefs* to her *Craftinefs ;* That, *that* He would join *Craftinefs* to his *Swiftnefs :* To Whom *Jupiter* thus *anfwered;* We have beftowed Gifts to all *living Creatures,* from *the Beginning* of the World, *out of* our *moft liberal* Bofom ; *but* to have given *All* to One *would have been* the Injury *of Others.*

MOR.

Hæc *Fabula* indicat, *Deum* effe largitum *fua* Munera

MOR.

This *Fable* fhows, that *God* has given *his* Gifts

Munera *ita* æquali *Lance*, ut *Quifque* debeat *effe* contentus *fuâ* Sorte.

Gifts *with fo* equal *a Balance*, that *Every One* ought *to be* content *with his own* Lot.

FABLE CLVI.

De Equo *inculto*, fed *veloci*, & *cæteris* irridentibus *Eum*.

Of the Horfe *ugly*, but *fwift*, and *the reft* mocking *Him*.

COmplures *Equi* fuerant *adducti* ad *Circenfes* Ludos, *ornati* pulcherrimis *Phaleris*, præter *Unum*, Quem *cæteri* irridebant, *ut* incultum, & ineptum *ad* tale *Certamen*; nec *opinabantur*, futurum unquam Victorem. *Sed* ubi *Tempus* currendi *advenit*, &, *Signo* Tubæ dato, cuncti *exfiliêre è Carcere*, tum *demum* innotuit, *quantò* Hic *paulò* antè *irrifus* fuperaret *cæteros* Velocitate; *etenim*, omnibus *aliis* relictis *poft* Se *longo* intervallo, *affecutus eft* Palmam.

MANY *Horfes* were brought to *the Circenfian* Games, *adorned* with moft beautiful *Trappings*, except *One*, Whom *the reft* laughed at, *as* ugly, and unfit *for* fuch *an Engagement*; nor *did They think*, that He would be *ever* Victor. *But* when *the Time* of running *approached*, and, *the Signal* of the Trumpet *being given*, all *leaped* from *the Goal*, then *at laft* it appeared, *by how much* This *a little* before *derided* excelled *the reft* in Swiftnefs; *for*, all *the others* being left *behind* Him *at a long* Diftance, *He gained* the Victory.

MOR.

Fabula fignificat, Homines *non judicandos* ex *Habitu*, fed *ex* Virtute.

MOR.

The Fable *fignifies*, that Men *are not to be* judged by *Habit*, but *by* Virtue.

FABLE

FABLE CLVII.

De Ruſtico *admiſſo* ad *Juriſconſultum* per *Vocem* Hædi.

Of the Countryman *admitted* to the Lawyer by the Voice of the Kid.

QUidam *Ruſticus*, implicitus *gravi* Lite, *acceſſit* ad *quendam* Juriſconſultum, *ut*, Eo *Patrono*, explicaret *Se.* At *Ille* impeditus *aliis* Negotiis *jubet* renunciari, *Se* nunc *non poſſe* vacare *Illi;* quare *abiret* rediturus *alias.* Ruſticus, *Qui* fidebat *Ei* plurimùm, *ut* veteri & fido *Amico*, nunquam *admittebatur.* Tandem *deferens* Hædum *adhuc* lactantem, & pinguem, *Secum*, ſtabat *ante* Fores *Juriſperiti*, & *vellicans* Hædum, *coëgit* Illum *balare.* Janitor, *Qui* ſolebat *admittere* Eos, *Qui* portarent *Dona*, ex *Precepto.* Heri, *Voce* Hædi *auditâ*, illico *aperiens* Januam, *jubet* Hominem *introïre.* Tunc *Ruſticus*, converſus *ad* Hædum, *inquit*, Mi *Hædule*, ago *Gratias* Tibi, *Quæ* effeciſti *has* Fores *tam* faciles *Mihi.*

A Certain *Countryman*, entangled *in a heavy* Suit, *went* to a *certain* Lawyer, *that*, He being *Patron*, He might unfold *Himſelf.* But *He* hindered *with other* Affairs *orders Him* to be told, *that He* now *was not able* to be at Leiſure *for Him;* wherefore *He ſhould go away* to return *another Time.* The Countryman, *Who* truſted *to Him* very much, *as* an old *and* faithful *Friend*, never *was admitted.* At length *bringing* a Kid *as yet* ſucking, *and* fat, *with Him*, He ſtood *before* the Doors *of the Lawyer*, and *plucking* the Kid, *forced* Him *to bleat.* The Porter, *Who* was wont *to admit* Thoſe, *Who* brought *Gifts*, by *the Command* of his Maſter, *the Voice* of the Kid *being heard*, preſently *opening* the Gate, *orders* the Man *to enter.* Then *the Countryman*, having turned *to* the Kid, *ſaid*, My *little Kid*, I give *Thanks* to Thee, *Who* haſt made *theſe* Doors ſo eaſy *to me.*

MOR.

Fabula *indicat*, nullas *Res* eſſe *tam* duras & difficiles,

MOR.

The Fable *ſhows*, that no *Things* are ſo hard and difficult,

tiles, *Quas* Munera *non* cult, *Which* Gifts *do not*
aperiunt. *open.*

FABLE CLVIII.

De Sene *dejiciente* *Of* the old Man *driving down*
Saxis *Juvenem* with Stones *the young Man*
diripientem *Poma* Sibi. stealing *Apples* from Him.

Quidam *Senex* orabat *Juvenem* diripientem *Poma* Sibi *blandis* Verbis, *ut* descenderet *ex* Arbore, *nec* vellet *auferre* suas *Res;* sed *cùm* funderet *Verba* incassùm, *Juvene* contemnente *ejus* Ætatem *&* Verba, inquit, Audio, *esse* aliquam *Virtutem* non *tantùm* in *Verbis,* verùm *etiam* in *Herbis;* igitur *cœpit* vellere *Gramen,* & *jacere* in *Illum;* Quod *Juvenis* conspicatus *ridebat* vehementer, *&* arbitrabatur *Senem* delirare, *Qui* crederet, *Se* posse *depellere* Eum *ex* Arbore. *Tunc* Senex, *cupiens* experiri *Omnia,* inquit, *Quando* Verba *&* Herbæ *valent* Nil *adversus* Raptorem *mearum* Rerum, *agam* Eum Lapidibus, *in Quibus* quoq; dicunt *esse* *Virtutem;* & *jaciens* Lapides, *Quibus* impleverat *Gremium,* coëgit *Illum* descendere, *&* abire.

A Certain *old Man* besought a *young Man* stealing *Apples* from Him *with fair* Words, *that* He would descend *out of* the Tree, *nor* would *take away* his *Things;* but *when* He poured out *Words* in vain, *the young Man* despising his Age *and* Words, *He said,* I hear, *that there is* some *Virtue* not *only* in *Words,* but *also* in *Herbs;* therefore *He began* to pull *the Grafs,* and *to throw it* at Him; Which *the young Man* having seen *laughed* vehemently, *and* thought *the old Man* to doat, *Who* believed, *that He* was able *to drive down* Him *out of* the Tree. *Then* the old Man, *defiring* to try *all Things,* said, *when* Words *and* Herbs *avail* Nothing *against* the Stealer *of my* Things, *I will drive* Him *with Stones,* in *Which* also *They say* that there is *Virtue;* and *throwing* Stones, *with which* He had filled *his Lap,* he forced *Him* to descend, *and* to go away.

_Mor.

Q

MOR.

Hæc *Fabula* indicat, *Omnia* tentanda *Sapienti,* priufquam confugiat ad *Auxilium* Armorum.

MOR.

This *Fable* fhows, *that all Things* are to be tried *by a wife Man,* before that *He fleeth* to *the Help* of Arms.

FABLE CLIX.

De Lufciniâ *pollicente* Accipitri *Cantum* pro fuâ Vitâ.

Of the Nightingale *promifing* to the Hawk *a Song* for *her* Life.

Lufciniâ *comprehenfâ* à *famelico* Accipitre, *cùm* intelligeret, *Se* fore *devorandam* ab *Eo,* rogabat *Eum* blandè, *ut* dimitteret *Se,* pollicita, *Sefe* relaturam *ingentem* Mercedem *pro* tanto *Beneficio.* Autem *cùm* Accipiter *rogaret,* Quid *Gratie* poffet *referre* Sibi; *inquit,* Demulcebo tuas Aures *dulcibus* Cantibus. *Accipiter* refpondit, *Malo,* demulceas *meum* Ventrem; *poffum* vivere *fine* tuis Cantibus, fed *non* fine Cibo.

THE Nightingale *being caught* by a *hungry* Hawk, *when* She underftood *that She* fhould be *devoured* by *Him,* afked *Him* fairly, *that* He would difmifs *Her,* having promifed, *that She* would return a *vaft* Reward *for* fo great *a Benefit.* But *when* the Hawk *afked,* What *Favour* She was able *to return* to Him; *She faid,* I will foften thy Ears *with fweet* Songs. *The Hawk* anfwered, *I had rather,* thou fhouldeft foften *my* Belly; I *am able* to live *without* thy Songs, but *net* without Meat.

MOR.

Hæc *Fabula* docet, *utilia* anteponenda *jucundis.*

MOR.

This *Fable* teacheth, *that profitable Things* are to be preferred *to pleafant.*

FABLE CLX.

De Leone *eligente* Porcum
Socium Sibi.

Of the Lion *choosing* the Hog
a *Companion* for Himself.

LE-O, *cùm* vellet
adsciscere Socios *Sibi*,
& *multa* Animalia *optarent*
adjungere *Sese* Illi, &
expofcerent *Id* Votis &
Precibus, *cæteris* fpretis,
voluit inire
Societatem folùm *cum* Porco.
Autem rogatus *Caufam*,
refpondit, *Quia* hoc *Animal* eſt *adeò* fidum, *ut* nunquam *relinqueret* fuos *Amicos*
& *Socios* in *ullo*, quantumvis
magno, Difcrimine.

THE LION, *when* He would
get Companions *to Himfelf*,
and *many* Animals *wiſhed*
to join *Themfelves* to Him, and
required *It* with Vows *and*
Prayers, *the others* being defpifed,
He was willing to enter into
Society only *with* the Hog.
But being aſked *the Caufe*,
He anfwered, *Becaufe* this *Animal* is *fo* faithful, *that* He never *would leave* his *Friends*
and *Companions* in *any*, altho'
great, Danger.

MOR.

MOR.

Hæc *Fabula* docet,
Amicitiam Eorum *appeten-
dam*, Qui *Tempore* Adver-
fitatis *non referunt* Pedem
à præſtando *Auxilio*.

This *Fable* teaches,
that the Friendſhip of thofe *is to be
defired*, Who *in the Time* of Ad-
verfity *do not. draw back* a Foot
from affording *Affiſtance*.

FABLE CLXI.

De Culice *petente* Cibum &
Hofpitium *ab* Ape.

Of the Gnat *aſking* Meat *and*
Lodging *of* the Bee.

CUM *Culex* hyberno
Tempore conjiceret, *Se*
periturum *Frigore* &
Fame, acceſſit *ad* Alvearia
Apum *petens* Cibum &
Hofpitium *ab* Eis ; *Quæ*
ſi *fuiſſet confecutus* ab *Eis*
pro-

WHen *the Gnat* in the Winter
Time conjeĉtured, *that He*
ſhould periſh *with Cold* and
Hunger, He went *to* the Hives
of the Bees *aſking* Meat *and*
Lodging *from* Them ; *Which*
if *He ſhould obtain* from *Them*
He pro-

promittebat, *Se* edocturum *Filios* Eorum *Artem* Muficæ. *Tunc* quædam *Apis* refpondit, *At* Ego *mallem*, quòd *mei* Liberi *edifcant* meam *Artem*, Quæ *poterit* eximere *Eos* à *Periculo* Famis & Frigoris.

He promifed, *that He* would teach *the Children* of Them *the Art* of Mufick. *Then* a certain *Bee* anfwered, *But* I *had rather*, that *my* Children *fhould learn* my *Art*, Which *will be able* to exempt *Them* from *the Danger* of Hunger *and* Cold.

MOR.

Hæc *Fabula* admonet nos, ut *erudiamus* noftros *Liberos* his *Artibus*, Quæ valent *vindicare* Eos *ab* Inopiâ.

MOR.

This *Fable* admonifhes Us, that *We infruct* our *Children* in thofe *Arts*, Which are able *to defend* Them *from* Want.

FABLE CLXII.

De Afino *Tubicine*, & *Lepore* Tabellario.

Of the Afs *the Trumpeter*, and *the Hare* the Letter-Carrier.

LEO, *Rex* Quadrupe-dum, *pugnaturus* adverfus *Volucres*, inftruebat *fuas* Acies: *Autem* inter-rogatus *ab* Urfo, *Quid* Iner-tia *Afini*, aut *Timidi-tas* Leporis *conferret* Victo-riam *Ei*, Quos *cernebat* adeffe *ibi* inter *Ceteros*, refpondit, *Afinus*, Clangore *fuæ* Tubæ, *concitabit* Milites *ad* Pugnam ; *verò* Lepus *fan-getur* Officio *Tabellarii* ob *Celeritatem* Pedum.

THE Lion, *the King* of the four-footed Beaft, *about to fight* againft *the Birds*, difpofed *his* Troops : *But* being afk-ed *by* the Bear, *How* the Slug-gifhnefs *of the Afs*, or *the Fearful-nefs* of the Hare *would bring* Victo-ry *to Him*, Whom *He* faw to be prefent *there* among *the reft*, He anfwered, *The Afs*, with the Sound *of his* Trumpet, *will roufe* the Soldiers *to* the Fight ; *but* the Hare *will per-form* the Office *of a Letter-Bearer* thro' *the Swiftnefs* of his Feet.

MOR.

Fabula *fignificat*, Nemi-nem *effe* adeò *contemptibilem*, Qui

MOR.

The Fable *fignifies*, that no One is fo *contemptible*, Who

Qui *non poſſit* prodeſſe *Nobis* in *aliqua* Re.

Who *cannot* be profitable *to Us* in *ſome* Thing.

FABLE CLXIII.

De Accipitribus *Inimicis* inter *Se,* Quos *Columbæ* compoſuerunt.

Of the Hawks *Enemies* among *Themſelves,* Whom the *Doves* reconciled.

ACcipitres *Inimici* inter *Se* decertabant *quotidie,* & *occupati* ſuis *Invidiis* minimè *infeſtabant* alias *Aves.* Columbæ *dolentes,* Legatis *miſſis,* compoſuêre *Eos :* Sed *Illi,* ubi *ſunt* effecti *Amici* inter *Se,* non deſinebant *vexare* & occidere cæteras *imbecilliores* Aves, *&* maximè *Columbas.* Tum *Columbæ* dicebant, *Quantò* erat *Diſcordia* Accipitrum *melior* Nobis, *quàm* Concordia.

THE Hawks *Enemies* among *Themſelves* contended *daily,* and b͟uſied with their own *Enmities* they very little *infeſted* the other *Birds.* The Doves *grieving,* Ambaſſadors *being ſent,* reconciled *Them :* But *They,* when *They were* made *Friends* among *Themſelves,* did not leave off *to vex* and *kill* the other *weaker* Birds, *and* moſtly *the Doves.* Then *the* Doves ſaid, *By how* much was *the Diſcord* of the Hawks *better* to Us, *than* their Agreement.

MOR.

Hæc *Fabula* admonet, *Odia* malorum *Civium* inter *Se* potiùs *alenda,* quàm *extinguenda,* ut, *dum* certant *inter Se, permittant* bonos *Vires* vivere *quietè.*

MOR.

This *Fable* admoniſhes, that *the Hatreds* of bad *Citizens* among *Themſelves* rather *are to be* nouriſhed than *extinguiſhed,* that, *whilſt* They contend *among* Themſelves, *They may permit* good *Men* to live *quietly.*

FABLE

FABLE CLXIV.

De Sene *volente* differre *Mortem.*

Of the old Man *being willing* to defer *Death.*

QUidam *Senex* rogabat *Mortem,* Quæ *advenerat* ereptura *Eum* è *Vitâ,* ut *deferret,* dum *conderet* fuum *Teftamentum,* & *præpararet* cætera *neceffaria* ad *tantum* Iter. *Cui* Mors *inquit,* Cur *monitus* toties *à Me non præparáfti* Te ? *Et,* cùm *Ille* diceret, *quòd* nunquam *viderat* Eam *antea,* inquit, *Cùm* quotidie *rapiebam* non *modò* tuos *Æquales,* Quorum *Nulli* ferè *jam* reftant, *verùm* etiam *Juvenes,* Pueros, & Infantes, *nonne admonebam* Te *tuæ* Mortalitatis ? *Cùm* fentiebas *tuos* Oculos *tabefcere,* tuum *Auditum* minui, & tuos *cæteros* Senfus *deficere* indies, *nonne* dicebam *Tibi,* Me *effe* propinquam ? & *negas,* Te *effe* admonitum ? *quare* non eft *differendum* ulteriùs.

A Certain *old Man* afked *Death,* Who came to fnatch *Him* out of *Life,* that *He would defer it,* till *He* made his *Will,* and *prepared* the other *neceffary Things* for *fo great* a Journey. *To whom* Death *faid,* Why *warned* fo often *by* Me *haft thou not prepared* Thyfelf ? *And,* when *He* faid, *that* He never *had feen* Him *before,* He faid, *When* daily *I fnatched away* not *only* thy *Equals,* of Which *None* almoft *now* remain, *but* alfo *Young Men,* Boys, *and* Infants, *did not I admonifb* Thee *of thy* Mortality ? *When* Thou perceivedft *thine* Eyes *to grow dim,* thy *Hearing* to be leffened, *and* thy *other* Senfes *to decay* daily, *did I not* fay *to Thee,* that *I was* near ? and *doft Thou deny,* that Thou *haft been* admonifhed ? *wherefore* it is not *to be deferred* longer.

MOR.

Hæc *Fabula* indicat, *quòd* debemus *vivere,* quafi *femper* cernamus *Mortem* adeffe.

MOR.

This *Fable* fhows, *that* We ought *to live* as if *always* We faw *Death* to be prefent.

FABLE

FABLE CLXV.

De Avaro *Viro* alloquente *Sacculum* Nummi.

Of the covetous *Man* speaking to *the* Bag of Money.

QUidam *avarus* Vir *moriturus,* & *relicturus* ingentem *Acervum* Aureorum *malè* partum, *interrogabat* Sacculum *Nummorum,* Quem *juſſit* afferri *Sibi,* Quibus *eſſet* allaturus *Voluptatem?* Cui *Sacculus* inquit, *Tuis* Hæredibus, *Qui* profundent *Nummos* quæſitos *à* Te *tanto* Sudore, *in* Scortis & Conviviis; & Dæmonibus, *Qui* mancipabunt *tuam* Animam *æternis* Suppliciis.

A Certain *covetous* Man *about to die,* and *about to* leave a vaſt *Heap* of golden Pieces *ill* gotten, *aſked* a Bag of *Monies,* which *he commanded* to be brought *to Him,* to whom *He was about* to bear *Pleaſure?* To Whom *the Bag* ſaid, *To thine* Heirs, *Who* will ſpend *the Monies* gotten *by* Thee *with ſo great* Sweat, *upon* Whores *and* Feaſts; *and* to the Devils, *Who* will torment *thy* Soul *with eternal* Puniſhments.

Mor.

Hæc *Fabula* indicat *eſſe* ſtultiſſimum *laborare* in *Eis,* Quæ · *ſint* allatura *Gaudium* Aliis, *autem* Tormenta *Nobis.*

Mor.

This *Fable* ſhows it *to be* a moſt fooliſh Thing *to labour* in *thoſe Things,* Which *may be* about to bear *Joy* to Others, *but* Torments *to Us.*

FABLE.

F A B L E CLXVI.

De Vulpe & Capro.

Of the Fox and the He-Goat.

VUlpes & Caper *siti-bundi* defcenderunt in quendam *Puteum* ; in *Quo* cùm *perbibiffent*, Vulpes ait Capro *circumfpicienti* Reditum, *Caper*, efto *bono* Animo, *namq;* excogitavi, quo *pacto* uterque *fimus* reduces. *Siquidem* Tu eriges Te *rectum*, prioribus *Pedibus* admotis *ad* Parietem, & reclinabis *tua* Cornua, *Mento* adducto ad Pectus, *Ego* tranfiliens per tua *Terga* & *Cornua*, & *evadens* extra *Puteum*, educam *Te* ifthinc *poftea*. Cujus *Confilio* Capro *habente* Fidem, *atq;* obtemperante, *ut* Illa *jube-bat*, Ipfa *profiliit* è *Puteo*, ac *deinde* geftiebat *præ* Gaudio *in* Margine *Putei*, & *exultabat*, habens *Nihil* Curæ *de* Hirco. *Caterùm*, cùm *incufaretur* ab *Hirco*, ut *fædifraga*, refpondit, *Enimvero*, Hirce, *fi* effet *Tibi* tantum *Senfûs* in *Mente* quantum *eft* Setarum *in* Mento, non *de-fcendiffes* in *Puteum*, priufquam *habuiffes* *explo-ratum* de *Reditu*.

A FOX *and* a Goat *being thir-sty* defcended *into* a certain *Well* ; in *Which* when *They* had *well drank*, the Fox *fays* to the Goat *looking about for* a Return, Goat, be *of good* Cheer, *for* I have thought *by what Means* We both *may be* brought back. *If truly* Thou *wilt raife up* Thyfelf *ftrait*, thy fore-*Feet* being fet *to* the Wall, *and* wilt lean forward *thy* Horns, *thy Chin* being drawn *to* thy Breaft, *I* leaping *over* thy *Back* and *Horns*, and *efcaping* out of *the Well* will bring out *Thee* thence *afterwards*. To whofe *Counfel* the Goat *having* Faith, and obeying, *as* She *com-manded*, She *leaped* out of *the Well*, and *then* jumped *for* Joy *upon* the Brink *of the Well*, and *rejoiced*, having *no* Care *of* the Goat. *But*, when *She was accufed* by *the Goat*, as a *League-Breaker*, She anfwered, *Indeed* Goat, *if* there had been *to Thee* as much of *Senfe* in *thy Mind* as *there is* of Hairs on thy Chin, *thou wouldft not have defcended* into *the Well*, before that *thou hadft examin-ed* about *a Return*.

MOR.

Mor.	Mor.
Hæc Fabula innuit, prudentem Virum debere explorare Finem, antequam veniet ad peragendam Rem.	This Fable hints, that a prudent Man ought to examine the End, before that He comes to do the Thing.

FABLE CLXVII.

De Gallis & Perdice.   *Of* the Cocks *and* the Partridge.

CUM *Quidam* haberet *Gallos* Domi, *mercatus eſt* Perdicem, & dedit *Eam* in *Societatem* Gallorum alendam, & *faginandam* unà *cum* Eis. Galli *quiſque* pro *Se* mordebant & abigebant *Eam*. Autem *Perdix* afflictabatur *apud* Se, *exiſtimans* talia inferri Sibi à Gallis, quòd ſuum *Genus* eſſet alienum ab *Illorum* Genere. *Verò* ubi *non* multò *pòſt* aſpexit *Illos* pugnantes inter Se, & mutuò *percutientes*, recreata à Mœrore & Triſtitiâ, *inquit*, Equidem *pòſt* Hæc *non* af-*flictabor* ampliùs, *videns* Eos dimicantes etiam *inter* Se.

WHEN *a certain* Man had Cocks at Home, *He bought* a Partridge, and gave *Her* into *the* Company of the Cocks to be *fed*, and *fattened* together *with* Them. The Cocks *every* one for *Himſelf* bit *and* drove away *Her*. But the *Partridge* was afflicted *with* Herſelf, *thinking* that ſuch things *were offered* to Her *by* the Cocks, *becauſe* her *Kind* was *different* from *their* Kind. *But* when *not* much *after* She ſaw *Them* fighting *amongſt* Themſelves, *and* mutually *ſtriking*, recovered *from* Grief *and* Sadneſs, *She ſaid*, Truly *after* theſe Things *I ſhall not be afflicted* more, *ſeeing* Them fighting even *amongſt* Themſelves.

Mor.	Mor.
Hæc Fabula innuit, prudentes Viros debere ferre Contumelias illatas ab Alienigenis, *Quos* vident ne abſtinere ab Injuriâ Domeſticorum.	This Fable hints, that prudent Men ought to bear the Contumelies offered by Foreigners, Whom They ſee not to abſtain from the Injury of their own Countrymen.

R   FABLE

FABLE CLXVIII.

De Jactatore.

QUidam *Vir* peregrinatus *aliquandiu*, cùm *fuiſſet* reverſus *Domum* iterum, *cùm* jactabundus prædicaret *multa* alia *geſta* a *Se* viriliter *in* diverſis *Regionibus*, tum *verò* Id maximè, quòd *Rhodi* ſuperâſſet *Omnes* ſaliendo : *Rhodios*, Qui *adfuerant*, eſſe *Teſtes* ejuſdem *Rei :* Unus *Eorum*, Qui *aderant*, reſpondens illi inquit, O *Homo*, ſi *Iſtud* eſt verum, Quod *loqueris*, Quid *Opus* eſt *Tibi* Teſtibus? *Ecce* Rhodium ! *Ecce* hic *Certamen* ſaliendi !

Of the Boaster.

A Certain *Man* having travelled *a long while*, when He *was* returned *Home* again, *both* boaſting told *many* other Things *carried on* by *Him* manfully *in* divers *Regions*, and *truly* That *eſpecially*, that *at Rhodes* He had excelled *All* in leaping ; *that the Rhodians*, Who *had been preſent*, were *Witneſſes* of the ſame *Thing :* One *of Them*, Who *were preſent*, anſwering him ſaid, O *Man*, if *That* is true, Which *you ſpeak*, What *Need* is there *to You* of Witneſſes? *Behold* a Rhodian ! *Behold* here a *Trial* of leaping.

Mor.

Hæc *Fabula* indicat, quòd, ubi *vera* Teſtimonia *adſunt*, eſt *nihil* *Opus* *Verbis*.

Mor.

This *Fable* ſhows, that, where *true* Teſtimonies are preſent, there is *no* *Need* of *Words*.

FABLE CLXIX.

De Viro *tentante* Apollinem.

QUidam *facinoroſus* Vir *contulit* Se *Delphos* tentaturus *Apollinem*, & *habens* Paſſerculum *ſub* Pallio, *Quem* tenebat *ſuo* Pugno,

Of the Man *tempting* Apollo.

A Certain *wicked* Man *betook* Himſelf *to Delphos* about to tempt *Apollo*, and *having* a Sparrow *under* his Cloak, *Which* He held *in his* Fiſt,

Pugno, & accedens *ad* Tripodas, *interrogabat* Eum *dicens*, Quod *habeo* in *meâ* Dextrâ, *vivitne*, an *eſt* mortuum ? *Prolaturus* Paſſerculum *vivum*, ſi *Ille* reſpondiſſet, *mortuum :* rurſus *prolaturus* mortuum, *ſi* reſpondiſſet, *vivum ;* etenim *occidiſſet* ·' Eum *ſtatim* ſub *Pallio* clam, *priuſquam* proferret. *At* Deus, *intelligens* ſubdolam *Calliditatem* Hominis, *dixit*, O *Conſultor*, facito *Utrum* mavis *facere ;* etenim *eſt* penes *Te ;* & proferto *ſive* vivum, *ſive* mortuum, *Quod* habes *in* tuis *Manibus*.

Fiſt, *and* going *to* the Trevet, *He* aſked Him *ſaying*, What *I* have in *my* Right Hand, *liveth it*, or *is it* dead? *About to pluck forth* theSparrow *alive*, if *He* had anſwered, *dead :* again *about to pluck it forth* dead, *if* He had anſwered, *alive ;* for *He would have killed* It *preſently* under *the Cloak* privily, *before that* He plucked it out. *But the* God, *underſtanding* the deceitful *Craftineſs* of the Man, *ſaid*, O *Conſulter*, do Thou *Whether* Thou art more willing *to do ;* for *it is* in the Power *of Thee ; and* pluck out *either* ' alive, *or* dead, *What* Thou haſt *in* thy *Hands*.

MOR.

Hæc *Fabula* innuit, *Nihil* latere, *neque* fallere *divinam* Mentem.

MOR.

This *Fable* hints, *that* Nothing lies hid from, *nor* deceives *the divine* Mind.

FABLE CLXX.

De Piſcatore & Smaride.

Of the Fiſherman *and* the Sprat.

Quidam *Piſcator*, Retibus *dimiſſis* in *Mare*, extulit *puſillam* Smaridem, *Que* ſic *obſecrabat* Piſcatorem ; *Noli* capere *Me* tam *puſillam* in *præſentiâ ;* ſine *Me* abire & creſcere *ut* poſtea *potiaris* Me *ſic* adultâ *cum* majori *Commodo.* Cui *Piſcator*

A Certain *Fiſherman*, his Nets *being let down* into *the Sea*, brought out *a ſmall* Sprat, *Which* thus *beſought* the Fiſherman ; *Be not willing* to take *Me* ſo little at *preſent ;* ſuffer *Me* to go away, *and* to grow, *that* afterwards *Thou mayſt* obtain Me *ſo grown* up *with* greater *Advantage.* To whom *the Fiſherman*

ter inquit, *Verò* Ego *essem* amens, *si* omitterem *Lucrum* licèt *exiguum*, Quod habeo *inter* meas *Manus*, Spe *futuri*   Boni *quamvis* magni.

erman said, *But* I *should be* mad, *if* I should omit *a Gain* altho' *small*, Which I have *between* my *Hands*, for the Hope *of a future* Good *altho'* great.

MOR.

Hæc *Fabula* indicat *Eum* esse *stolidum*, Qui *propter* Spem *majoris* Commodi *non* amplectitur Rem *&* præsentem *&* certam, *licèt* parvam.

MOR.

This   *Fable* shows *Him* to be *foolish*, Who *for* Hope *of a greater* Advantage *does not embrace* a Thing *both* present *and* certain, *although* small.

FABLE CLXXI.

De Equo *&* Asino.

Of the Horse *and* the Ass.

QUidam *Vir* habebat *Equum* & *Asinum*; autem *dum* faciunt *Iter*, Asinus *inquit* Equo, *Si* vis, *Me* esse *salvum*, leva *Me* Parte *mei* Oneris: *Equo* non *obsequente* Illius *Verbis*, Asinus *cadens* sub *Onere* moritur. *Tunc* Dominus *Jumentorum* imponit *Equo* omnes *Sarcinas*, Quas *Asinus* portabat, *&* simul *Corium*, Quod *exuerat* à *mortuo* Asino: *Quo* Onere *Equus* depressus *&* gemens inquit, Væ *Mihi* infelicissimo *Jumentorum!* Quid *Mali* evenit *misero* Mihi! *Nam* recusans *Partem*, nunc *porto* totum Onus,

ACertain *Man* had *a Horse* and *an Ass*; but *whilst* they make *a Journey*, the Ass *says* to the Horse, *If* You are willing, *that I* be *safe*, lighten *Me* of a Part *of my* Burden: *The Horse* not *obeying* His *Words*, the Ass *falling* under *the Burden* dies. *Then* the Master *of the Beasts* puts on *the Horse* all *the Packs*, Which *the Ass* carried, *and* at the same Time *the Hide*, Which *He had stripped off* from *the dead* Ass: *With which* Burden *the Horse* depressed *and* groaning said, Woe *to Me* most unhappy *of Beasts!* What an *Evil* has happened *to wretched* Me! *For* refusing *a Part*, now *I* carry the whole *Burden,*

Onus, & *infuper* Illius *Corium.* | *Burden,* and *moreover* his Hide.

MOR. | MOR.

Hæc *Fabula* innuit, *majores* debere *effe* Partcipes *in* minoribus *Laboribus,* ut *Utriq;* fint *incolumes.* | This *Fable* hints, that the greater ought *to be* Partakers *in* the leffer Labours, that *Both* may be fafe.

FABLE CLXXII.

De TUBICINE. | *Of* the TRUMPETER.

Quidam *Tubicen,* interceptus *ab* Hoftibus *in* Militiâ, *proclamabat* ad *Eos,* Qui *circumfiftebant,* O *Viri,* Nolite *occidere* Me *innocuum* & *infontem;* etenim *nunquam* occidi *Ullum;* quippe *habeo* Nihil *aliud,* quàm hanc Tubam. *Ad* Quem *Illi* refponderunt *viciffim* cum *Clamore;* Verò *Tu* trucidaberis *magis* hoc *ipfo;* quòd *cùm* Tu *Ipfe* nequeas *dimicare,* potes *impellere* Cæteros *ad* Certamen. | A Certain *Trumpeter,* taken *by* the Enemies *in* the War, *cried out* to *Them,* Who *ftood about,* O *Men,* Be not willing *to kill* Me *harmlefs* and *innocent;* for *never* have I killed *any One;* for I *have* Nothing *elfe,* than this Trumpet. *To* Whom They anfwered *in* Turn with *a Noife;* But Thou fhalt be flain *rather* on this fame *Account;* becaufe *when* Thou *Thyfelf* can'ft not fight, Thou art able *to drive* the Reft *to* the Engagement.

MOR. | MOR.

Hæc *Fabula* innuit, *quòd* peccant *præter* cæteros, Qui *perfuadent* malis *&* improbis *Principibus* ad *agendum* iniquè. | This *Fable* hints, that They fin *beyond* Others, Who *perfuade* bad and wicked *Princes* to *act* unjuftly.

FABLE

FABLE CLXXIII.

De Vaticinatore.

VAticinator sedens in Foro *sermocinabatur* ; Cui *Quidam* denunciat, *Ejus* Fores *esse* effractas, & Omnia *direpta*, Quæ *fuissent* in *Domo*. Vaticinator, *gemens* & *properans* Cursu, *recipiebat* Se *Domum :* Quem *Quidam* intuens *currentem*, inquit, *O Tu, Qui* promittis, *Te* divinaturum *aliena* Negotia, *certè* Ipse *non divinâsti* tua.

MOR.

Hæc *Fabula* spectat *ad* Eos, *Qui* non *rectè* administrantes *suas* Res, *conantur* providere & consulere *Alienis*, Quæ *non pertinent* ad *Eos*.

Of the Fortune-teller.

A Fortune-teller fitting in the Market *discoursed ;* To whom *One* declares, *that his* Doors *were* broke open, *and* all Things *taken away,* Which *had been* in *the House.* The Fortune-teller, *sighing* and *hasting* in his Pace, *betook* Himself *Home :* Whom a *certain Man* perceiving *running,* said, *O Thou, Who* promiseth, *that Thou* wilt divine *others'* Affairs, *surely* Thyself *hast not divined* thine own.

MOR.

This *Fable* looks *to* Them, *Who,* not *rightly* administering *their own* Affairs, *endeavour* to foresee *and* consult *for other Men's,* Which *do not belong* to *Them.*

FABLE CLXXIV.

De Puero & Matre.

QUidam *Puer* in *Scholâ* furatus *Libellum,* attulit *suæ* Matri ; *à* Quâ *non* castigatus, *quotidie* furabatur *magis* atque *magis ;* Autem *Progressu* Temporis *cœpit* furari *majora*. Tandem *deprehensus*

Of the Boy *and* his Mother.

A Certain *Boy* in *School* having stolen *a little Book,* brought it *to his* Mother ; *by* Whom *not* being chastised, *daily* He stole *more* and *more ;* But *in Progress* of Time *He began* to steal greater *Things.* At last *being apprehended*

henſus à *Magiſtratu*, duce-batur *ad* Supplicium. *Verò* Matre *ſequente*, ac *vociſe-rante*, Ille *rogavit*, ut *lice-ret* Sibi *loqui* pauliſper *cum* Eâ *ad* Aurem. *Illo* per-miſſo, & Matre *properante*, & *admovente* Aurem *ad* Os *Filii*, evulſit *Auriculam* Matris *ſuis* Dentibus. *Cùm* Mater, & cæteri, *Qui* adſtabant, *increparent* Eum, *non* modò *ut* Furem, *ſed* etiam, *ut* impium *in* ſuam *Parentem*, inquit, *Hæc* fuit *Cauſa* mei *Exitii* ; etenim *ſi* caſtigâſſet *Me* ob *Libellum*, Quem *furatus ſum* priùs, *feciſſem* Nîl *ulteriùs* ; nunc *ducor* ad *Supplicium*.

prehended by *the Magiſtrate*, He was led to Puniſhment. But the Mother *following*, and *crying*, He *aſked*, that *it might be law-ful* for Him *to ſpeak* a little *with* Her *in* her Ear. *He* being per-mitted, *and* the Mother *haſtening*, and *moving* her Ear *to* the Mouth of *the Son*, He tore off *the Ear* of his Mother *with his* Teeth. *When* the Mother *and* the Others, *Who* ſtood about, *blamed* Him, *not* only *as* a Thief, but alſo, *as* impious *to* his *Parent*, He ſaid, *She* was *the Cauſe* of my *Deſtruction* ; for *if* She had chaſtiſed *Me* for *the little Book*, Which *I ſtole* firſt, *I had done* Nothing *further* ; now *I am* led to *Puniſhment.*

MOR.

Hæc *Fabula* indicat, *quòd* Qui *non* coërcentur inter *Initia* peccandi, evadunt *ad majora* Flagitia.

MOR.

This *Fable* ſhows, that They Who *are not reſtrained* at *the Beginnings* of ſinning, go on to greater Crimes.

FABLE CLXXV.

De Hircis & Capellis.

Of the HeGoats *and* the SheGoats.

CUM *Capellæ* obtinu-iſſent *Barbam* à *Jove*, Hirci *cæperunt* offendi, *quia* Mulieres *haberent* parem *Honorem* cum *Eis.* Jupiter *inquit*, Sinite *Illas* frui *vanâ* Gloriâ, & uſurpare *Ornatum* veſtræ *Dig-*

WHEN *the SheGoats* had ob-tained *a Beard* from *Jupiter*, the He-Goats *began* to be offended, *becauſe* the Females *had* equal *Honour* with *Them.* Jupiter *ſaid*, Suffer ye *Them* to enjoy *the vain* Glory, and to uſurp *the Ornament* of your *Dig-*

Dignitatis, dum *non æquent* veſtram. *Virtutem.*

Dignity, whilſt *They do not equal* your *Virtue.*

MOR.

Hæc *Fabula* edocet *Te,* ut *feras* Illos *uſurpare* tuum *Ornatum,* Qui *ſunt* inferiores *Tibi* in *Virtute.*

MOR.

This *Fable* teaches *Thee,* that *thou may'ſt bear* Thoſe *to uſurp* thy *Ornament,* Who are inferiors *to Thee* in *Virtue.*

FABLE CLXXVI.

De Filio *cujuſdam* Senis & Leone.

Of the Son *of a certain* old Man *and* a Lion.

Q Uidam *Senior* habebat *unicum* Filium *gene-roſi* Spiritûs, & Amatorem *venaticorum* Canum. *Viderat* Hunc *per* Quietem *trucidari* à *Leone.* Igitur *territus,* ne *fortè* aliquando *Eventus* ſequeretur *hoc* Somnium, *extruxit* quandam *politiſſi-mam,* & *amæniſſimam* Domum ; *inducens* Filium *illùc,* aſſiduus *Cuſtos* ade-rat *Illi.* Depinxerat *Domo* omne *Genus* Ani-malium *ad* Delectationem *Filii,* cum *Quibus* etiam *Leonem.* Adoleſcens in-ſpiciens Hæc, *contrahebat* Moleſtiam *Eò* magis. *Autem* quodam *Tempore,* adſtans *propius* Leoni, *inquit,* O *truculentiſſima* Fera, *aſſervor* in *hâc* Domo *propter* inane Somnium *mei* Patris : *Quid* faciam *Tibi?* Et *ita* di-cens,

A Certain *elderly Man* had an *only* Son *of a gene-rous* Spirit, and a Lover *of hunting* Dogs. He *had, ſeen* Him *in* a. Dream *to be killed* by *a Lion.* Therefore *afraid,* left *by Chance* ſometime *an Event* ſhould follow *this* Dream, He *built* a certain *very* fine, and *moſt pleaſant* Houſe ; *bringing* his Son *thither,* a daily *Guardian* was pre-ſent *to Him.* He had painted *in the Houſe* every *Kind* of Ani-mals *for* the Delight *of his Son,* with *Which* alſo a *Lion.* The Youth *look-ing on* theſe Things, *contracted* Trouble *by ſo much* the more. *But* on a certain *Time,* ſtanding *nearer* to the Lion, He *ſaid,* O *moſt cruel* wild Beaſt, *I am kept up* in *this* Houſe *for* a vain Dream *of my* Father : *What* ſhall I do *to Thee?* And *ſo* ſay-ing,

cens, *incuſſit* Manum *Parieti,* volens *eruere* Oculum *Leonis,* & *offende-bat* in *Clavo,* Qui *latebat* illìc, quâ Percuſſione *Manus* emarcuit, & Sanies *ſuccrevit,* & *Febris* ſubſe-cuta eſt, & brevi *Tempore* mortuus eſt. *Ita* Leo *occidit* Adoleſcentem, *Arte* Patris *juvante* Nihil.

ing, *He ſtruck* his Hand *on the Wall,* willing *to pluck out* the Eye *of the Lion,* and *He hit* it on *a Nail,* Which *lay hid* there, *with which* Blow *the Hand* rankled, *and* the Matter *grew under,* and *a Fever* fol-lowed, *and* in a ſhort *Time* He died. *Thus* the Lion *killed* the Youth, *the Art* of the Father *availing* Nothing.

Mor.

Hæc *Fabula* indicat, Neminem *poſſe* devitare *Quæ* ſunt *ventura.*

Mor.

This *Fable* ſhows, that no Man *is able* to avoid *thoſe Things Which* are *to come.*

FABLE CLXXVII.

De Vulpe & Rubo.

Of the Fox *and* the Bramble.

VUlpes, *cùm* aſcende-ret *quandam* Sepem, ut *vitaret* Periculum *Quod* videbat *imminere* Sibi, *comprehendit* Rubum *Manibus,* atque *perfodit* Volam Senti-bus ; & cùm foret *ſaucia* graviter, inquit, ge-mens, *Rubo, Cùm* confuge-rim ad *Te,* ut *juve-ris* Me, *Tu* nocuiſti Mihi. *Cui* Rubus *ait,* Vulpes, *erráſti,* Quæ *putáſti* capere *Me* pa-ri *Dolo* quo *conſuevi-ſti* capere *cetera.*

THE Fox, *when* She got up upon *a certain* Hedge, that *She might avoid* a Danger *Which* She ſaw *to hang over* Her, *catched hold of* a Bramble *with her Hands,* and *pricked* the Hollow of her Hand *with the Thorns* ; and *when* She was *wounded* grievouſly, *ſhe ſaid,* groan-ing, *to the Bramble, When* I have fled to *Thee,* that *Thou mighteſt have helped* Me, *Thou* haſt hurt Me. *To whom* the Bramble *ſays,* O Fox, *Thou haſt erred,* Who *haſt thought* to take *Me* with the like *Deceit* with which *Thou haſt uſed* to take *other Things.*

Mor.

S

MOR.

Fabula *significat*, quòd *est* stultum *implorare* Auxilium *ab* Illis, *Quibus* est *datum* à *Naturâ* potiùs *obesse*, quàm *prodesse*.

MOR.

The Fable *signifies*, that it is a foolish Thing *to implore* Help *from* Them, *to Whom* it is *given by Nature* rather to *hurt*, than *to profit*.

FABLE CLXXVIII.

De Vulpe *&* Crocodilo.

Of the Fox *and the* Crocodile.

VUlpes *&* Crocodilus *contendebant* de *Nobilitate.* Cùm *Crocodilus* adduceret *Multa* pro *Se*, & *jactaret* Se *supra* Modum *de* Splendore *suorum* Progenitorum ; *Vulpes* subridens, ait Ei, *Heus*, Amice, *etsi* quidem *Tu* non dixeris *Hoc*, apparet *clarè* ex *tuo* Corio, quòd jam *multis* Annis *fuisti* denudatus *Splendore* tuorum *Progenitorum*.

THE Fox *and* the Crocodile *contended* concerning *their Nobility.* When *the Crocodile* brought *many Things* for *Himself*, and *boasted* Himself beyond Measure *concerning* the Splendour *of his* Ancestors ; *the Fox* smiling, *said* to Him, *So Ho,* Friend, *although* indeed *Thou* hadst not have said *This*, it appears *clearly* by *thy* Skin, *that* now many Years *Thou hast been* deprived *of the Splendour* of thy *Ancestors.*

MOR.

Fabula *significat,* quòd *Res* ipsa *potissimùm* refellit *mendaces* Homines.

MOR.

The Fable *signifies*, that the *Thing* itself *chiefly* refutes *lying* Men.

FABLE CLXXIX.

De Vulpe *&* Venatoribus.   *Of* the Fox *and* the Hunters.

VUlpes, *effugiens* Ve-
natores, *ac* jam *defeſſa*
currendo *per* Viam,
Caſu reperit *Lignatorem,*
Quem *rogat,* ut *abſcondat*
Se *in* quoquo *Loco.* Ille
oſtendit Tectorium ; *Vulpes*
ingrediens *Id,* abſcondit *Se*
in *quodam* Angulo. *Vena-
tores* adveniunt, *rogant*
Lignatorem, *ſi* videret
Vulpem. *Lignator* negat
Verbis quidem, *Se* vi-
diſſe ; *verò* oſtendit
Locum Manu, *ubi*
Vulpes *latebat ; verò Vena-
tores,* Re *non* percep-
tâ, *ſtatim* abeunt.
Vulpes, ut *proſpicit*
Illos *abiiſſe,* egredi-
ens *Tectorio,* recedit *tacitè.*
Lignator *criminatur*
Vulpem, quòd, *cùm fecerit*
Eum *ſalvum,* ageret *Nihil*
Gratiarum Sibi. *Tunc*
Vulpes, *convertens* Se, *ait*
tacitè *Illi,* Heus, *Amice,*
ſi *habuiſſes* Opera
Manuum, & *Mores* ſimiles
tuis Verbis, *perſolveres*
meritas *Gratias* Tibi.

THE Fox, *flying from* the Hunters, *and* now *tired*
with running *along* the Way,
by Chance found *a Wood-Cutter,*
Whom *He aſks,* that *He may hide*
Himſelf *in* any *Place.* He
ſhowed the Cottage ; *The Fox*
entering *It,* hides *Himſelf*
in *a certain* Corner. *The Hunters* come up, *aſk*
the Wood-Cutter, *if* He faw
the Fox. *The Wood-Cutter* denies
in Words indeed, *that He* had
ſeen Him ; *but* He ſhowed
the Place with his Hand, *where*
the Fox *lay hid ;* but *the Hunters,* the Thing *not* being perceived, *immediately* go away.
The Fox, as ſoon as *He perceives*
Them *to be gone away,* coming
out of *the Cottage,* retires *ſilently.*
The Wood-Cutter *accuſes*
the Fox, *that,* when *He had made*
Him *ſafe,* He gave *no*
Thanks to Him. *Then*
the Fox, *turning* Himſelf, *ſays*
ſoftly *to Him,* Hark ye, *Friend,*
if *thou wouldſt have had* the Work
of *thy Hands,* and *thy Morals* like
to *thy* Words, *I would* pay
the deſerved *Thanks* to thee.

MOR.
Fabula *ſignificat,* quòd
nequam Homo, *etſi* pollicetur *bona,* tamen *præ-
ſtat* mala *&* improba.

MOR.
The Fable *ſignifies,* that
a wicked Man, *altho'* He promiſes *good Things,* yet *He per-
formeth* bad *and* wicked Things.

FABLE

FABLE CLXXX.

De Cane *vocato* ad Cænam.

Of the Dog *invited* to Supper.

QUidam *Vir*, cùm pa-ráſſet opiparam *Cæ-nam*, vocavit quendam Amicum *Domum ;* Ejus *Canis* quoque *invitavit* Canem *Alterius* ad *Cæ-nam.* Canis *ingreſſus,* cùm *videret* tantas *Dapes* apparatas, *lætus*, ait *Secum,* Sanè *explebo* Me *ita* hodie, quòd non indigebo *comedere* cras. *Verò* Coquus *conſpiciens*, tacitus *cepit* per *Caudam,* atque *rotans* terque *quaterque,* projecit *Illum* per *Feneſtram.* Ille *attonitus* aſſurgens *Humo,* dum *fugit* clamans, *cæteri* Canes *accurrunt* Ei, atque rogant, *quàm* opiparè *cæ-naverit :* At *Ille* languens ait, Ita *explevi* Me *Potu* & *Dapibus,* quòd cùm exiverim, *non vidi* Viam.

A Certain *Man,* when *He* had prepared a dainty *Sup-per,* invited a certain Friend *Home ;* His *Dog* alſo invited the Dog *of the other Man* to *Sup-per.* The Dog *having entered,* when *He ſaw* ſo great *Dainties* prepared, *joyful,* ſays *with Himſelf,* Truly *I ſhall fill* Myſelf *ſo* To-Day, that I ſhall not want *to eat* To-morrow. *But* the Cook *ſeeing Him,* ſilent *took Him* by *the Tail,* and *whirling Him* both three *and four Times,* threw *Him* thro' *the Window.* He *amazed* riſing up *from the Ground,* whilſt *He flies* crying, *the other* Dogs *run up* to Him, and aſk, *how* daintily *He had ſup-ped :* But *He* languiſhing ſays, So *have I filled* Myſelf *with Drink* and *Dainties,* that, *when* I came out, *I ſaw not* the Way.

Mor.

Fabula *ſignificat,* mul-ta *cadere* inter *Culicem* & *Labra.*

Mor.

The Fable *ſignifies,* that many Things *fall* between *the Cup* and *the Lips.*

FABLE

FABLE CLXXXI.

De Aquilâ & Homine.   *Of* the Eagle *and* the Man.

CUM *quidam* Homo *cepiſſet* Aquilam, Pennis Alarum *avulſis* Ei, *dimiſit* Eam *morari* inter *Gallinas.* Deinde *Quidam,* merca-tus, *munit* Alas Pennis : tum *Aquila* volans *capit* Leporem, & fert *Illum* ſuo *Benefaƈtori.* Quam *Rem* Vulpes *conſpi-ciens,* ait *Homini,* No-li *habere* hanc *Aquilam* Hoſpitio, *ne* venetur *Te,* æquè *ac* Leporem. *Tum* Homo *item* evulſit *Pennas* Aquilæ.

WHEN *a certain* Man *had taken* an Eagle, *the* Feathers of the Wings *being plucked* from Her, *He diſmiſſed* Her *to dwell* among *the Hens.* Afterwards *a certain* Man, having purchaſed Her, *fortifies,* her Wings *with* Feathers : then *the* Eagle flying *takes* a Hare, *and* bears *Him* to her *Benefaƈtor.* Which *Thing* a Fox *perceiv-ing,* He ſays *to the* Man, Be un-willing *to have* this *Eagle* in Entertainment, *leſt* She hunt *Thee,* as well *as* the Hare. *Then* the Man *alſo* plucked off *the Feathers* from the Eagle.

MOR.

Hæc *Fabula* ſignificat, *quòd* Benefaƈtores *quidem* ſunt remunerandi, *verò* improbi *omnino* vitandi.

MOR.

This *Fable* ſignifies, *that* Benefaƈtors *indeed* are to be requited, *but* the Wicked *altogether* to be avoided.

FABLE CLXXXII.

De Agricolâ.   *Of* the Huſbandman.

QUidam *Homo,* exiſtens *Agricola,* cùm *cog-noſceret* adeſſe *Finem* Vitæ *Sibi,* & *cuperet* Filios *fieri* peritos *in* Cultu *Agrorum,* vocavit *Eos,* atq; *inquit,* Filii, *Ego* decedo *è* Vitâ ;

A Certain Man, *being* a Huſbandman, when *He knew* that there was *an* End of Life *to Him,* and *deſired* his Sons *to become* ſkilful *in* the Tilling *of* Lands, called *Them,* and ſaid, O Sons, *I* depart *out of* Life ;

Vitâ ; *omnia* mea *Bona* funt *confita* in *Vineâ*. Illi, *poſt* Obitum *Patris*, putantes *reperire* hunc *Theſaurum* in *Vineâ*, Ligonibus, *Marris*, ac *Bidentibus* fumptis, *funditus* effodiunt *Vineam*, & *non inveniunt* Theſaurum ; verò, *cùm* Vinea *ſuit* probè *eſſoſſa*, produxit *longè* plures *Fructus* ſolito, *atq;* fecit *Illos* divites.	Life ; *all* my *Goods* are *placed* in *the Vineyard*. They, *after* the Death *of the Father*, thinking *to find* this *Treaſure* in the *Vineyard*, Spades, *Mattocks*, and *Prongs* being taken, *entirely* dig up *the Vineyard*, and *do not find* the Treaſure ; but, *when* the Vine *was* well *dug up*, it produced *by far* more *Fruits* than uſual, *and* made *Them* rich.

Mor.	Mor.
Hæc *Fabula* ſignificat, *quòd* aſſiduus *Labor* parit *Theſaurum*.	This *Fable* ſignifies, *that* daily *Labour* bringeth forth *Treoſure*.

F A B L E CLXXXIII.

De quodam *Piſcatore.*	*Of* a certain *Fiſherman.*
QUidam *Piſcator* inexpertus *piſcandi*, Reti ac Tibiis *aſſumptis*, accedit *juxta* Littus *Maris*, atq; *ſuperexiſtens* quodam *Saxo* cœpit *imprimis* tubicinare, *putans*, Se *capturum eſſe* Piſces *facilè* Cantu ; *verùm* cùm *conſequeretur* nullum *Effectum* Cantu, *Tibiis* depoſitis, *dimiſit* Rete *in* Mare, ac cepit *perplures* Piſces ; *ſed* cùm *extraheret* Piſces *è* Reti, *atque* perſpiceret *Eos* ſaltantes, ait non *inſalſè*, O *improba* Animalia, *cùm* tubicinarem, *noluiſtis* ſaltare ; *nunc*	A Certain *Fiſherman* unſkilful *of Fiſhing*, his Net *and* Pipes *being taken*, goes near the Shore *of the Sea*, and *ſtanding up* on a certain *Rock* He began *at firſt* to pipe, *thinking*, that He *ſhould take* Fiſhes *eaſily* with a Tune ; *but* when *He* obtained no *Effect* with a Tune, *the Pipes* being laid down, He *let down* the Net *into* the Sea, *and* took very many Fiſhes ; *but* when He drew the Fiſhes *out* of the Net, and perceived *Them* dancing, He *ſays*, not *unwittily*, O *wicked* Animals, *when* I piped, *Ye were unwilling* to dance ; *now*

nunc quia *ceſſo* tubicinare, *ſaltatis* continuò.

now becauſe *I ceaſe* to pipe, *Ye dance* continually.

Mor.

Hæc *Fabula* docet, *quòd Omnia* fiunt *probè*, Quæ fiunt ſuo *Tempore.*

Mor.

This *Fable* ſhows, *that All Things* are done *well*, Which *are done* in their own *Seaſon.*

FABLE CLXXXIV.

De quibuſdam *Piſcatoribus.*

Of certain *Fiſhermen.*

Piſcatores *profecti* piſcatum, & defeſſi *piſcando* diu, *præterea* oppreſſi *Fame* & *Marore*, quòd *cepiſſent* Nihil, *tùm* decernant *abire*, ecce, *quidam* Piſcis *fugiens* Aliam *inſequentem* Se *ſaltat* in *Naviculam.* Piſcatores *admodum* læti *comprehendunt* Illum, *ac* vendunt *in* Urbe *grandi* Pretio.

Fiſhermen *having gone* to fiſh, *and* tired *with fiſhing* a long while, *beſides* oppreſſed *with Hunger* and *Grief*, becauſe *They* had *taken* Nothing, *when* They reſolve *to go away*, behold, *a certain* Fiſh *flying* another *purſuing* Him *leaps* into *the Boat.* The Fiſhermen *very* joyful *take* Him, *and* ſell Him *in* the City *at a great* Price.

Mor.

Hæc *Fabula* indicat, *quòd* Fortuna *exhibet* Id *frequentiùs*, Quod *Ars* non *poteſt efficere.*

Mor.

This *Fable* ſhows, *that* Fortune *offers* That *very frequently*, Which *Art* is not able *to effect.*

FABLE

FABLE CLXXXV.

De Inope & infirmo.   *Of* the poor *and* infirm Man.

QUidam *Pauper,* cùm *ægrotaret,* vovit Diis, quòd, *si* liberaretur *ab* eo *Morbo,* immolaret *centum* Boves. *Quod* Dii *volentes* experiri, *facilè* reddunt *Sanitatem* Illi. *Igitur* liber *à* Morbo, cùm non haberet *Boves,* quia *erat* pauper, *collegit* Ossa *centum* Boûm, & deponens *super* Altare, *inquit,* Ecce, nunc persolvo *Votum,* Quod *vovi* Vobis. Dii audientes *Hoc* assistunt *Ei* in *Somniis,* atq; *inquiunt,* pergito *ad* Littus *Maris ;* etenim *ibi* reperies *centum* Talenta *Auri* semoto *Loco.* Ille *expergefactus,* memor *Somnii,* dum *pergit* ad *Littus,* incidit *in* Latrones, *Qui* spoliant & verberant *Eum.*

A Certain *poor Man,* when *He was sick* vowed *to the Gods,* that, *if* He should be freed *from* that *Disease,* He would sacrifice *a hundred* Oxen. *Which* the Gods *willing* to try, *easily* restore *Health* to Him. *Therefore* free *from* the *Disease, when* he had not *the Oxen, because he was* poor, *He* gathered the Bones *of a hundred* Oxen, *and* putting them down upon the Altar, *He said,* Behold, *now* I pay *the Vow,* Which *I vowed* to You. *The Gods* hearing *This* stand before *him* in *Dreams,* and *say,* Go *to* the Shore *of the Sea ;* for *there* Thou shalt find *a hundred* Talents *of Gold* in a secret *Place.* He *having arose,* mindful *of the Dream,* whilst *He goes* on to *the Shore,* falls *among* Thieves, *Who* rob *and* beat *Him.*

MOR.

Hæc *Fabula* indicat, *quòd* Mendaces *accipiant* Præmia *Mendaciorum.*

MOR.

This *Fable* shows, *that* Liars *receive* the Rewards *of Lies.*

FABLE

De Piscatoribus.

Of the Fishermen.

QUIDAM *Piscatores* trahebant *Rete* Mari ; *Quod* cùm *sentirent* esse grave, lætabantur magnopere, putantes *fuisse* multos *Pisces* ; sed, *ut* traxissent *Rete* in *Terram,* cùm *perspiciunt* paucos *Pisces* quidem, *verò* ingens *Saxum* inesse *Reti,* fiunt *tristes.* Quidam *ex* Illis, *jam* grandis *Ætate,* inquit *prudenter* Sociis, *Estote* quietis *Animis ;* quippe *Mæstitia* est Soror Lætitiæ ; *etenim* oportet *Nos* prospicere *futuros* Casus, *&* ut *Quis* ferat illos *leviùs,* persuadere *Sibi* esse eventuros.

CERTAIN *Fishermen* drew *their Net* out of the Sea; *Which* when *they perceived* to be *heavy,* They rejoiced *greatly,* thinking *that there were* many *Fishes* ; but, *as soon as* They had dragged *the Net* unto *the Land,* when *They perceive* few *Fishes* indeed, *but* a vast *Stone* to be *in the Net,* They become *sad.* A certain One *of* Them, *now* great *by Age,* says *prudently* to his Companions, *Be Ye* of quiet *Minds* ; for *Sorrow* is *the Sister* of Gladness ; *for* it behoveth *Us* to foresee *future* Mischances, *and* that *any Man* may bear Them *more lightly,* to persuade *Himself* that They will come to pass.

Mor.

Mor.

Hæc Fabula *significat,* quòd *Qui* reminiscitur *humanæ* Sortis, *afficitur* minimè *in* adversis.

This *Fable signifies,* that *He who* remembereth human Lot, is *affected* the least *in* adverse Things.

T

FABLE

FABLE CLXXXVII.

De Catâ *mutatâ* in *Fœminam.*

Of the She-Cat *being changed into* a *Woman.*

QUædam *Cata,* capta Amore cujuſdam ſpecioſi Adoleſcentis, oravit Venerem, *ut* mutaret *Eam* in *Fœminam.* Venus *miſerta* Illius *mutavit* Eam *in* Formam *Fœminæ;* Quam, *cùm* eſſet *valde* formoſa, *Amator* adduxit *Domum.* Sed *cùm* federent *ſimul* in *Cubiculo,* Venus *volens* experiri, *ſi,* Facie *mutatâ,* mutáſſet *& Mores, conſtituit* Murem *in* Medium; *Quam* cùm, *Illa* proſpexit, *oblita* Formæ *& Amoris, perſecuta eſt Murem, ut* cape- ret; *ſuper* quâ *Re* Venus *indignata,* denuo *mutavit* Eam *in* priorem *Formam* Catæ.

A Certain *Cat,* taken *with the Love* of a certain *beautiful* Young Man, *beſought* Venus, *that* She would change *Her* into *a Woman.* Venus *having pitied* Her *changed* Her into the Shape *of a Woman;* Whom, *when* She was *very* beautiful, *the* Lover led Home. But *when* They ſat *together* in *the* Chamber, Venus *willing* to try, *if,* the Face *being changed,* She had changed *alſo* her Morals, *placed* a Mouſe *in* the Mid- dle; *Which* when She ſaw, *having forgot* her Shape *and* Love, She *purſued* the Mouſe, *that* She might take Her; *upon* which *Thing* Venus *being* angry, again *changed* Her *into* the former *Shape* of a Cat.

MOR.

Fabula *ſignificat,* quòd *Homo,* licèt *mutet* Perſonam, *tamen* retinet *eoſdem* Mores.

MOR.

The Fable *ſignifies,* that a *Man,* altho' *He may change* his Perſon, *yet* retains *the ſame* Manners.

FABLE

FABLE CLXXXVIII.

De duobus *Inimicis.*   *Of* the two *Enemies.*

DUO *Quidam* habentes *Inimicitias* inter *Se* navigabant *unâ* in *Navi.* Et *cùm* Alter *non pateretur* Alterum *flare* in *eodem* Loco, *Unus* sedit *in* Puppi, *Alter* in *Prorâ. Autem,* Tempeftate *ortâ,* cùm *Navis* eſſet *in* Periculo, *Qui*ſedebat *in* Proiâ *rogat* Gubernatorem *Navis,* Quæ *Pars* Navis *feret* ſubmerſa *priùs ;* & *cùm* Gubernator *dixiſſet* Puppim, *Ille* ait, *Mors* nunc *non eſt* adeò *moleſta* Mihi, *ſi* perſpicio meum *Inimicum* mori *priùs.*

TWO *certain Men* having *Enmities* between *Themſelves* ſailed *together* in *a Ship.* And *when* the One *would not ſuffer* the Other *to ſtand* in *the ſame* Place, *One* ſat *at* the Head, *the Other* at *the Stern.' But* a Tempeſt *having aroſe,* when *the Ship* was *in* Danger, *He that* ſat *at* the Prow *aſks* the Governor *of the Ship,* What *Part* of the Ship *would be* ſunk *firſt ;* and *when* the Pilot *had ſaid* the Stern, *He* ſaid, *Death* now *is not* ſo *troubleſome* to Me, *if* I perceive' my *Enemy* to die *firſt.*

MOR.   MOR.

Hæc *Fabula* redarguit *Inimicitias* Hominum ; *cùm* Inimicus *ſæpius* eligit *perdere* Seipſum, *ut* per*dat Inimicum.*

This *Fable* reproves *the Enmities* of Men ; *when* one Enemy *very often* chpoſes *to deſtroy* Himſelf, *that* He may deſtroy *his Enemy.*

FABLE CLXXXIX.

De Cane & Fabro.   *Of* the Dog *and* the Smith.

QUidam *Faber* habebat *Canem,* Qui, *dum* Ipſe *cudebat* Ferrum, *dormiebat* continuò ; *verò* cùm *manducabat,* Canis *ſtatim* aſſurgebat, & ſine

A Certain *Smith* had a *Dog,* Which, *whilſt* He *ſtruck* the Iron, *ſlept* continually ; *but* when *He eat,* the Dog *immediately* roſe up, *and* without

Mo-   *De-*

Morâ corrodebat *Quæ erant dejeĉta* fub *Menfâ,* ceu *Offa,* & *Alia* hujufmodi. *Quam* Rem *Faber* animadvertens, *ait ad Canem,* Heus, *Mifer,* nefcio *Quid* faciam ; *Qui,* dum *cudo* Ferrum, *dormis* continuò, *& teneris Segnitie ;* rurfus *cùm* moveo *Dentes,* ftatim *furgis,* & *applaudis* Mihi *Caudâ.*

Delay gnawed *thofe things which* were *thrown down* under *the Table,* as *Bones,* and *other Things* of this Kind. *Which* Thing *the* Smith minding, *He fays* to *the Dog,* So Ho, *Wretch,* I know not *What* I fhall do ; *Who,* whilft *I ftrike* the Iron, *fleepeft* continually, *and* art poffeffed *with Sloth ;* again *when* I move *my Teeth,* prefently *Thou rifeft,* and *flattereft* Me *with thy Tail.*

MOR.

Fabula *fignificat,* quòd *Socordes* & *Somnolenti,* Qui *vivunt* ex *Laboribus* aliorum, *funt* coërcendi *gravi* Cenfurâ.

MOR.

The Fable *fignifies,* that *the* Slothful and *Drowfy,* Who live out of *the Labours* of Others, are to be reftrained *with a heavy* Cenfure.

FABLE CXC.

De quâdam *Mulâ.*

Of a certain *Mule.*

QUædam *Mula,* effeĉta *pinguis* nimio *Hordeo,* lafciviebat *nimiâ* Pinguedine, *inquiens* Secum, *Equus* fuit *meus* Pater, *Qui* erat *celerrimus* Curfu, *&* Ego *fum* fimilis *Ei -* per *Omnia.* Parum *pòft* contigit, quòd oportuit *Mulam* currere *quantùm* potuit ; *fed* cùm *ceffavit* Curfu, *inquit,* Heu ! *Miferam* Me, *Quæ* putabam *Me* effe Sobolem Equi ! *At* nunc *me-*

A Certain *Mule,* being made *fat* with too much *Barley,* wantoned *with too much* Fatnefs, *faying* with Herfelf, *A Horfe* was my Father, *Who* was *fwifteft* in the Race, *and* I *am* like *Him* in *all Things.* A little *after* It happened, *that* It behoved *the Mule* to run *as much as* She could ; but when *She ceafed* from Running, She faid, Alas ! *wretched* Me, *Who* thought *Myfelf* to be *the Offspring* of the Horfe ! *But* now *I re-*

memini Patrem *fuiſſe* *I remember* that my Father *was* Aſinum. an Aſs.

MOR.

Fabula *ſignificat*, quòd *Stulti* non agnoſcunt *Se-ipſos* in *proſperis* ; ſed *in* adverſis *perſæpe* recognoſcunt *ſuos* Errores.

MOR.

The Fable *ſignifies*, that *Fools* do not know *Themſelves* in *proſperous Things* ; but *in* adverſe Things *very often* They again know *their* Errors.

F A B L E   CXCI.

De Medico &
Mortuo.

Of the Phyſician *and*
the dead Man.

Quidam *Medicus*, Qui *curaverat* Ægrotum, *Qui* paulò *pòſt* moriebatur, *aiebat* Illis, *Qui* efferebant *Funus*, Si *iſte* Vir abſtinuiſſet Vino, & fuiſſet uſus *Clyſteribus*, non fuiſſet *mortuus*. Quidam *ex* His, *Qui* aderant, *ait* Medico *haud* infacetè, *Heus*, Medice, *iſta* Conſilia *fuerunt* dicenda, *cùm* quibant *prodeſſe*, non *nunc*, cùm *valent* Nil.

A Certain *Phyſician*, Who *had looked after* a ſick Man, *Who* a little *after* died, ſaid to Them, *Who* bore *the Funeral*, If *that* Man *had* abſtained from Wine, *and* had uſed *Clyſters*, He would not have been *dead*. A certain One *of* Theſe, *Who* were preſent, *ſays* to the Phyſician *not* unwittily, *So Ho*, Phyſician, *thoſe* Counſels *were* to be told, *when* They were able *to profit*, not *now*, when *They avail* Nothing.

MOR.

Fabula *ſignificat*, quòd *ubi* Conſilium *non prodeſt*, dare *Id* eo *Tempore* eſt *ſanè* deludere *Amicum*.

MOR.

The Fable *ſignifies*, that *when* Counſel *does not profit*, to give *It* at that *Time* is *truly* to play upon *a Friend*.

F A B L E

FABLE CXCII.

De Cane & Lupo.

CUM *Canis* dormiret *ante* Aulam, *Lupus* superveniens *statim* cepit *Eum*, & cùm vellet *occidere* Eum, *Canis* orabat, *ne occideret* Eum, *inquiens*, Heus, mi Lupe, *nunc* noli *occidere* Me ; *nam*, ut *vides*, sum *tenuis*, gracilis, & macilentus ; *sed* meus *Herus* est facturus *Nuptias*, ubi, si *expectabis* parum, *Ego* manducans *opiparè*, atq; *factus* pinguior, ero utilior *Tibi*. Lupus *habens* Fidem *his* Verbis *dimisit* Canem. *Post* paucos *Dies* Lupus *accedens*, cùm *reperit* Canem *dormientem* Domi, *stans* ante Aulam, rogat *Canem*, ut *præstaret* Promissa *Sibi*. Canis *inquit*, Heus, Lupe, si *cepisses* Me *ante* Aulam, non *expectaveris* Nuptias *frustrà*.

Of the Dog and the Wolf.

WHEN *the Dog* slept *before* the Hall, *the Wolf* coming upon Him, *presently* took *Him ;* and *when* He was willing *to slay* Him, *the Dog* besought Him, *that he would not kill* Him, *saying*, So Ho, *my* Wolf, *now* be unwilling *to kill* Me ; *for*, as you *see*, I am *thin*, lean, and slender ; but my *Master* is about to make *a Wedding*, when, if *you will wait* a little, *I* eating daintily, and *being become* fatter, *shall be* more advantageous *to Thee*. The Wolf *having* Faith in *these* Words *dismissed* the Dog. *After* a few *Days* the Wolf *coming*, when *He found* the Dog *sleeping* at Home, *standing* before *the Hall*, asks *the Dog*, that He *would perform* his Promises *to Him*. The Dog *says*, Hark ye, *Wolf*, if *Thou hadst taken* Me *before* the Hall, *Thou wouldst not have expected* the Wedding *in vain*.

MOR.

Hæc *Fabula* indicat, quòd *Sapiens*, cùm *semel* vitaverit *Periculum*, continuò *cavet* in *futuro*.

MOR.

This *Fable* shows, that *a wise Man*, when once He hath avoided *a Danger*, continually *takes Care* for *the future*.

FABLE

FABLE CXCIII.

De Cane & Gallo.

Of the Dog *and* the Cock.

CAnis & Gallus *Socii* faciebant *Iter ;* autem *Vesperi* superveniente, *Gallus* dormiebat *inter* Ramos *Arboris ;* at *Canis* ad *Radicem.* Cùm *Gallus,* ut *assolet,* cantabat *Noctu,* Vulpes *audivit* Eum, accurrit, & *stans* inferiùs *rogabat,* ut *descenderet* ad *Se,* quòd *cuperet* complecti *Animal* adeò *commendabile* Cantu ; *autem,* cùm *Is* dixisset, *ut* priùs *excitaret* Janitorem *dormientem* ad *Radicem,* ut *descenderet,* cùm *Ille* aperuisset ; *Illo* quærente, *ut* vocaret *Ipsum,* Canis *prosiliens* dilaceravit *Vulpem.*

A Dog *and* a Cock *Companions* made *a* *Journey ;* but *Evening* coming on, *the* Cock slept *among* the Branches *of a Tree ;* but *the Dog* at *the* Root. When *the* Cock, *as* He *is* wont, crowed *in the Night,* a Fox *heard* Him, *runs* to *him,* and *standing* below *asked,* that *He* would *come down* to *Him,* because *He* desired to embrace *an* Animal *so* commendable for Song ; *but,* when *He* had said, *that* first *He should wake* the Porter *sleeping* at *the* Root, that *He* might *come down,* when *He* had opened ; *He* asked, *that* *He* would call *Him,* the Dog *leaping* out tore *the Fox.*

MOR.

Fabula *significat,* prudentes *Homines* mittere *Inimicos* potentiores *quàm* Se, ad fortiores *Astu.*

MOR.

The Fable *signifies,* that prudent *Men* send *Enemies* more powerful *than* Themselves, *to* the more brave *by Craft.*

FABLE

FABLE CXCIV.

De Ranis.

DUÆ *Ranæ* pascebantur *in* Palude; *autem* Æstate *Palude* siccatâ, *quærebant* aliam; *ceterùm* invenerunt *profundum* Puteum; *Quo viso, Altera* dixit *Alteri*, Heus *Tu*, descendamus *in* hunc *Puteum*; Illa *respondens* ait, *Si* Aqua *aruerit* hic, *quomodo* ascendemus?

MOR.

Fabula *declarat*, quòd *nulle* Res *sunt* agendæ *inconsideratè*.

Of the Frogs.

TWO *Frogs* were fed *in* a Marsh; *but* in Summer *the Marsh* being dried up, *They sought* another; *but* They found *a deep* Well; *Which* being seen, *One* said *to the Other*, So ho *You*, let us descend *into* this *Well*; the Other *answering* says, *If* the Water *should dry up* here, *how* shall we get up?

MOR.

The Fable *declares*, that *no* Things *are* to be done *inconsiderately*.

FABLE CXCV.

De Leone & Urso.

LEO & Ursus, *quum* cepissent *magnum* Hinnulum, *pugnabant* de Eo, & *vulnerati* graviter *à* seipsis *jacebant* defatigati. *Vulpes*, videns *Eos* prostratos, & Hinnulum *jacentem* in *Medio*, rapuit Hunc, & *fugiebat.* Illi *videbant*, sed quia non potuerant *surgere*, dicebant, *Heu!* miseros Nos, quia *laboravimus* Vulpi.

Of the Lion and the Bear.

THE Lion *and* the Bear, *when* They had taken *a great* Fawn, *fought* about *Him*, and *wounded* grievously *by* one another *they lay down* tired. *A Fox*, seeing *Them* laid down, *and* the Fawn *lying* in *the Middle*, snatched *Him*, and *ran away.* They *saw* Him, but *because* They could not *rise*, They said, *Alas!* wretched *Us*, because *We have laboured* for the Fox.

MOR.

Mor.

Fabula *significat,* quòd dum Alii *laborant,* Alii *potiuntur* Prædâ.

Mor.

The Fable *fignifies,* that *whilft* Some *labour,* Others *enjoy* the Prey.

F A B L E CXCVI.

De Cassita.

Of the Lark.

CAffitâ, *capta* Laqueo, *dicebat* plorans, Hei! Mihi *mifera* & *infelici,* non furripui *Aurum* neque *Argentum* cujufquam; *autem* Granum *Tritici* fuit *Caufa* meæ *Mortis.*

THE Lark, *taken* in a Snare, *faid lamenting,* Alas! to Me *miferable* and *unhappy,* I have not taken away *the Gold* nor *the Silver* of any One; but a Grain *of Wheat* has been *the Caufe* of my *Death.*

Mor.

Fabula *tendit* in *Eos,* Qui *fubeunt* magnum *Periculum* ob *inutile* Lucrum.

Mor.

The Fable *tends* to *Them,* Who *undergo* great *Danger* for *unprofitable* Gain.

F A B L E CXCVII.

De Leone *confecto* Senio.

Of the Lion *worn out* with Age.

CUM· *Leo* fenuiffet, *nec* poffet *quærere* Victum, *machinabatur* Viam, qui Alimenta *haud deeffent* Sibi. *Igitur* ingreffus Speluncam, jacens, *fimulabat* Se *vehementer* ægrotare. *Animalia,* putantia *Se* verè *ægrotare,* accedebant ad Eum *Gratiâ* vifitandi; *Qua* Leo *capiens* mandu-cabat *fingulatim.* Càm jam

WHen the Lion was grown old, nor could *get* his Living, *He contrived* a Way, *how* Provifions *fhould not be wanting* to Him. *Therefore* having entered *the Den,* lying down, *He feign-ed* Himfelf *vehemently* to be fick. *The living Creatures,* thinking *Him* verily *to be fick,* went *to* Him *for the Sake* of vifiting Him; *Whom* the Lion *taking* eat up *fingly.* When now

U

jam occidiſſet _multa_ Animalia, _Vulpes, Arte Leenis_ cognitâ, _accedens_ ad _Aditum_ Speluncæ, _ſtans_ exteriùs, _rogat_ Leonem _quomodo_ valeret. _Leo_ reſpondens _blandè_ Ei _ait,_ Filia _Vulpes,_ cur _non ingrederis_ intrò _ad_ Me ? _Vulpes_ ait _non_ illepidè, _Quoniam,_ mi _Here,_ cerno _equidem_ perplura _Veſtigia_ Animalium _ingredientium,_ ſed _nulla_ Veſtigia _Eorum_ egredientium.

now He had killed _many_ Animals, _The Fox,_ the Art _of the Lion_ being known, _coming_ to _the Entrance_ of the Cave, _ſtanding_ without, _aſks_ the Lion _how_ He did. _The Lion_ anſwering _fairly_ to Him _ſaid,_ Daughter _Fox,_ why _doſt Thou not enter_ in _to_ Me ? _The Fox_ ſaid _not_ unwittily, _Becauſe,_ my _Maſter,_ I perceive _indeed_ very many _Footſteps_ of Animals _entering in,_ but _no_ Footſteps _of Them_ coming out.

MOR.

Fabula _ſignificat,_ quòd _prudens_ Homo, _Qui_ providet _imminentia_ Pericula, _facilè_ devitat _Illa._

MOR.

The Fable _ſignifies,_ that a _prudent_ Man, _Who_ foreſees _imminent_ Dangers, _eaſily_ avoids _Them._

FABLE CXCVIII.

_De_ Leone & Tauro.

_Of_ the Lion _and_ the Bull.

LEO _ſequens_ ingentem _Taurum_ per _Inſidias,_ cùm _acceſſit_ propè, _vocavit_ Eum _ad_ Cœnam, _inquiens,_ Amice, _occidi_ Ovem, _cœnabis_ Mecum _hodie,_ ſi _placet_ Tibi. _Poſtquam_ diſcubuiſſent, _Taurus_ conſpiciens _plures_ Lebetes, & Obeliſcos _paratos,_ & adeſſe nullam _Ovem_ Illi, _voluit_ decedere ; _Quem_ Leo _perſpiciens_ jam _abeuntem,_ rogavit, _cur_ abiret. _Taurus_ reſpondit, _Equidem_
non

A LION _following_ a great Bull by _Treachery,_ when _He_ came near, _invited_ Him _to_ Supper, _ſaying,_ Friend, _I have killed_ a Sheep, _You ſhall ſup_ with Me _To-Day,_ if _it pleaſes_ You. _As ſoon as_ They had ſat down, _the Bull_ ſeeing _many_ Cauldrons, _and_ Spits _ready,_ and _that there was_ no _Sheep_ for Him, _was willing_ to depart ; _Whom_ the Lion _perceiving_ now _going away,_ aſked Him, _why_ He would go. _The_ Bull anſwered, _Truly_ I do

non abeo *de* Nihilo,	I do not go away *for* Nothing,
cùm videam *Inftrumenta*	*when* I fee *Inftruments*
parata *non* ad *coquendum*	prepared *not* to *drefs*
Ovem, *fed* Taurum.	a Sheep, *but* a Bull.

MOR.	MOR.
Fabula *fignificat,* quòd	The Fable *fignifies,* that
Artes improborum *non*	the *Arts* of the Wicked *do not*
latent prudentes.	lie *hid from* the prudent.

FABLE CXCIX.

De Ægroto *&* Me-dico.	*Of* the Sick Man *and* the Phyfician.

ÆGER, *rogatus* à *Medico* de *fuâ* Salute, *refpondit,* Se *fudâffe* violenter ; *Medicus* ait, *Id* fuiffe *bonum ;* rogatus *ab* eodem *Medico* fecundò, *quomodo* inveniebat *Se,* Ægrotus *inquit,* Se *fuiffe* comprênfum *vehementi* Frigore : *Medicus* quoque *ait,* Id *fore* ad *Salutem.* Interrogatus *tertiò* ab *eodem,* quomodo *reperiebat* Se, *Ægrotus* *inquit,* Se *non potuiffe* digerere *fine* magnâ *Difficultate.* Medicus *ait* rurfus, *Id* fuiffe *optimum* ad *Salutem ;* deinde, *eùm* Quidam *Domefticorum* interrogaret *Ægrotum,* quomodo *valeret,* ait *Ille,* ut *Medicus* ait, *funt* Mihi *multa* & *optima* Signa *ad*

THE Sick Man *being afked* by the *Phyfician* about *his* Health, *anfwered,* That he *had fweated* violently ; *the Phyfician* fays, *that That* was *good ;* afked *by* the fame *Phyfician* a fecond time, *how* He found *Himfelf,* the fick Man *faid,* that He *was* feized *with a vehement* Coldnefs ; *The Phyfician* alfo *fays,* that That *was* for *his* Health. Afked a *third time* by *the fame,* how *He found* Himfelf, *the fick Man faid,* that He *was not able* to digeft *without* great *Difficulty.* The Phyfician *fays* again, *that That* was *the beft* for *his* Health ; *afterwards, when* fome One *of his Domefticks* afked *the* fick *Man,* how He *did,* fays *He,* as *the Phyfician* fays, *there are* to Me *many* and *the beft* Signs *for*

ad Salutem, *tamen* dispe-
reo *illis* Signis.

for Health, *yet* I pe-
rish *by those* Signs.

MOR.

Fabula indicat, *Assenta-
tores* esse culpandos.

MOR.

The Fable shows, *that Flatter-
ers* are to be blamed.

FABLE CC.

De quodam LIGNATORE.

Of a certain WOOD-CUTTER.

DUM quidam *Ligna-
tor* scindebat *Lignum
juxta* Flumen, *dicatum* Deo
Mercurio, Securis *Casu*
decidit *in* Flumen. *Igitur*
affectus *multo* Mœrore,
considebat gemens *juxta*
Ripam *Fluminis*. Mer-
curius, *motus* Misericordiâ,
apparuit *Lignario*, &
rogavit Causam *sui* Fletûs;
Quam simul *ac* didicit,
afferens auream *Securim*,
rogavit, *utrùm* esset
Illa, Quam *perdiderat*. At
Pauper negavit *esse*
suam. *Secundò* Mercurius
detulit alteram, *argenteam*;
Quam, *cùm* Pauper
negaret quoque *esse* suam,
postremò Mercurius *detulit*
ligneam; *cùm* Pau-
per *assentiret*, Illam *esse*
suam, *Mercurius*, cognoscens
Illum esse *Hominem* verum
& justum, *dedit* Omnes *Sibi*
Dono. *Igitur* Ligna-
rius, *accedens* ad *Socios*,
declarat *Quid* acciderat
Sibi.

WHILST a certain *Wood-
Cutter* cleaved *Wood
near* a River, *dedicated* to the God
Mercury, his Ax *by chance*
fell *into* the River. *Therefore*
affected *with much* Grief,
He sat down sighing *near*
the Bank *of the River*. Mercury, *moved* with Pity,
appeared *to the Wood-Cutter*, and
asked the Cause *of his* Weeping;
Which as soon *as* He learnt,
bringing to him a golden *Ax*,
He asked, *Whether* It was
That, Which *he had lost*. But
the poor *Man* denied *that it was*
his. *A second Time* Mercury
brought another, *a silver One*;
Which, *when* the poor Man
denied also *to be* his,
at last Mercury *reached*
the wooden One; *when* the Poor
Man *agreed*, that That *was*
his, *Mercury*, knowing
Him to be *a Man* true
and just, *gave* Them All *to Him*
for a Gift. *Therefore* the Wood-
Cutter, *coming to his Companions*,
declares *What* had happened
to Him.

Sibi. Unus è Sociis *volens* experiri *Id,* cùm *accessisset* ad *Flumen,* dejecit Securim in *Aquam,* deinde confedit flens *in* Ripâ ; *Causam* Cujus *Fletûs* cùm *Mercurius* audivisset, *offerens* auream *Securim,* rogavit, *Illane* effet, *Quam* perdiderat : *Quam,* cùm *assereret* 'esse *suam,* Mercurius, *ejus* Impudentiâ *cognitâ,* nec *tradidit* Ei auream, nec *suam.*

to *Him.* One *of* his Companions *willing* to try *It,* when *He came* to *the River,* threw *his Ax* into *the Water,* then *He sat* weeping *on* the Bank ; *the Cause* of Whose *Weeping* when *Mercury* had heard, *bringing* a golden *Ax,* He asked, *Whether That* was *It, Which* He had lost : *Which,* when *He asserted* to be *his own,* Mercury, *his* Impudence *being known,* neither *delivered* to Him the golden One, nor *his own.*

MOR.

Fabula *significat,* quòd quantò Deus *est* propitior *Probis,* existit *inferstior* Improbis.

MOR.

The Fable *signifies,* that by *how much* God is more propitious *to the Honest,* He is *the more infestuous* to the Wicked.

FABLE CCI.

De Medico, *Qui* curàbat *Insanos.*

Of the Physician, *Who* cured *the Mad.*

PLures *colloquebantur* de *superfluâ* Curâ *Eorum, Qui* alunt *Canes* ad *Aucupium.* Quidam *ex* Iis *inquit,* Stultus *Mediolani* risit *Hos* rectè. *Cùm* Fabula *posceretur,* inquit, *Fuit* Medicus, *Civis* Mediolani, *Qui* suscipiebat *sanare* infanos, *delatos* ad *Se* intra *certum* Tempus : autem Curatio erat hujus *Modi ;* habebat *Domi* Aream, *&* in *eâ* Lacunam *fœtidæ*

MANY *talked* of the *superfluous* Care *of Them, Who* feed *Dogs* for *Fowling.* A certain Man *of* Them *says,* The Fool *of Mediolanum* laughed at *These* rightly. *When* the Story *was demanded,* He said, *There was* a Physician, *a Citizen* of Mediolanum, *Who* undertook *to cure* the Mad, *brought to Him* within *a certain* Time : *but* the Cure *was* of this Manner ; He had at Home a Court, *and* in *it* a Pond *of stink-*

fœtidæ Aquæ, in Quâ
ligavit Eos nudos ad
Palum, Alios usq; ad Genua,
Alios usque ad Ventrem,
Nonnullos profundiùs, se-
cundum Gradum Infaniæ ;
ac tamdiu macerabat Eos
Aquâ, quoad viderentur
fani Mente. Quidam
eft allatus inter Cæteros,
Quem pofuit in Aquam
ufque ad Femur, Qui cœ-
pit refipifcere poft quindecim
Dies, & rogare fuum Me-
dicum, ut reduceretur
ex Aquâ ; Ille exemit
Hominem à Cruciatu, tamen
eâ Conditione, ne' egrederetur Aream. Cùm
paruiffet aliquot Diebus,
permifit, ut perambula-
ret totam Domum ; at
ut non egrederetur exterio-
rem Januam ; (Sociis,
Qui erant multi, relictis in
Aquâ ;) paruit Manda-
tis Medici diligen-
ter ; verò ftans fuper Li-
men quodam Tempore ; (nam
non audebat egredi,) vidit
Juvenem venientem in Equo
cum duobus Canibus, &
Accipitre ; motus Novi-
tate Rei ; (etenim non tenebat Memoriâ
Quæ viderat
ante Infaniam ; cùm
Jubenis acceffiffet, Ille
inquit, Heus, Tu, oro, re-
fponde Mibi paucis: Quid
eft Hoc, Quo vehe-
ris ? Inquit, eft Equus.
Tum

of ftinking Water, in Which
He bound Them naked to
a Stake, Some up to the Knees,
Others up to the Belly,
fome more deeply, accord-
ing to the Degree of Madnefs ;
and fo long He ftarved Them
in the Water, till They feemed
found in Mind. A certain Man
was brought among the Reft,
Whom He put into the Water
up to the Thigh ; Who be-
gan to repent after fifteen
Days, and to afk his Phy-
fician, that He might be brought
out of the Water ; He took out
the Man from the Torment, yet
on that Condition, that He fhould
not go out of the Court. When
He had obeyed fome Days,
He permitted, that He might
walk over the whole Houfe ; but
that he fhould not go out of the outward Gate ; (his Companions,
Who were many, being left in
the Water ;) He obeyed the Commands of the Phyfician diligently ; but ftanding upon the Threfh-
old on a certain Time ; (for
He did not dare to go out,) He faw
a Young Man coming on a Horfe
with two Dogs, and
a Hawk ; moved with the No-
velty of the Thing ; (for He did not
retain in Memory
the Things Which He had feen
before his Madnefs ;) when
the Young Man came near, He
faid, So ho, You, I pray, anfwer Me in a few Things : What
is This, on Which Thou art carried ? Says He, It is a Horfe.
Then

Tum *deinceps*, Quid *voca-tur* Hoc, *Quod* geftas *Manu*, & in quâ *Re* uteris? *Ille* refpondit, *eft* Accipiter, & aptus *Captui* Perdicum. *Tum* Infanus *petit*, & *Hi*, Qui *comitantur* Te, *Qui* funt, & Quid *profunt* Tibi? *Ait*, Sunt *Canes*, & apti Au-cupio, ad inveftigandum *Aves.* Autem *hæ* Aves, *Caufâ* capiendi *Quas* paras *tot* Res, cujus *Pretii* funt, fi *con-feras* Capturam *totius* Anni *in* unum? *Cùm* re-fpondiffet *parvum*, nefcio quid, & *quòd* non ex-cederet *fex* Aureos, *Infanus* rogat, *Quænam* fit *Impenfa* Equi, Canum, & *Accipitris?* affirmavit *Im-penfam* Eorum *effe* quotan-nis *quinquaginta* Aureos. *Tum* admiratus *Stultitiam* Juvenis, *inquit*, oro, *abi* hine *ocyùs*, antequam *Medicus* redeat *Domum;* nam *fi* Hic *compererit* Te, *conjiciet* Te *in* fuam *Lacunam*, veluti *infaniffi-mum* Omnium, & collo-cabit *Te* in *Aquâ* ufque *ad* Mentum.

Then *afterwards*, What *is call-ed* This, *Which* thou beareft on thine *Hand*, and *in* what *Thing* doft thou ufe it? *He* anfwered, *it is* a Hawk, *and* fit for the *catching* of Partridges. *Then* the Madman *afks*, and *Thefe*, That *accompany* Thee, What are they, *and* What do they *profit* to Thee? *He fays*, They are *Dogs*, and *fit* for Fowl-ing, to trace the *Birds.* But *thefe* Birds, for the *Sake* of catching *Which* You prepare *fo many* Things, of what *Price* are They, if *You* put *together* the Catching *of a whole* Year *into* one? *When* He had an-fwered *a little*, I know not-*what*, and *that* it could not ex-ceed *fix* Guineas, *the Madman* afks, *What* may be *the Expence* of the Horfe, *of the Dogs*, and of the *Hawk?* He affirmed *the Ex-*pence of Them *to be* year-ly *fifty* Guineas. *Then* having admired *the Folly* of the Young Man, *fays he*, I pray, go hence *quickly*, before that the *Phyfician* return Home; for *if* He *fhould find* Thee, He *will* throw Thee *into* his *Pond*, as the *moft* mad of all Men, *and* He will place *Thee* in *the Water* up *to* the Chin.

Mor.
Hæc *Fabula* oftendit, *multas* Infanias *effe* quotidie inobfervatas.

Mor.
This *Fable* fhows, *many* Madneffes *to be* daily unobferved.

F A B L E.

FABLE CCII.

De obſtinatâ Muliere, Quæ vocavit Virum pediculoſum.

QUædam, Mulier, ſupra Modum contraria Viro, ita, ut vellet eſſe ſuperior, ſemel in gravi Altercatione cum Eo vocavit Eum pediculoſum. Ille, ut retractaret illud Verbum, contundebat Uxorem, cædens Illam Pugnis & Calcibus. Quò magis cædebatur, eò plùs vocavit Illum pediculoſum. Vir tandem laſſus verberando Illam, ut ſuperaret Pertinaciam Uxoris, dimiſit in Flumen per Funem, dicens, Se ſuffocaturum Eam, ſi non abſtineret talibus Verbis. Illa perſtabat nihilà minùs continuare illud Verbum, quamvis fixa uſque ad Mentum in Aquâ. Tum Vir demerſit Eam in Flumen, ita ut non poſſet loqui ampliùs, tentans ſi poſſet avertere Eam à Pertinaciâ Timore Mortis. At Illa, Facultate loquendi ademptâ, exprimebat Digitis, Quod nequibat Ore: Nam, Manibus erectis ſupra Caput, Unguibus utriuſque Pollicis conjunctis, dedit quod Opprobrium potuit Viro, illo Geſtu.

MOR.

Hæc Fabula indicat, quòd Quidam retinebunt ſuam Pertinaciam etiam Periculo Mortis.

Of the obſtinate Woman, Who called her Huſband louſy.

A Certain Woman, above meaſure contrary to her Huſband, ſo that ſhe would be uppermoſt, once in a heavy Quarrel with Him called Him louſy. He, that She might retract that Word, bruiſed his Wife, beating Her with his Fiſts and Heels. By how much the more ſhe was beaten by ſo much the more ſhe called Him louſy. The Man at length tired with beating Her, that He might overcome the Obſtinacy of his Wife, let her down into a River by a Rope, ſaying, that He would ſuffocate Her, if She would not abſtain from ſuch Words. She perſiſted in nothing the leſs to continue that Word, altho' fixed up to the Chin in the Water. Then the Man plunged Her into the River, ſo that She could not ſpeak more, trying if He could avert Her from her Obſtinacy by the Fear of Death. But She, the Faculty of ſpeaking being taken away, expreſſed with her Fingers, What She could not with her Mouth: For, her Hands being raiſed above her Head, the Nails of each Thumb being joined, She gave what Reproach She could to her Huſband, by that Geſture.

MOR.

This Fable ſhows, that Some will retain their Obſtinacy even at the Hazard of Death.

FINIS.

www.ingramcontent.com/pod-product-compliance
Lightning Source LLC
Chambersburg PA
CBHW021110020726
47500CB00003B/698